WALKING THROUGH FIRE

WALKING THROUGH FIRE

RANDHIR KHARE

NIYOGI
BOOKS

Published by

NIYOGI BOOKS

D-78, Okhla Industrial Area, Phase-I
New Delhi-110 020, INDIA
Tel: 91-11-26816301, 49327000
Fax: 91-11-26810483, 26813830
email: niyogibooks@gmail.com
website: www.niyogibooks.com

Cover and Book Design: PealiDezine
Editor: Nandita Jaishankar / Niyogi Books

ISBN: 978-93-81523-15-5
Publication: 2012

Printed at: Niyogi Offset Pvt. Ltd., New Delhi, India.

For Susan, Lavanya and Raghuvir
in gratitude for all that they have given me

Contents

Prologue

Sean ran up the spiral staircase in the dark, stumbling as he hurtled forward, until he crashed headlong into a pile of dilapidated crates stacked against the wall on the first landing. He lay there in a heap, heart slamming against his ribs, tears streaming down his face, blood from a cut on his lower lip dripping on to his dirty vest. He could feel a strange darkness welling up from within. It wasn't fear or sadness or even a sense of helplessness. It was rage—pure, desperate rage. He sat up with his back against the splintered pile of wood and stared at the palms of his small bony hands. Clenching his fists, he stabbed the air with them. *No, no, I won't let it happen, I won't. I'm going to save Mum. I'll save her. You are not going to let her kill herself, Dad, you are not going to make her die. I'll kill you first. I'll kill you first, you hear me? You hear me? I hate you, I hate you, I hate you!* He continued to punch the air until his right fist slammed against a wrought iron bar of the staircase. A sharp pain shot up along his arm. He sobbed as he felt the darkness in him pour out into the night. Then he was calm and raised himself till he was standing and step by step, began climbing the spiral stairs again. This time, it was as if he was in a dream. It was the aftermath of his fit of rage—there was really nothing more that he could use against his father. Nothing at all.

Once on the roof, he stopped to catch his breath. Across, in the adjoining building, he could see the Morrisons sitting down to a normal family dinner and in the apartment beside theirs, old man

Davidson practised on his violin. But none of that for him. Just the strangely fascinating terror that loomed before him—the prospect of his mother leaping to her death. He watched her standing on the wall at the corner near the large rusty water tank, resting against it with one arm. She was swaying like the tired mast of a battered barge on the Hooghly, her crumpled lilac dress fluttering sails in the wet river wind. A stream of warm piss ran down the inside of his thighs.

He heard his voice saying, *Mum, please don't jump. Please don't jump. What will I do without you? Please don't jump. I'll tell Dad not to hit you anymore and not to call you bad names. Please. I'll do anything to make you happy again. I promise I won't be sick ever again so that you don't have to stay awake all night and cook special food for me. Please don't jump.*

Imelda wasn't listening to him. She was staring blankly out across the rooftops all around.

When Sean's legs finally began to move, he found himself standing close to her, clutching on to her feet. Ages seemed to pass before she finally went down on her haunches and sat there quietly. Then she arranged herself so that she sat on the wall. Her son climbed up beside her and she pulled him close. He could smell the familiar fragrance of her body: spices, talcum powder and eau de cologne. Blood from her nose dripped down on to the back of his hand. He didn't wipe it off.

After a while she rested an arm lightly on his shoulder. *Don't be frightened. All of this will finally pass and you will grow up and forget what has happened and you will marry and have children and they will marry and have children. Life goes on. I know this is too much for you to understand. I'm sorry for putting you through it, I really am. But once I'm gone, Sean, maybe things will be easier, much easier. Maybe I'm wrong. I don't know.*

What am I going to do without you? he asked, frightened and already feeling abandoned.

Do you want to come with me?

I'm scared.

Let's pray then, maybe it will help you feel better.

So they prayed. Imelda's voice trailed off but he went on. He prayed that she wouldn't be beaten anymore, that his father would get a job, that he wouldn't get sick anymore, that his mother would change her mind and remain alive. Then the boy burst into tears and cried violently. His body shook and he lost his balance and toppled forward. She lunged at him and grabbed his left arm.

Hanging there by one arm, he struggled to grab on to the water pipe that jutted out of the wall but it broke the moment he caught it. *You aren't going to die, you aren't going to die. I won't let you die*, his mother kept saying. He was sure she was wrong and prepared himself for the final plunge, frightened of the physical experience of hitting the street below. What would the impact feel like? Would there be any sensation at all? *Pray, pray, come on son, pray*, Imelda whispered hoarsely.

There is nothing to pray for, he kept repeating to himself, *nothing to pray for. No God and no angels to help. Nothing. No one. Just Mum.* He tried to look up at her face as he dangled there but didn't succeed. His body became very still and he waited for the drop but instead he felt the tug of his mother's hand that lifted him gently until he reached the parapet. He grabbed on to it with his right hand when his mother let go of her grip on him. A surge of power forced him to haul himself on to the parapet and then the wall. His mother had fallen over and sat slumped on the floor of the roof. Climbing down, he sat beside her.

I'm sorry, I'm sorry, son. She sat with her back resting against the wall, her hand gently stroking his hair. *I nearly lost you. If I had, I would have jumped after you. We would have been in Heaven together.*

There is no Heaven, he heard his voice, barely a whisper.

Don't say that. It's not the way a good Catholic should talk.

Then why do I get sick so often? Why does Dad hit you as if you are a punching bag?

That's not Heaven's fault, son.

Then whose fault is it? Whose fault is it?

Ours. Our fault.

What have we done wrong? What have I done wrong?

You haven't done wrong. I have. I made the wrong choices.

What choices? I don't understand.

Let it be. You are alive. I am alive. That's what is important.

And he is alive. And we are all living in Hell.

Now let's pray, son, let's pray.

Sean sat in silence, listening to his mother pray. He felt nothing.

When Imelda was done, she quietly got up with her son and walked back to the spiral staircase. Afraid that she would find her husband waiting for them at the front door, she slipped into the apartment through the bathroom door of her daughter Nora's room. The young woman sat crouched, sobbing in one corner, her face and arms bruised and bleeding, the room in a complete state of disarray. Her father had intercepted a love letter on its way out. Just a simple, innocuous love letter with little pink flowers painted along the margins. What was so criminal about an eighteen year old writing a love letter to her 'boyfriend'? At least she had someone to love. And someone who loved her. In those desperate times, that in itself was a blessing.

Nora wasn't the sort who wanted too much out of life. Her dreams were simple ones: get through college, settle into a teacher's job, marry, raise a family of her own. That's it. No more, no less. Lancy was her man. Hard working, sincere, with a great sense of humour, he could sing like Harry Belafonte. His favourite number was *Come Back Liza.*

The funny thing was that her father didn't mind the guy when they were in each other's company. In fact he'd sing along with him. But once he'd gone, he'd criticise Lancy and reduce him to the status of an ordinary good-for-nothing. No one could understand the logic. *I don't like the fellow, that's all.* Gordon would dismiss further discussion.

Then how come you sing with him? Phillip, her younger brother, would persist.

Shut up, you squirt. I sing with him because I'm being civil. That's all. We have to be civil when people come home. Meet them on the street and you can behave with them as you choose. But at home you just have to be civil—that's what matters most.

Sean walked over to Nora. Kissing her on her bloodstained hand, he whispered, *I'm sorry.*

What are you sorry about? she asked brokenly. *This is not your fault. It's him. It's his fault. He's a mad man. Why are you saying sorry?*

I should have defended you.

What can you do against that brute?

Don't say that, Imelda interjected. Whatever the circumstance, she would jump to her husband's defence automatically, almost without thinking. *He's your father.*

What has he done to earn that position?

He's your father and my husband. Don't talk about him like that. She sat down on the edge of the bed and putting her arms around both her children, wept.

Gordon appeared at the doorway and stood there looking at them. Alone. Helpless. Now that his rage had passed, he was embarrassed. A bumbling, almost awkward, stream of words tumbled out. *I went down the road and picked up some strawberry ice cream since it's your birthday and you like strawberry ice cream. Nora? Don't you like it too?* He stood there like a child who was trying to make up for the mistakes that he'd made, holding a box of ice cream which had already begun to melt. Just a short while earlier, he had gone crazy, wrecking the birthday meal which Nora had made for Imelda.

He's my fourth child, Imelda had once said. *I have to take care of him in a very special way by understanding him and coping with his moods that swing from one extreme to the other.*

But he makes no effort with you, Nora had replied. *He gives you nothing in return. What is he to you? What Mum? What do you get from him?*

He is my destiny.

Sean couldn't understand the conversation. All he saw was an unreliable person who he wanted to love and trust, wanted to depend on but was baffled by the man's unpredictable behaviour and was beginning to hate him.

Imelda got up, the blood drying on her birthday dress and took the box of ice cream out of his hands and went off to put it in a bowl. He remained there staring down at his children. Nora began to shiver.

When he left, she calmed down and slipped into sleep. The boy wiped the blood off her nose and hands with a wet towel and covered her with a sheet. Flicking off the light, he stood at the doorway of her room wondering what was happening in the rest of the house.

A deathly silence had fallen. He walked out onto the veranda and found his mother at the dining table, face down on her hands, asleep. She had not managed to get the ice cream to a bowl and left the box on the table. The contents had oozed out and trickled across the table, dripping down on the floor. A puddle of fluorescent pink had formed at her feet. She was beyond caring.

Gordon was already asleep in the bedroom and his snoring echoed through the house, bouncing from wall to wall and out of the door into the night.

The only one awake, he peeled off his pee-soaked shorts, threw them in a corner and lay down on the cool cement floor and tried to sleep. But sleep brought dreams. He felt himself toppling off the roof with his mother and as his body fell he saw the ground rush up to meet him. Then the dream repeated itself and he saw her floating away over the rooftops and found himself howling at a sinking moon. Another butted in—he sat and watched her leap into the void, her night dress ballooning out and carrying her down gently and when her feet touched the ground she looked up at him and laughed, *you should have been a girl, Sean, then you'd have a nightie on and you could float down like me. Boys don't float, they fall like stones with a thud.*

Something startled him out of his sleep. A wail that sounded like an air raid siren. Bolt upright. He yelled, *Mum, Mum, the Chinks are coming, the Chinks are coming!* Imelda shot out of her chair and scrambled over to Nora's room.

Up, get up, we got to get downstairs! They are coming, they are coming! she called out as if the yellow hoard was on its way up the flight of wooden stairs. A moment later, the three of them went staggering down the stairs.

But there was no sign of Gordon. Despite his wife's incessant calls, he snored on. When they were halfway down the stairs, he called out, *Where are my trousers? Where are my trousers?*

The entire neighbourhood was awake outside and the crowd stood and waited in the dark. Planes droned overhead. No one seemed to be breathing.

The Chinese don't have any planes I'm told, old Gerry Upham said from the crowd gathered out in the dark. *Just plenty of men like bloody ants. And all they can do is let them loose. So I don't know why we're worried. Unless they grow wings, ha ha. These are our bloody planes doing their usual rounds.*

Shut up Gerry, Sarah his wife enjoyed putting him down. *You never know when's the right time for a joke.*

This is no joke, it's for real. The fellows don't even have enough guns. One weapon for every ten soldiers. One chap dies and the other takes his gun. Then when he gets popped off, there's someone else to take his place. I'm sure they've even started eating each other up.

No one found that funny because most of the crowd out there that night were actually struggling to feed themselves and their families. Almost all of them were Anglo Indians who were either unemployed or were working hard on low wages. In Calcutta, the booming 50s were over and the 60s had started with a fizz and pop...and then silence. A long painful silence when Anglos started losing their jobs. Indians who were more qualified had started to elbow them out. Those who were teachers were found to be under-qualified, 'engineers' were now regarded as mechanics and a host of other able but 'untrained' workers and junior officers agreed to stay on lower wages. But those in the railways, the merchant navy, in night clubs and maybe the police hung on. And if one couldn't fit in where the jobs were going then that was the end of the road. Most of the group huddled out there in the dark were the doomed variety...waiting to get away to Canada, England and Australia. Many would die waiting.

Gordon turned up a while later and stood staring at the crowd. *I wouldn't worry if I were you. This must be one of their drills. The Chinks are busy making money in their chow shops. We're not going to get any trouble from them. Besides, there are no dog fights in this war. It's all ground combat. That must be a ship's hooter.*

Sounded like a siren to me, chimed Gerry, *maybe you're right.*

That means we drink from the same bottle Gerry, he muttered.

Not sure about that, the fellow shot back, *I brew my own stuff.*

Everyone ignored them.

The crowd stood huddled together, waiting for a supposed all clear but it never came. People started slipping away, returning to their homes. It was only when Sean got back that he discovered he had forgotten to put on his pants.

It was 1962. Sean was eleven. India and China were busy beating the hell out of each other on the border way up. The Chinese started it off by attacking an Indian border patrol north of the MacMohan Line, at least that's what the papers said and then one thing led to another and a lot of blood was shed. Though it seemed far off from Calcutta, the war was on everyone's lips. It was something to talk about, something to worry about, a diversion. In fact, a lot of families during that time stopped frequenting Chinese restaurants because they were afraid they'd get poisoned.

All sorts of theories did the rounds and quickly became local legends. One said that Mrs Fu who ran a hole in the wall eatery on Bentick Street was feeding pork to Muslims and beef to Hindus to destroy their faith. Another said that the Wongs in Park Lane were spiking their soups with a strange concoction that made the skin look yellow and the eyes narrower than usual.

But Sean and his family had a special fondness for Chinese food. That's because it was neither here nor there. Besides that, there was plenty on a plate with lots of non-veg thrown in. And it was cheap. Overseas on Wellesley Street was that sort of place that's why they never ran out of business. The stuff they dished up may have been oily but there was a lot of it; heaps of veggies and chunks of meat. Only God knew where the meat came from. If there was a God around during those years, that is.

Nothing of course like the popular Ching Wi's where the family would have a meal in the mid 50s. Their food was quite something. The place was on Central Avenue. It was a great watering hole for small families with maybe a friend or two thrown in. Everyone called the owner John because they couldn't be bothered to find out his real name. He was a squat Chinaman who had a mouthful of perfectly shaped teeth. His cropped hair stuck out in all directions and his bright piggy eyes gleamed deep set in his round greasy face. Everything about him was porker, even the smell that his body gave off was like pig's fat. Gordon called him WB, wild boar—when he was in a jovial mood and talked about the great holidays he'd take the family on when he got his first salary after he landed a job. And when he was in a bad mood he'd snap, John this and John that. And John had this amazing way of responding appropriately—jovial when Gordon was jovial and businesslike when he was in a bad mood. But when he was sour and drunk he'd refer to the owner as that bloody Chinaman or the chow-eating porker.

Most times the family dinner would start with Gordon in a humorous mood and end with him arguing over the bill. On occasions he'd pick an argument with someone at another table and push it into a fight. And John would try to break it up and get shoved around and a few glasses would break and punches would fly and Imelda and the three kids would be in the 'family room', a cabin with half swinging doors, and she would say, *Eat up now. Don't waste your food. So many people out there go hungry.*

At those times, the fellow with a black tie playing the fiddle on the steps outside would change to a real happy number and pitch in a few words. John would go out and tell him, *Shsh now dey fieteen. Can't you see mun? Dey fieteen.*

Sean's earliest memory of a Ching Wi meal went back to the time when he was possibly around four. A boy out with his family for a meal which had ended in a brawl. No one had the time or inclination to ask what he felt. Scared? Confused? Whatever the feeling must have been it nevertheless couldn't have been very nice for the boy to see his father breaking up furniture in a public place. By the time Imelda had managed to get her husband out, he was a wreck. Even cabs wouldn't stop for them. Then back home, he grumbled all night, finally falling asleep when early morning rickshaw bells rattled their way down Sudder Street.

He remembered vaguely that when his Dad was employed, family dinners out were few and far between. He'd be off with his friends and his wife would spend the night wondering if he'd ever return.

No one dared ask him how on earth he could take his family out for dinner when he was unemployed. Quite simple. He'd sell or pawn household possessions to raise the money. When he was employed, he'd stock up the house again. When he lost his job he'd rapidly pawn and sell things till the house was stripped bare. Once, they were reduced to three plates and they had to take turns at the table...until the table went too and never came back. They ended up on the floor, a plate propped up on their knees, shovelling morsels into their mouths. One night, when the family was virtually eating off the floor, Gordon decided to spin a few shikar yarns about the time he was lost in some wilderness somewhere and was forced to eat raw meat soaked for an hour in booze. *Jasper liked it so much that when we got back he started eating raw meat soaked in vodka. That's not unusual, the Japs eat raw fish all the time. Give them half a chance and they'll wallop the fish in your aquarium.* When he had got his listeners laughing, he waxed on about exotic cuisines. He was a fund of information, some authentic and lots just made up...all reeled off with the snappy style of a nightclub entertainer.

And while they were all there eating on the floor with their backs resting against peeling walls, listening to him share his experiences of high living and sophisticated eating in posh restaurants he began narrating a story about the time when he and Imelda had gone to a Company dinner where they met some outrageously bad mannered Italians. *They were Russians*, she corrected him, *not Italians.*

Italians, he insisted and pushed his plate across the floor towards her.

Italians are loud but not bad mannered. Russians are awful.

He stretched across, picked up his plate half full of food and threw it at the wall above her head. When it hit the wall, shards of china scattered like shrapnel. The food dripped down on her head, over her face and down the front of her clothes.

Okay, they were Italians. She was visibly nervous.

You don't have to behave like you're doing me a favour by agreeing with me. You turned the mood of a perfectly good meal upside down by spoiling my story. So what if they were Italians or Russians or Yugoslavians or Belgians or from the Congo? It was my story and you ruined it! He sat there like a spoilt child trapped in the enormous body of a street fighter.

I didn't mean to, I was just correcting the facts in your story, she tried pacifying him.

Who cares about the facts? A story is a story. It doesn't make a difference whether it's true or false. The problem with you is that you are constantly putting me down, trying to prove me wrong. You are a goody-two-shoes, a fake angel with plaster of paris wings. I'm tired of being put down. He stormed off and they heard him banging around in the next room.

He's looking for where the money's hidden, Imelda said softly. *He's going out when he finds it.*

Gordon left the house and came back after a few hours, beat his wife silly and then fell asleep in a drunken stupor. Sean saw dried blood speckled on the walls of their room the next morning. She spent the day in bed.

Once when he was employed he bought a gramophone on instalments but soon after that he lost his job and couldn't get past the third instalment so the manager from the store came to collect the payments. He avoided her by escaping through the window down a ladder. But when she began insisting that they'd have to carry off the machine, he sent his family out of the house and met her alone and charmed her off her feet. He sold the gramophone to someone else just when they were shifting out of the house.

He had charm. There was a magnetism about the man that stopped conversations when he walked into a room. It wasn't just his striking good looks but also the ease with which he could slip his way into women's hearts and beds. But when it came to his wife and family, he presented extremes, veering from one mood to another. Tender, loving, violent, savage, spiteful, supportive, caring, impetuous. The swings were frightening. The violence was inevitable. Blood was the only image that Sean could associate with his father.

Now, decades later, he sat staring at the red which had dripped down the front of his shirt from his nose. The familiar smell of blood seemed to comfort him.

Is she related to you? asked the uniformed man staring down at him.

Who?

That one there. The dead one, he said pointing to the body at his feet. *Is she related to you? What's your name?*

The man threw questions at him by the handful and they seemed to land around him like marbles that went bouncing off across the bloodstained floors of the hospital's emergency ward. The marbles kept bouncing until he could take it no more and raised his palms to his face and cried into them. They took him away on a stretcher, the uniformed man walking alongside him, throwing more marbles at him. *Just tell me your name, what's your name? Who is she?*

The smell of blood hung reassuringly around him and for some inexplicable reason drew him into the folds of memory, protecting him. Or was it the last review of his life? He didn't know. He couldn't tell.

Images of his childhood surfaced, enveloping him.

Little Elliot Road Times

The Little Elliot Road apartment was the first proper home we stayed in after we shifted from Grandpa's home in Kanpur in 1954. The earlier one was a dingy place on Sudder Street. This was so much better. It was a compact apartment with a number of rooms. All except one had windows that opened out on to various views of the locality around. Not particularly pleasant views—just acres of low rooftops. Far to the right was a wood depot and to the left a few three storied buildings with little bungalows tucked cozily in between. And below, just outside on three sides there was an open ground that was gravelly and skinned our knees and elbows whenever we tumbled about. A gnarled old mango tree with a twisted trunk stood in the far corner of the compound. There were stories about this tree that did the rounds. One claimed that the person who had built the apartment block went bankrupt and hung himself from one of its stout branches and the tree stopped bearing fruit the next year. Another said that it was inhabited by the spirit of an old woman that would materialise at night and roam the property crying softly. Mum claimed to have heard her weeping on a couple of occasions.

Near the front gate stood an uninspiring silk cotton tree that burst into waxy red blooms in spring. In its heyday it was said to have been covered in flowers that gave way to giant pods. When they burst, the air would fill thickly with wisps of floating cotton.

The jackfruit tree beside the boundary wall to the west of the property was enormous, with branches stretching far and wide. Every year when the fruits were swollen and ready to be harvested, they would be expertly removed, stored for a week and then cut open and shared amongst all the families in the block. Baboo Da, a vegetable vendor, was the fellow who would do the harvesting. I would hang around with a gang of children and watch him carefully remove the heavy fruit clinging to the trunk of the tree. He had a long curved knife to do the job and slathered his hands and the blade with oil to ward off the stickiness of the sap. When the fruits were ready to be cut open, he'd be back again to do the job. We watched in fascination as the blade sank into the prickly hide of the fruit and ran deep along its length until the inside was revealed...perfect compartments which contained fleshy yellow fruit that exuded a heady fragrance. Not everyone, though, considered it to be a fragrance. The Tuckers refused to accept their share because they said that their entire apartment would get so filled with the stench that they'd have to burn "those Hindu joss sticks" to clear the air. And they were certainly not going to do that. James Tucker, fondly known as J Uncle by kids in the block, was a toffee-nosed Catholic who considered anything vaguely Hindu as a hindrance on the pathway to Paradise. *I see it this way,* he'd sniff affectedly, *we are the only ones who will go up. The rest will just stay right here and vanish into thin air.* The other families, a number of them belonging to one Christian denomination or the other, weren't rabid and had learnt to be more accommodating.

It was surprising how many families there were crammed into that block which was like a veritable bee's hive, with some living in small flats tucked into every nook and cranny. The Tuckers were on our floor. James Tucker was a tall, lean fellow with stooping shoulders and a bald head that gleamed like a polished egg. His wife Mary Lou Tucker looked like a man. She had a moustache and a mole on her right jaw which had a few stiff black hairs standing up around it. They had adopted the son of a poor widow and brought the boy, Billy, up with lots of love, good clothes and more food than his body actually needed. The little fellow had the run of the house and his elderly foster parents doted on him. Every second evening was a tea party and all the kids of the neighbourhood would turn up at their house and have a great time tucking into the sumptuous spread laid out on the table. One day his sister arrived. The Tuckers apparently tried to adopt her too, but didn't succeed. She'd stay, have a good time and then vanish. She was much older than all of us. Wanda, that's what her name was. Wanda. And she had all the young fellows in the area hanging around in the courtyard outside the building, like dogs waiting for a go.

Then something terrible happened. Whilst we were busy having one of our tea parties someone arrived at their front door and gave Mary Lou a message. She staggered back and fainted on the couch. James went next and turned away after reading the message, holding his head as if he had suddenly developed an awful headache. The lady of the house got up and led Billy into the bedroom. James followed them. I stopped eating, wondering what the hell was going on. The others kept at the food. Alan, the guy who lived down the road, picked up the jar of Kraft Cheese Spread, stuffed his pockets with little heart shaped cookies and walked off. A couple of the others flicked things too. Soon I was the last fellow at the table. I sat there, waiting for them to return.

Sometime later Billy came running out of the room and sat down next to me. He stared at his plate and suddenly said, *My sister died. She's gone to Heaven.* Then he howled like a frightened puppy. I left because I didn't know what to say or do. The three of them pushed off that night and we didn't see them for a long time. Their locked front door seemed ghostly. I was always scared to walk past it in case the ghost of little Billy's sister reached out to snatch me. So then the entire floor, with the exception of our apartment was a ghost floor...I say this because the other two front doors had large padlocks on them and legends clung to the fate of their residents.

On the ground floor there was the Rozario family, husband and wife, who put up *The Rozario Family* on a ceramic name tile on their small front gate. Bach and Beethoven billowed out through their blue frilly curtained windows. Beside them were the Smiths, Coleen and Percy, a tiny couple who looked distinctly like twins. Their aged beagle looked like a relative. Aunty Coleen loved to make pickles and set out row upon row of jars just outside their window in the sun. The dog guarded them through the day. Every Christmas we were given a small jar of pickle with a thank you card attached to it. We could never make out what the 'thank you' was for. But that didn't matter really, the pickle was delicious.

After their place came the flat that Peggy the air hostess occupied. She threw wild parties and had strange men drop in whenever she was in town. She was quite a looker—slim, tall and angular with lustrous dark hair tied tight in a bun and large, limpid eyes. Her name was always spoken in whispers and a sidelong glance here and there, a furtive grin and raised eyebrows. Even though at that age I didn't understand the implications of their behaviour, I nevertheless understood that no one really knew what to do with her.

On the other side of the building on the ground floor were the Chongs and old Bullman. The Chongs were a family of eleven noisy brats with equally noisy parents. They had left China a couple of years before and had come to Calcutta to seek their fortune. Their neighbour 'old Bullman' was an ancient version of Desperate Dan. That Anglo had made his fortune, they said, shaking down people on behalf of money lenders. Sometimes a friend of his would visit him and bring along his air gun. He'd stand many paces away and point the gun at the open palm of Bullman's outstretched hand. It was a strange sight with the big fellow standing there with his arms stretched out like he was being crucified. Then bang the gun would go and he'd jerk his hand back, catching the pellet. I don't know why the fellows played the game. They'd go at it for hours and when it got dark they'd push off to Le Farer's bar on Elliot Road for a few shots and come back late, singing loudly.

The entire first floor was occupied by the Kaiser family. At least that's what I remember them being called. They were a mysterious lot who came and went like shadows. Whole books could have been written about what the neighbours had to say. True or false wasn't the issue. The stories themselves would take your breath away. Some said that they had friends in the underworld, others that they bought and sold people...and others still that they landed up as shipwrecked survivors in Diamond Harbour and found their way to Calcutta to seek their fortune. They looked distinctively Middle Eastern. The mother of them all, at least that's what we called her, was a huge woman who was all wrapped up in colourful loose silky garments. Everyone called her Kaiser Aunty.

We children were terrified of her. If we didn't obey the elders we'd be warned, *Kaiser Aunty will wrap you up in a big shawl and carry you off to a place from where you'll never return. Shhh! Can you hear those footsteps? There. That's Kaiser Aunty. She won't take no for an answer. If she walks into the house and asks for you then we'll have to hand you over. You understand? Kaiser Aunty will get you.* Uncle William even made up a song about her and he'd perform it when he was drunk. And everyone would laugh.

Then one evening, my playtime over, I was headed up the stairs when I saw Kaiser Aunty standing on the landing. I stopped dead in my tracks, scared out of my wits. When she started descending I turned and ran for my life, tripping and falling down the stairs. I blacked out. When I opened my eyes I found myself staring into the darkness of her face under the shawl. She picked me up, dusted my clothes and walked out. I staggered up the stairs, weeping with fright.

That was Christmas time, I remember, one of the three big times of the year. We spent a whole week decorating the tree with colourful baubles from New Market and we went off to midnight mass wrapped in warm clothes and hair well pomaded. It was quite another feeling being there amongst hundreds of other people attending mass together. Small as I was I could feel the specialness in the air and everyone looked so happy there and the bells rang and there were clouds of incense and the choir sang its heart out and Dad patted me on the head and smiled and everyone, yes everyone, really felt that Christ had just been born.

We ate all the next day as droves of friends and cousins dropped in with sweets and cakes and fruits and glugged some wine on the sly. The evening was for presents and Santa Claus (who was usually Uncle William dressed up) handed out the gifts.

Yes, that's the way Christmas went. Easter of course, was quite another type of occasion. Nahoums in New Market was the place we'd get our hot cross buns, Easter eggs and marzipan sweets from. I still remember the fellow behind the counter. Actually there were a couple of them and they all looked alike...gaunt, pale with large noses and nasal accents. *Take the mutton patties,* they'd say, *so fresh that they'll melt in your mouth.* Mum would supplement what we bought with homemade stuff like poottoo rice and dol dol. Easter Breakfast dissolved into Easter Lunch and then everyone would fall asleep and wake up in the evening and the elders would start drinking. Friends would come in from everywhere. Usually fair-weather friends like the Haleys, the Feltons, the Potsmans, Hughrice and others. They'd come, they'd eat and drink and slip into the shadows.

Apart from being a cop Ted Haley was also an ace freeloader. He'd turn up with a couple of friends and hang on till the booze got over. One day Dad decided to offer them a deadly concoction of mixed drinks and after just two shots they staggered around all over the place and finally had to be carried home. They didn't show up for a long time after that.

Diwali was filled with bombs, rockets and a host of other fireworks. Usually Dr Das, the family physician would join us. He'd bring along a large basket of crackers and we'd have a great time.

Calcutta of the 50s was quite another sort of place to be—more cosmopolitan, more flexible, relaxed. People were not afraid to be themselves. At least the people who Mum and Dad knew. Even in times when we were slipping down the ladder, we could still see a bit of the city's colour and revel in it. Every evening Anglo-Indian minstrels roamed the streets singly or in twos and threes singing and strumming on their guitars. You could stand at your window and listen to them and if you liked what they sang throw money down to them. Or if you didn't like what they sang you could ask them to sing something else. If they couldn't do that, they'd usually go away. Some persisted and people would be forced to throw a mug of water on them and chase them off.

There was a singer named Jimmy Lantern, a small fellow, who'd roam the by-lanes crooning in a rich deep voice. Everyone who heard him was amazed by the voice that flowed out of such a wee little fellow. He sang all of Dad's favourites and was once invited to croon at his birthday party. *Happy to do that,* he said, *but I won't come up to your home.*

Why's that? Dad wanted to know. And when he wanted to know something, he was like a hyena, he sank his teeth in and never let go until he got an answer which he believed to be true.

I'm a street singer, the man said quickly.

So just imagine you're on the street and sing, the hyena persisted.

I don't sing inside houses, mister.

There must be another reason. Dad wasn't going to give up. *Stop being such a stubborn fellow, dress up and come. You'll make more money in one evening than you've done all these years. You can relax after that. I've got friends in high places. They have contacts. And who knows, maybe you'll make it into one of the nightclubs on Park Street.*

Don't think so mister. Not with clothes like these and a face like this.

He stepped out of the shadows and stood under the streetlight. Dad let go of my hand when he saw the man. A frayed rag of a tie hung around a scrawny neck which supported a large misshapen head and a face with a deep scar that ran all the way along from the right corner of his mouth to above his right eyebrow. His clothes hung on him just as discarded garments hang on a scarecrow. *Well? What did I just say mister?*

Dad was so taken aback that he said perhaps what he didn't mean to say. *I'd never imagine that such a beautiful voice could come out of someone like you.*

Sorry mister. I just told you. I am not worth backing.

Maybe you'd make a good playback singer, Dad said limply.

I'm happy as I am.

Maybe you have a friend who can come along? Dad put his foot into his mouth.

You mean someone who can sing as well as me but is better looking? When's your party?

This Friday. Eight.

The man slipped into the shadows and a few minutes later we heard his voice waft into the night air.

How would you like to be
Down by the Seine with me?
Under the bridges of Paris with you
To make my dreams come true...
Darling I'll hold you tight....

Well, the man's friend didn't turn up for the party but at around ten we heard the man with a golden voice crooning his heart out from the street outside the front gate. The moon was full and the air was crisp and clear. Dad sent Mum and me down with a packed meal and a small bundle of notes but when we got there, he had left.

Even though I was still a child, the incident and the man had a profound impact on me. Strangely, I always thought of him along with Dad. There was some hidden connection. He also made me start thinking more about the many others who roamed the streets vending their talents and their wares. Early morning the Bakarkhani wallas would come around with their baskets on their heads wailing, *Baaa-kar-khaanee-wala, Baaa-kar-khaanee-wala.* The white flour parathas cooked in goat's fat were popular for breakfast. The other was a Tibetan bun baked with a piece of meat inside. Then there were the Alu Puri wallas and the Chat wallas and Puchka wallas. Calcutta's street vendors loved singing, hawking their delicacies with their very own melodies. Each area had its own brand of songsters. When our family fortunes were bright and our stomachs were full their voices sounded enchanting and entertaining. But when we had slipped down the ladder and had nothing at all, their voices became haunting. When there is no money and no hope of laying your hands on any food, the cry of Bakarkhani wallas and all the others loosen the tongue and make it float in a pool of saliva and the stomach begins to burn. *Drink cool water and you'll feel better,* Mum would say. *The more water the better. This is a good time to flush your insides.*

When I was a little older and we had hit really dire straits, I remember slipping out of the house by seven to go "window eating". I'd turn up at Khana Walla Khan's kathi kebab joint on Elliot Road and sitting on a small wooden crate would watch Mushtaq Khan prepare the *sigri*, expertly spreading coal chunks over its open mouth, setting a flame from beneath and sending up plumes which burnt my nose, watered my eyes and made me cough. Once he'd get the smoke under control and the coals had begun to glow, he'd lay skewered meat in rows across the glow, turning the rods slowly over the *sigri* mouth till they were cooked tender. Stripping the juicy pieces off the rods he'd pass them to Vilayat, a scrawny young man with a perpetual half open mouth and a forehead dripping perspiration. He was the fellow who did the final flourish, folding the succulent meat into white flour parathas along with sliced onions and green chillies, finally half rolling each in white grease paper he'd stack them up according to orders in newspaper bags. I got lucky once when Vilayat, taking pity on me while Mushtaq was busy with a customer, gave me a piece of meat wrapped in half a paratha. Nothing had ever tasted so good till then. But mostly, Mushtaq had no patience for my sniffing around. *Don't stare so hard, boy,* he would grunt, *they'll vanish and you'll have nothing to look at.*

Kathi Begum

During those Little Elliot Road years, life was still a little kind. That's the time when both Aunt Katherine, Dad's eldest sister, and Grandpa would come visiting. On one occasion when they arrived together, Grandpa from Kanpur and Aunt Katherine from Patna, the house was filled with food and music and laughter. Dad was in a particularly good mood and decided to take us all off for a picnic to the Botanical Gardens.

It was a beautiful day and the sky was so blue that it seemed like sadness had never existed. The two women had put together a big hamper and all we did was stuff our faces and loll around. In an hour or so Nora got bored and sprawling out with a book, went to sleep. Phillip, for the first time in our life together, decided to invite me for a ramble around the place. He led the way, picking up stones and chucking them at the trees. I followed him, imitating his action. It wasn't easy to copy him exactly because he was a big made, tough fellow who swung his arms and leapt into the air every time he threw a stone. I tried to follow his action and ended up falling on my face. Then he stopped and stepping back showed me how to do it. *This way, duckling*, he said with a grin. *Take a deep breath and then grip the stone and swing your arm around like this. Not just your arm but your whole body and when you throw you must behave like you are throwing your whole body with the stone, like this, whoooooooosh.*

I watched his athletic body spin in the air and the stone sail off into the trees. A moment later we heard an almighty thump. The stone had knocked a large green mango off its stem and brought it down out of the cluster of leaves. We gasped then whooped with delight and charged off to pick it up. Nearing the mango, we stopped. *Easy,* he whispered, *there's a watchman there, he's looking this way. Let's pretend we're playing a game.* So we chased each other around a bit and then fell over on the grass and wrestled. Tired, we threw ourselves on our backs in the tall grass and lay there looking up into the branches. Bright sunlight streamed through the foliage and fell in splashes around us. The mango lay between our heads and we could smell the sharp fresh tangy fragrance which lingered in the air around us.

It was all so happy and peaceful that I could have lay there forever. *I know I'm a bad brother,* Phillip suddenly said, running his fingers through his closely cropped hair, his tanned profile, sharp against the bright green background.

I didn't understand entirely what he was trying to say. *I've never liked you,* he continued. *Never liked you at all. You know why? Because you're everyone's pet duckling. You always have been. I'm the one no one likes. I'm big and strong so everyone thinks they can tell me what they want to and I'm not to complain. You, you are small and mamby-pamby and say sweet things to everyone and they think you are cute. Grandpa and Aunt Katherine love you. You are their teddy bear. And me? They just chase me away. You know in Kanpur in Grandpa's house, he'd hit me with a stick every time he caught me breaking guavas. A big stick, the one he chased snakes away with. And you – he'd put you on his knee and rock you about the place. He never ever did that with me. Remember the time he got a photograph taken with you? He called a fellow with a big special camera who did the job. I never liked you ever since you were born. Not because of you but because of everyone else. Now there's no one here. There's just you and I so let's have a good time and pretend we're not brothers.*

So we pretended that we were friends. Got up, pocketed the mango and ran off, taking turns in chasing each other and sometimes wrestling on the grass. When we got back to the others it was time for another round of face stuffing. Later, we slipped off and quietly swung into the branches of a banyan tree. As usual, Phillip was stronger and swifter and he vanished up the branches. I tried to follow him and losing my balance toppled over and landed on my back on the grassy floor. I lay there quite still, a little stunned. Grandpa turned up and bending down gently made me sit up, *Are you hurt?* He asked.

No, said the voice from the branches up above. *He's dead.*

Shut up, snapped the old man.

I'm God, the voice replied, *and you don't tell God to shut up. I'm sending my angels down to carry away the dead duckling.*

Come down you little rascal, snapped Grandpa.

Come and get me, come and get me.

A moment later Dad turned up and scaled the tree and collaring Phillip, brought him down. *Why did you push your little brother off a branch?* he asked angrily.

I didn't, I didn't, he squealed.

He didn't, I said.

I did, he changed his line. *It was all a joke. To toughen the fellow up. He's such a baby.*

Now don't you ever do that again, you hear me? You hear me? Don't you ever do that again, Dad warned him.

I'll try not to.

And what's this in your pocket? Take it out and show me. A mango? You've been stealing mangoes? I've had enough of you.

Just one, Dad.

What do you mean by just one? You stole a mango. You aren't supposed to break anything here. This is the Botanical Gardens. You hear me?

You can't expect him to be an angel, Gordon. Boys will be boys. Just let him be. Let the boy be. It was Aunt Katherine. *Now you come here Phillip,* she said.

I watched Aunt Katherine lead him away. *Are you okay?* Dad asked me.

Yes, he's fine, Grandpa replied.

Dad walked back to the picnic spot and Grandpa and I sat in the tall grass, quietly. Some time later Phillip returned with a football. *Look what Aunt Katherine gave us,* he said with a broad grin. *Come on.*

So off we went and played into the afternoon.

When the light changed into a drowsy lukewarm, we boarded a country boat and rowed down the Hooghly river, following the curving bank. The boatmen, two wiry characters, sang their way along and stopped when they had reached the ghat near Howrah bridge. We climbed off and headed for a large cab that rattled us home. Once home, Dad was a lot more sober than usual because his elder sister was visiting. He was scared of her. Whenever she came visiting, he'd be on his best behaviour and become a gem of a husband and father. To his good fortune, he usually had a job when she came to stay, so he managed to keep out of her way.

Aunt Katherine was an enormous woman with a wicked sense of humour, fiercely loyal, loud and all-encompassing. She filled the room whenever she entered and bowled her way through the toughest of arguments. Nothing seemed too difficult to handle once she had laid her hefty hands on it. Back in Patna she was somewhat of a local legend. When her husband Sajjid Sahab, a civil rights activist, was gunned down in the streets during a demonstration, she started a school in his memory, *for unfortunate Muslim kids* she'd often say. And their parents loved her for it. *Kathi Begum,* they called her. *The mother of the unwanted, the voice of the silent, the champion of the misunderstood. The negotiator.* These terms of course are refined English versions of the raw originals, smelling of passion and respect.

A month rarely went by without a report from Patna via the grapevine about the Begum's latest achievement. One piled on the other creating a formidable mountain that grew from being a curiosity to a threat. There was the time when the inmates of the prison climbed on to the tiled roof in the pouring rain and refused to come down, protesting against the communal behaviour of the warden. When all efforts to bring them down failed, the Begum was called in.

Gaping policeman watched the enormous woman scale ladder after ladder until she reached the roof, cheered on by the protestors. After an hour's negotiation which appeared to the audience down below more like a long lost mother being reunited with her family, she turned to the crowd and delivered what appeared to be an impassioned speech. Though the blasts of rain, thunder and lightning overshadowed the sound of her words they nevertheless heightened the drama that she so powerfully orchestrated.

When the performance was over, she guided them all down safely, handing them over to the prison authorities who didn't know exactly how to respond to her success. Unused to being respectful and appreciative of women, they called her *sir.* Her maids received her at the gate and she rode her tonga home, waving regally to people who cheered her on her way. The local press had a great time the next day, pulling the prison administration to shreds, instigating the suspension of the warden.

We had heard this story several times over, along with many others. But this was like the mother of all her exploits. Grandpa told the story like a criminal lawyer would. Facts, details, highlights, observations, quietly and firmly presented, his small body sitting elegantly in his armchair, stabbing the air with his right forefinger, leaning forward and staring at his listeners, pausing and then smiling almost triumphantly as if he was once more back in some district court on the verge of splitting a case wide open. He was such a quiet and composed man, it really was a miracle how he had survived his numerous children.

Uncle William's version was far more dramatic than Grandpa's. That's probably because it had been enhanced by six pegs of Triple X rum. And he'd end by claiming that he was going to convert to Islam and move to Patna. So typical of him. A man of riotous excess. Five marriages, three live-ins and innumerable one night stands, Uncle had a special way with women. Nobody was quite sure what they found in this fellow who had an enormous head balancing on a lanky body and arms and legs so long that one missed his body sometimes. But they loved him all the same. Harold, his brother, was more the short stocky sort of chap and when something excited him he'd jump up and down, throwing the pitch of his voice at the roof. His versions of Aunt Katherine's escapade were punctuated with a rapid slapping of his forehead and interjections of *fixed them, fixed them good and proper!*

Dad's version was reserved for times when only our family was around and he was in one of his drunken, sentimental moods. Mum said nothing, only smiled wistfully to herself.

Anyway, the long and the short of the story was that the Muslim population of Patna wanted her to stand for the State elections. She toyed with the idea and often made up speeches and delivered them when she was alone in her room. Actually she wasn't really alone because I was usually there with her. She called me her pet pup whenever she visited. I'd lie there in her bed, pretending to sleep, watching her through half-shut eyes. She'd stand in front of the long mirror and smile and grunt and wave her arms about and flex her muscles, and swear and curse and grin and wave.

Once when she caught me watching, *what do you think my pup? Will you vote for me?*

Yes.

That's why you are my pup. I'm going to carry you off with me. I'm going to tell that irresponsible father of yours that I'm going to take you away and make you into a politician. You've got the seeds in there. How about it? Want to be a leader? I'll make you a leader. I'll make you into someone special. Sean, I'll make you a revolutionary. Know what a revolutionary is? Well, he's someone who won't take shit from anyone, knows what he wants and goes out there and makes life better, at any cost. You've got it in you. But of course you have to get bigger and stronger. And you know how you get bigger and stronger? Eat lots of vegetables along with meat.

I disliked vegetables because I didn't like the way they were cooked at home. So she would go off to the local market and pick up all sorts of greens and come back and cook them up. She was also a fabulous cook and could turn out delicious tandoori delicacies to supplement the large bowl of boiled vegetables that she'd place before me. She'd produce kebabs and parathas on her own sigri which was made with mud and an old damaged metal bucket. Beef, mutton and chicken were transformed into delectable platefuls of kebabs and lumps of dough into eight layered parathas. After every three chunks of boiled pumpkin I was given a piece of kebab and paratha. If I fared well, she'd take me off to Colombo Stores in New Market and buy me small glass animals filled with coloured water.

Whenever she returned to Patna, the glass animals were my only companions. Each of them had a name. In fact I'd talk to Popo the penguin when Dad shouted drunkenly in the next room, ask Simba the lion to come and help when Mum was being beaten black and blue, cradle Zaza the zebra when Phillip once went missing. They may not have been able to do anything to help but the fact that they were there was enough.

No one could really understand why Aunt Katherine found me special. I remember Aunt Katherine's last visit. She had come to stay with us for nearly a month and had to leave a week earlier as there were some legal problems regarding the boundaries of her property. A day before her departure, we found ourselves the only ones seated at the breakfast table. She was in a particularly agitated mood and kept mumbling curses. Then she stopped suddenly and raised her heavy hand and brought it down on a fly on the table top with such force that my plate bounced, sending the fried egg into the air.

Flies! I can't stand them! she grunted. *They remind me of all the people I have to deal with. Nothing but irritating flies buzzing about.* The yolk of the egg had splashed all over the table, its dripping yellow glistening in the morning light. *But you aren't a fly. There's something different in you, boy. I've told you that before so I'm not going to say it again. You hear me?*

I nodded and looked at the glisten of the egg yolk slowly fading.

Sorry, I frightened you. That's the sort of person I am. Like iron. But you aren't going to be like iron. If you try hard enough, you'll be tough. But not like iron. I think you'll end up another sort of revolutionary. The dreamer kind. Who knows? You may even start writing. I know. I can see it in you.

I felt a little stupid and out of place listening to her as if she was talking to someone much older than I was. That's what was so confusing. Either I was treated like a baby or an adult by everyone around. Including her. I wasn't given a chance to be myself. I wasn't really allowed to grow up like a child grows up, step by step, moment by moment, experience by experience. Instead I was pushed backwards and forwards at everyone's convenience. I had no choice.

Well, what's going on in that little head of yours?

Nothing.

Surely something's going on.

I looked at her sitting there with her large hands placed firmly on either side of her plate, her broad shoulders set back and relaxed, in command, her enormous brown eyes set into a large tanned oval face and her hair tied back in a neat bun. She looked at me as if she was waiting for me to respond so that she could ambush me. But I said nothing, just kept staring at her.

I sometimes feel that there's a hell of a lot going on inside that head of yours. Maybe I'm wrong and it's just the way you use those eyes of yours. I mean the way you look, your stare. It's so deep, like it goes right in. The way you are looking at me. What do you see inside?

I let my eyes take over and looked deep into her eyes and I saw nothing. Nothing. It was all blank and dark and very lonely.

So, what do you see?

Nothing.

You mean I'm dead?

I didn't reply.

I *don't know what you are going to do with your life*, she said, putting a piece of burnt toast, something she relished, into her mouth, *but you'll surely get somewhere*. She paused and cleared her throat, looked into my eyes, her own suddenly filling with tears. *I know that I'm not going to be there when that happens. I'm not going to be there*, she said quietly.

That night I couldn't sleep and she lay beside me and told me stories of her life as a child in Kanpur, the mother she once had and the maid who brought her up as her very own. *We owe so much to other people that we never really get a chance to repay them for their love and kindness. You know Sean, life is a gift that most of us don't know what to do with...and who to thank. So we end up taking it for granted. Go to sleep now, I'm bothering you too much. Before I say sleep well I just want to tell you something. Remember, if you ever need me, just call out and I'll be there.*

But how will you hear me if you are far away?

I will. You'll see.

An hour before she had to leave to catch her train a fire broke out in the wood depot nearby. We could see the flames rise menacingly and the wind blew them across to the nearby buildings. A sheet of fire spread. There was smoke everywhere. I lay curled up on Aunt Katherine's metal trunk, imagining that I was safe.

Get up now, Mum held me by the hand. *Get up now and let's go down and drop Aunty to the cab.*

But when we reached the front gate, the cab had left because the fire was spreading and drivers had been ordered by the fire brigade to leave the street.

Aunt Katherine grabbed the tin trunk and hoisting it on to her head like a coolie, walked off through the smoke, not listening to our protests. We stood there helplessly watching her leave.

A few months later, in 1956, the Begum died. A right wing gang attacked her house one night, dragged her out and shot her thrice in the stomach, leaving her struggling in a pool of blood under a streetlight. No one intervened. They found her the next day outside her front door at the end of a metre wide bloody trail. She had crawled, dying, to her own home.

The police concluded that she had committed suicide and her burial was hurriedly performed. Uncle William swore over his own dead body that he'd rustle up a gang of toughs and take them down to Patna and finish off the bastards. Uncle Harold said that he'd have a question raised in Parliament. Of course he didn't really know how he was going to do that. Uncle Patrick took the cake. He started a Foundation in her memory for poor Muslim children. When he had raised 'enough' money, he went off to Kumaon where he bought himself some land, built a cosy bungalow and settled down to grow apples.

Her going left a void in our family. Just like a bullet hole does. Nobody knew exactly what to do with it. I was just five and didn't understand the meaning of dying. In fact, I was under the impression that humans were the only living beings who lived on forever and when there were too many people piled up in one place they were shunted off somewhere else...to other cities, other countries, other planets. How wrong I was. I had actually lost someone very dear to me, someone who believed that there was something special in me. Even though she often scared the daylights out of me, I had come to love her. Her passing made me realise that humans, however strong they might be, don't live on forever—and some die tragically before their time. I had lost a kindred soul, I had lost a friend and I began to feel fragile and exposed. If someone as big and strong and powerful as Aunt Katherine could get gunned down and be left to die pitifully, what chance did I have to survive? None at all. I could be blown away like a dried leaf.

I couldn't stand the sight of blood for some time after that. I couldn't eat meat and I wet my bed at night. Nightmares visited me so often that I hardly slept.

I think I'm getting braver about remembering even though it isn't easy at all and hurts like hell and is embarrassing. I'm pushing myself to remember and the more I remember, the closer I come to the essential truth about myself. Is it worth it now, lying here as I am, struggling to break through this pain? I am afraid to open my eyes. The last time I opened my eyes there were strange faces around me. Is it worth remembering anything about myself? Should I just let it all go and stop once and for all this search for meaning, for ablution? Must be the Catholic in me, this need to confess.

How did I get here? How did I get here? Will someone please tell me how I got here?

There is no answer just a soft murmur of voices. Sombre words balancing on some horizon far away.

I open my eyes and focus on the fellow sitting beside me.

You'll live, you'll be fine, he is saying. *Took time getting the pieces out of you. The last one went deep. Breathe easy now, breathe easy. You'll be fine.*

There's another fellow here too. He's the uniformed man. The one who has been by my side all the while. He doesn't ask any more questions, just sits there looking at me. Expressionless. He wants information from me. What if I let him into my world and drown him in all that I remember?

Something terrible happened, he says suddenly, noticing that my eyes have focussed on him and I appear to be alert and somewhat in control of my senses. *Something terrible happened. And you were there and saw it all. You were a part of it all. We need you to talk as soon as you are able.*

Time is running out. What's your name? Just tell me your name. Who is that woman you were with? The one who got shot.

Shot? What about me? Have I got shot?

Just tell us what happened. Anything that you can remember. You had a gun with you. A machine pistol. Where…

I close my eyes and try to shut him out but his voice continues coming at me. Those wretched marbles are bouncing all over the place. I search for the comforting smell of blood to open that secret door and sink back into memory, be cushioned by its certainty… however hurting, however overwhelming…

I'm going back now. I am receding. Going back. I feel safe there. Memory. Memory. Memory.

Living and Dying

Not long after Aunt Katherine's death, when Uncle Patrick and Uncle William were visiting our Little Elliot Road apartment, an argument broke out at the dining table over some jewellery and cash that she had kept with Dad. It had vanished and his brothers wanted an explanation.

You! shouted Uncle William, *you stole the jewellery and the cash. You used it on your women!*

That's enough, whispered Grandpa, *can't you see that you are insulting him in front of his family?*

It's high time everyone got to know the real Gordon. The blighter's been bullshitting all of us for far too long. And you spoilt him, Uncle William accused Grandpa.

I didn't spoil him. He never really had a mother and you boys were of no help. Can't you accept that once and for all? Grandpa's voice had an edge to it.

You spoilt him, persisted Uncle William.

Don't bully an old man, Mum interrupted.

Imelda, keep out of it, Dad said sharply.

Come on children let's go to bed. You shouldn't be here when adults are arguing, she said softly.

Stay right here all of you, Dad banged on the table. *Stay right here!*

You need to hide behind your family, eh? Uncle Patrick butted in.

Shut up, Dad splashed his soup all over his brother's shirt. *You aren't in a position to talk Patrick. You've been raising money in Katherine's name. A Trust? Ha! Trust! My big fat toe!*

Uncle Patrick threw his plateful of mutton curry and rice in Dad's face.

Will you stop this nonsense? shouted Grandpa.

You touch my Dad and I'll kill you! said Phillip lifting a butter knife.

Me too, Nora pitched in.

I don't believe what I'm hearing! Uncle William stood up and started trying to lift the table from his end to turn it over.

What do you think you are doing? Mum sounded anxious.

Come on out, come on out! his brothers shouted at Dad. *Let's sort this out downstairs.*

When the three of them were walking out, Phillip threw the butter knife at Uncle Patrick. He didn't turn around, just kept going.

After a big commotion downstairs, the three returned, faces bloodied, shirts torn. They collapsed, one on the floor and two on the couches.

No one dared go near them.

All night they cursed each other.

The next morning Grandpa's blood pressure went through the roof. Three days later his heart condition got worse. In a week, the doctor wanted to shift him to a hospital.

He said that he wanted to die.

That declaration seemed to scare everyone off. Mum stayed by him and when he seemed to be sinking; we were sent over to the the Chongs downstairs whilst Mum patiently tended to him and Dad stood in the bedroom helplessly. He was too frightened to face his father's death.

One evening when dusk darkened the air, I managed to slip into Grandpa's room. He was alone and I did not want to disturb him so I stood quietly inside the doorway, listening to his laboured breathing.

Sean, is that you?

Yes, Grandpa.

Why are you standing there? Come in, come here, sit down beside me. Sit. That's it. Look at me. Don't be afraid to look at me. I don't have some sort of contagious disease! You aren't going to get infected if you look at me.

I looked at him.

Ah yes. That's it. That's my boy. There's magic in the way you look. When I first saw your newborn eyes I remember how certain I was that there was something special in you. You hear me?

Yes, Grandpa.

That's good. You will never really know how much Katherine loved you. You were her son more than anyone else's.

His wrinkled bony hands held mine, clutching on to them like a drowning man grips a straw.

I can't sit up son, there're these pipes and tubes stuck into me. They're trying to keep me alive. But there's nothing more to live for, nothing at all. Now go to the window and look out. Go on. Look out.

I skirted his bed and walked to the window.

What do you see?

I see buildings.

Not the buildings or the street below. Look carefully at the sky. Yes, the sky. What do you see there?

A star.

Yes, the star. Listen, it's telling you something. Can you hear it? Can you?

No, Grandpa.

Well, its saying—Sean, be like me. Everyone can see me but no one can touch me. I'm here and I am not here. I attach myself to no one and nothing. And still I shine brightly.

I stood there at the window and looked at the star, distant and yet visible. Yes, I said.

I returned to his bedside and sat down.

Don't hold on to anyone or anything Sean, everything passes away. Everything. Just live your best. You only have yourself and no-one else.

He closed his eyes and his breathing became uneven. Dad walked in and looked at me, surprised, opened his mouth to tell me something then closed it again. Instead he sat down in an arm chair and looked at me sadly. After a while, Grandpa stirred again.

Gordon, said Grandpa weakly, *I'm sorry that I neglected you. If you are what you are today it's because of me and my neglect. After your mother died I should have spent more time with you. You were the littlest. Just three. They bullied and battered you, your brothers. I did nothing. All I did was keep running away to the courts and the districts, leaving you to defend yourself. I failed.*

Don't say that, Dad said quietly. *That was long ago. That's all over now.*

Nothing is ever over. Nothing.

A silence settled on us.

I went to the window and looked out at the star hanging up there in the Calcutta sky. Behind me, a ghostly rattling sound began. It became a gurgle. Then a rattle again. Grandpa was choking. I was too frightened to turn around.

Dad went frantic. *Imelda, Imelda, he's going, he's going! Come fast. Hurry!*

She came running into the room and they wept and prayed as Grandpa's rattle became so loud that the hair on the back of my neck stood up on end and I began shivering. I couldn't pray.

Mum sounded frantic. *He's gone dear Jesus, he's gone. Jesus, Mary and Joseph, take his heart and his soul. I believe in God the Father Almighty, Creator of Heaven and Earth and in Jesus Christ his only son our Lord who was conceived by the power of the Holy Spirit, born of the Virgin Mary, suffered under Pontius Pilate, was crucified, died and was buried. On the third day he arose again from the dead...I believe in the Holy Catholic Church, the communion of saints, the forgiveness of sins, the resurrection of the body and life everlasting...*

Lights everywhere suddenly went off. It was pitch black. The sky was filled with stars. Dad picked me up in his arms and left the room.

Mum continued to babble prayers. Nora and Phillip stood clutching onto each other on the top of the flight of stairs, outside the front door, crying.

In the weeks that followed, our home was thrown into disarray. Dad went off to bury Grandpa in Kanpur and help to sort out his estate, whilst Mum wandered from room to room, ghostlike. She was as good as dead herself. I didn't understand her relationship with Grandpa then because I was far too young. Later, I came to understand what they meant to each other. She had entered his home as a young bride of sixteen and he had been like a father to her. She looked up to him and admired his determined spirit, his patience and generosity. He was her emotional anchor. She was the only one he really trusted. When we lived in the little cottage on his estate in Kanpur, Mum ensured that he was taken care of, that he got his meals on time, lived in a clean and comfortable home and was shielded from the avarice of his many children who seemed determined to strip him of his wealth. And it wasn't just his children alone. When news of his death reached Kanpur, before his body turned up there, his gardener cleaned out his entire library of books and sold them by weight to a waste paper merchant. A tragic end to an incredible life.

If Aunt Katherine made me feel wanted and special, Grandpa was my role model. Lawyer, traveller, brilliant speaker, rebel and guide—he was all that and more. A quiet, resolute man, he had lived his life just the way he had wanted to. The son of a zamindar of Tikamnagar, Narendra Prasad Varma was a reserved young fellow of twelve when he decided to leave home. He wasn't going to be part of the hell house that his home had been reduced to. Nor could he live with his violent father who had the habit of beating his farmhands silly and hanging some of them by their ankles from the old mango tree by the river. *This is the only language that they understand,* the man would say with a sneer. *They are thieves and shirkers and totally unreliable. Give them an inch and they'll take a hundred miles and run around the globe three times and leave you with nothing. They only understand the language of the stick.*

Bipin Prasad Varma, Grandpa's father, treated his family like his personal slaves, doing with them what he pleased. They were terrified of him. His two younger brothers fled the farm in fear of their lives and his sister ended her life in a well. As for his own family, well, he had a wife and kept her sister too. There were children everywhere. Grandpa would somehow have stayed on if it wasn't for the night that he saw his father rape the new bride of the youngest farmhand. A week later they found his body floating in the lake on the edge of the property.

Horrified, Grandpa fled to the dusty city of Kanpur. The kindness of strangers pulled him through until he ended up as office cleaner in the chambers of a prominent barrister of the time. He ate and slept and listened to things legal almost every moment of the day. From theft and murder to attacks on British officers, he heard them all. He was the silent listener, witness to the wheeling and dealing of the times. Even the so-called political activists who appeared to be fighting for the country's freedom were suspect. Often Barrister Ram Lal Choudhury would chat with Naren when the day's work was over while he sipped brandy from a bottle hidden in the drawer of his desk.

So Naren, what do you make of that case? Come on boy, let's have your opinion.

Reluctantly, he would express his point of view and when asked to explain further, he would methodically build up an argument in support of his view. Ram Lal was quickly impressed and saw in the runt of a teenager the mind and spirit of an astute lawyer. The more he listened to what the young fellow had to say, the more he was convinced that Naren was going to turn out a courtroom fox. So he got him through school and law college, made him his assistant and then launched him into a career in criminal law.

The young man took to his profession with ease and enthusiasm, specialising in crimes against rural labour, travelling deep into the interiors of Eastern Uttar Pradesh and parts of Bihar. Whilst his colleagues were busy raking in their earnings in the fast growing towns and cities, Grandpa settled for the agricultural heartlands, picking up cases and fighting them out for bags of rice, chickens and other farm produce. He travelled in ekkas, tongas, bullock carts, on bicycles and often on foot, spending the night under the open sky, in wayside glades. People often opened their doors to him and treated him with kindness that he knew he would never be able to repay. His persistence paid off and gradually the cash started trickling in.

All the while, his colleagues reminded him that it was time he started a family. But he adamantly remained single, settling instead for the company of a young widow who he often visited. Nothing came of it as Naren was a man who was constantly on the move with no desire to settle down—until he was bowled over by Iris O'Neil, the beautiful daughter of Patrick O'Neil, an indigo planter. Though it was one of those love at first sight stories, the occasion when they met wasn't a particularly pleasant one. It took place on the lawns of the O'Neil bungalow when Grandpa, representing his client, had set up a meeting for an out-of-court settlement. Patrick had been dragged to court for physically ill-treating his plantation workers. He had got away with it several times in the past but on this occasion, it was serious as two of them had died. When the matter was finally settled and compensation agreed upon, the young Indian got up to leave. That's when Iris appeared as if out of a dream, in flowing white, walking across the lawn towards them with a tray of tea. The sunlight set her auburn hair on fire and her deep green eyes settled on him.

Several chance encounters later, letters began passing between them, carried by none other than Himmat Ram the barber who specialised in home visits for haircuts and shaves. He was among the very few who visited both white and brown homes in Kanpur, pedalling from place to place in a crisp white trouser and jacket, lugging his little black box on the carrier of his bicycle.

The messenger pulled off a number of successful sorties until he was nabbed red-handed by the irate O'Neil who pummelled him silly and then proceeded to take his bicycle apart. After dealing with him he turned on his daughter who fled into her room and locked herself in. Three days of silence passed and on the fourth day when the door of the room was broken open they discovered that Iris had escaped through the window and run away. He quickly gathered a posse of toughs and arrived at Grandpa's home only to find that he wasn't there. They broke into the property and after a thorough search found no sign of his daughter.

The district machinery rolled into action and after a couple of weeks finally halted, sinking into inertia. There was no sign of either of them. They had eloped to Calcutta to marry in a Buddhist temple as she didn't want a Hindu marriage and he didn't want a Christian marriage. The honeymoon was spent on a friend's farm on the outskirts of Allahabad, extending from two weeks to a month and then six months. Grandpa's legal practice suffered and he started getting concerned about his finances so he convinced his reluctant wife to return to Kanpur. The wounds healed quickly and the dust settled down but neither Patrick O'Neil nor his wife had a clue that their daughter had married in a Buddhist temple. If they had, they would both have refused to meet her. At a stretch, being Hindu was more acceptable than being Buddhist.

When the first child was stillborn Iris went into a fit of mourning out of which she couldn't be rescued. It lasted months. She wasted away. Her parents were hysterical when they finally heard that their daughter had gotten married in a Buddhist temple. They wouldn't listen to Grandpa but called in the parish priest Father Paul instead. Their home was invaded by the priest and his retinue who sprinkled every nook and cranny with holy water.

The cleansing took three days with the enthusiastic priest drawing on all his knowledge of evil spirit chasing and putting on a dramatic performance. And after it was over, they all settled down to a long drink and a sumptuous meal.

A few days later, Iris was up and about. They married in the church. It was a quiet affair with Father Paul piously damning other faiths and encouraging the young couple to bring up their children as good Catholics even though one parent was a 'Hindoo'. Grandpa was far too deeply in love with his wild and beautiful Irish wife to argue. But when Katherine was born Iris announced that though she preferred the child to be baptised she had no objection if she chose to follow another faith when she became a teenager. Of course, the girl ended up marrying an Anglo-Indian drunk who beat her silly and drove her into the arms of another husband, accepting Islam.

Grandma and Grandpa produced babies like rabbits. There were twelve in all, and Dad was the youngest. And whilst he was busy in the courts she devoted herself to child rearing, bringing her children up like good Catholics but allowing them once they were teenagers to follow any faith they chose. And then she died of pneumonia just after Dad's third birthday. Aunt Katherine took charge and bullied her brothers into shape until she left home and life gave way to chaos once again. The eleven of them broke into gangs and marked off their territories, waging bitter battles, swinging from ceiling fans, jumping from sideboards, fencing like pirates on the enormous walnut wood dining table and finally falling asleep in various parts of the house. Dad's safe place was inside the large soiled linen basket. Once the house-cleaners carried the entire basket to the washing trough and dunked him in along with the linen to soak. Tangled with the sheets, he nearly drowned.

Afraid that his children would go astray when they grew up, Grandpa built several cottages on his estate. Many of his offspring stayed on for convenience. Dad and Mum lived in one of those cottages.

His children fleeced him and made no attempt to look after him. Mum being the youngest daughter-in-law was given the job of taking care of 'the old bugger'. Every day he sat in his room in the Kanpur courts desperately trying to compete with younger and smarter lawyers. In the evening he would return exhausted, down a stiff brandy or two, play patience, chat with Mum for a while and then settle down to a simple meal, retiring in the ancient house, alone. None of his family visited him. All he got from them were desperate notes requesting for money or some favour or the other.

He had no attachments. Just you, Mum told me years after he had passed away, laying her hand gently on my shoulder. *There was something between you two. I don't know what it was. You know, when you were born at home that rainy August evening, he stood outside in the garden with an umbrella, waiting patiently. And when he first saw you he said, just like baby Jesus in the manger. That was enough to send everyone present into a spin, Sean. They didn't like it one single bit. You were considered the favoured one after that. Your brother was furious, your sister sulked. And if you really want to know why you are so afraid of water it's because when you were a baby, your brother went into your room, picked you up and dropped you into a tub of water, holding your head under till your body went limp. You were dead, my son, and they brought you back.*

That means that Grandpa loved no one else.

He did. He had this great way of loving people. But he was never attached to anyone but you.

What about his father?

He was the only person he couldn't love. Even before he died, he said that he had always wished that he could have forgiven his father. He always wanted to be able to love and respect his father. He was a good man, your Grandpa. And I've sometimes seen a little of him in your father. I blame no one, not even your father for being the way he is. Because I know somewhere deep down inside he's a lost child. He was hammered into pulp by his eleven siblings. Sometimes I want to protect him from the world, from people, from women, from his own erring self. But he's like a criminal who doesn't want to reform and challenges himself with more daring crimes, hoping that he can destroy himself. He doesn't. He can't.

Mum's words sank into me like molten lead, passing deep into the very pit of my stomach and lay there along with other bits and pieces shoved down by the adult experiences of living. I didn't get a chance to grow up naturally but was forced to see the world through adult eyes, listen to it through adult ears. Touch, feel and think like an adult. In fact, I can't claim to have had much of a childhood. Whatever I did have consisted of a few precious moments snatched from the grubby paws of deprivation. Even then, whilst I enjoyed those moments there was always a bitter aftertaste. I couldn't believe that life was being kind to me. The two adults who made me feel special, who made me feel like a real child were Aunt Katherine and Grandpa.

Off to the Trenches

For weeks after Grandpa's death, Mum could hear his voice in her head and Dr Das was often called in to deal with her hysteria. Unable to cope with the stress, Dad started returning home late from work, sometimes even spending the night out. Occasionally, he would also call a few friends over for a drink. Sigrid, his boss's secretary, would often join them. Mum avoided such evenings. She'd either stay in bed or take us out for a film and dinner. On rare occasions, she'd decide to be sociable and join the party, only to start sagging after a couple of hours. The first signs that she was about to pass out was when she'd repeat herself when talking to someone. A blankness would spread across her face.

Sigrid was the first to notice these signals. She'd gently guide her away from the party and Nora would take her to bed. Mum rarely resisted and seemed to appreciate Sigrid's interceptions until she began to suspect that there was something fishy going on between Dad and her. And so she began to resist Sigrid's attention and would sit and look at Dad with a mixture of pity and disgust. This would infuriate him further.

Why do you look at me like that? What's wrong with you? Say something, woman! I've never understood this habit of yours.

But like always, she said nothing.

She was polite to Sigrid whenever she visited, but a certain coolness had settled into their friendship. And then, the inevitable happened—

Sigrid stayed over one night and Mum caught her with Dad on the couch. Mum said nothing, but went around the apartment switching on all the lights before returning to bed. Dad barged into the bedroom. *What's gotten into you, Imelda? Why have you put on all the lights? What you saw, it was nothing.* Then he noticed me peeping from under the covers on the bed. *What are you staring at?* After he left the room, I heard him switching off all the lights around the house. Mum lay on her back staring at the ceiling.

In the days that followed, Mum surfaced from her stupor and her fits of hysteria subsided. Life at home seemed 'normal' again even though all of us were aware that Dad was meeting Sigrid somewhere else. When he stayed out overnight, Mum never asked him for an explanation and he never provided one. Dad continued his affair with the tall, exquisite Scandinavian until the company they worked for hit a reef and was forced to sell out. Sigrid left for home and Dad was jobless.

That was the time, once again, that the family fortunes began to change. He'd spend entire nights sitting at the dining table, drinking and sobbing. It wasn't nice to see my father cry. He was a devastatingly handsome fellow with big broad shoulders, a distinguished aquiline nose and high forehead. So when that sort of a person collapsed from inside, it was a pathetic sight. He seemed to shrink.

Life at home went into a limbo of sorts and as resources rapidly dwindled, Dad decided that we should all move out of the apartment on Little Elliot Road as it was too expensive to maintain, considering that he was without a job. Whilst he was busy looking for a smaller apartment that was more affordable, we were packed off to Coimbatore to stay for a while with Mum's parents.

That was the first train journey I remember. Crammed into a packed compartment, we set off on a long slow chug by steam train that would take us three days and two nights all the way along the east coast of the country, crossing two States and into the third. We took turns at the window so many times that a well meaning and friendly family across allowed us to also sit at their window. Mum's angelic smile and huge mop of wavy hair disarmed them, but they probably felt sorry for her as well. She was having a tough time controlling Phillip. The fellow constantly jumped about the place, climbing up and down from one bunk to the other. I even saw some passengers snap at Phillip. One or two even pinched him hard. But that wouldn't stop the frisky chap.

Phillip and I shared the upper bunk and lay there staring at the dirty cream paint peeling off the roof of the carriage. *Why are you such a boring fellow?* he asked. *You're always doing the right thing. Such a goody-goody. Are you scared? You're such a sissy! You do all the right things because you want everyone to like you. That's why Grandpa liked you and Aunt Katherine liked you and no one gets angry with you. You think you are so smart. I should have got rid of you when I could.*

The way he talked scared me so I closed my eyes and pretended to go to sleep, eventually nodding off. I was woken up by a shout. It was the fellow below us who had been feeling sorry for Mum. *Arre! Your son up there has thrown a jhoota ice cream stick and cup on my wife! Madam this is not right. All this time we have sat quietly when he was misbehaving himself. Now this is the limit. Chee! Ask him to come down and apologise at once!*

Mum looked dumbstruck. The man's wife, a small woman wrapped up in an enormous sari, tried to pacify him but he ignored her. Their twins started crying loudly because they had been rudely woken up by his shouting. *Shut them up or I'll throw them out of the window,* he said to his wife. She was appalled. Then he looked up and straight into my eyes as I peered down at him.

So it was you! he said viciously. *I thought you were the better of the two. Come down and apologise.*

I didn't have time to explain that I didn't do it because I had been asleep. Turning to Phillip I found him pretending to sleep. It was obvious because I could see his eyelids moving as he struggled to keep them shut.

Come down at once, growled the man, as other passengers woke up and gathered around to see what was happening. I cowered under my shawl. He stood up and yanked the shawl off.

Don't bully the child, said one of the passengers. *Children are bound to make mistakes when their parents don't bring them up like proper Indians, in a cultured way. Let the boy be.*

But the fellow wouldn't have it that way. He wanted me down so I climbed down meekly and apologised for having thrown a dirty ice cream stick and cup at his wife.

Now go to bed and don't do any more mischief. And tell your brother to behave himself tomorrow morning or I'll lodge a complaint with the railway police.

The next morning Phillip behaved like an angel whilst I sat grumpily wondering what to do. Mum was so helpless that she could do nothing. Nora kept reading a book and refused to look up. As more and more people got on and off, the journey became increasingly interesting. The battered aluminium *thalis* with railway food came and went, followed by vendors hawking all sorts of eatables, from puffed rice to puris and bhaji to baskets of wild fruits and peanuts. Mum was on a tight budget and her stern looks as baskets of goodies passed by made us keep our silence.

There were three occasions during the journey when the compartment was so crowded that I could hardly breathe. Breaking out into a cold sweat, I gasped for air and felt life oozing out of me. *I can't breathe, I can't breathe, its stuffy,* I wheezed. My heart beat so hard that I thought it was going to explode. This had happened so many times before in other situations. It frightened me. I couldn't understand what was happening to me.

I had, I could sense, started to fear crowds and closed spaces.

It was quite pleasant when we reached Coimbatore. The rains were already over and the air tingled with freshness. The family house was an old fashioned bungalow on the outskirts of the city with a small front garden dense with hibiscus shrubs, a bougainvillea arching over the gate and a patch of unkempt grass. The garden at the back was considerably larger and it was bordered by more than a dozen fruit trees, mango and jack fruit being the most prominent. In the cool shade, in one corner Big Daddy, as we called Mum's father, had built himself a Grumpy Room in wood. He had painted it green and brown and left the windows open sometimes so that creatures from the garden could come in and out. One curious creeper with arrow-shaped leaves actually found its way into the room through a gap in one of the windows and had wound its way along one of the pipes on the wall. There was a rough hewn table and chair at one end and a book shelf which was on its last legs. At the other end stood a large wooden and metal trunk held together by worn out leather straps and an enormous lock. A large key hung from the wall. On the table lay a single book wrapped in printed cloth.

The bungalow had numerous small bedrooms, one cosier than the other and a large sitting room up front with a covered veranda that served also as a dining room at the back. This led on to the kitchen which was a long, endless room with pale green walls. It had one window which opened on to the garden. One of the larger rooms which had a view of the garden at the back had its door perpetually shut. It was referred to as 'Grand Mummy's Room'. But there was no sign of the woman. Whenever they mentioned her name or talked about her it was always in lowered voices. At first I thought that she was resting or had kicked the bucket but later I discovered that she wasn't in and was away in hospital being treated. I wasn't sure whose Grand Mummy she was so I just let it be.

When we arrived, we settled into our rooms—Phillip and I shared a room and Mum and Nora did the same. The first couple of days were 'catching up' time with Mum and Big Mummy either out shopping together, or in the kitchen or cleaning the house. Nora lazed around with her book and Phillip hopped over the low wall of the property and went off exploring other gardens. On the second day he was bitten by someone's guard dog and had to be put on a course of anti-rabies shots. I settled for climbing trees.

Alexander Harding, that is Big Daddy, was nothing like Grandpa. In fact, he was quite the opposite. He was a large expressive fellow who was prone to mood swings. Sometimes he'd laugh and sing and crack jokes and at other times he'd sink into himself and shut the world out. When he was between moods, he'd sit out quietly in an armchair watching over his garden.

To say that he was large was an understatement. He was a giant of a fellow who towered over me so he'd have to bend down a bit to get a proper look at my face. When we first arrived, he looked at me quizzically. *And who are you, little fella?* He grinned. I tried to turn and run but he quickly stooped down and scooped me up in his arms. He smelt of breakfast—fried eggs and toast and butter and sausages and a hint of the aroma of coffee. *So? What's your name?*

Sean, I replied.

Ah Sean, pleased to meet you. Then he put me down and walked me out into his garden. *Meet my little garden. And these are my children,* he said pointing to the shrubs and flowers skirting the front lawn. Then he took me to the rear of the house and said, *this is my big garden,* and pointing to the trees he said, *these are brothers and sisters and cousins.* After that I lost him because he had locked himself in his Grumpy Room and remained there, coming out only for his meals.

It's his moods, Big Mummy whispered. *They're coming on more often now. He's even started sleeping in his chair in the Grumpy Room, talking and shouting in his sleep. The other night he was sitting outside in the garden talking to someone. God alone knows who. I went out to have a look and found him fast asleep. Snoring. An hour later he was talking again. Well, I suppose that's what the war does.*

Big Daddy had been a Private in the British Army and had seen action in the hell holes of Mesopotamia during the First Great War.

Born into a family of traditional coach makers and crafters of horse trappings who traced their roots way back to the 'Herdings' mentioned in the Doomsday Book of Records and also to blacksmith families in and around Sherwood Forest, he never ever let go of his past. He had drawn an elaborate family tree which he had pasted on the inside of his cupboard door in his bedroom. *That's where I come from sonny boy,* he said, proudly, swinging open the door and showing me the enormous mass of squiggles which formed the tree.

Come on in sonny, he called one afternoon, standing at the doorway of his Grumpy Room. *Come on in, I've got something to show you.* I followed him in and he shut the door.

Take a look at what's on top of the trunk there, he said secretively. *Here's the magazine of a Turkish weapon. Here, feel it. This actually belonged to a Turk. But a dead one. And these here are bullets. Real bullets. The sort of bullets that killed our soldiers in Mespot. And this belt buckle is a Turkish belt buckle. Got it off a fellow my buddy shot in the chest. He fell like a stone straight into our trench. Billy cut his throat in case he started moving again and the rest of us got his belongings. I never liked killing you know, sonny. When I was a toddler, I didn't even like to kill a fly. My brothers would go off down to the river to catch fish but I couldn't even do that. And trapping birds and animals? No way. They called me 'Gander'. A big useless gander. I wanted to run away from it all. I wanted to run away from my family, my home, everything that I had grown up in. I didn't want to remain a coach maker's son...that too coaches for royalty. Royalty, pah, I hated royalty, with their noses in the air and all the bloody fanfare. When the war came I ran away and joined the lads, fudged my age...actually I was so big that I looked older than I was. Ha ha, little fellow, you're going to ask me why I joined the army when I was such a sissy. Good point. Right you are. But I went out to kill to prove myself...not because I liked killing. And something else too. I once dreamed that I was a crusader. You know who the crusaders were? Those fellows who went out in white with a big red cross on the front and back to fight for the Church against the Muslims. And a week in the trenches of Mespot and I became a killer. And here's proof.*

His eyes popped out of his head as he jabbed a finger in the direction of the bizarre array of war trophies that lay spread out on the floor all over the room. A silver lighter, a ring, a pocket notebook, a penknife and a host of other objects, even a bloodstained handkerchief.

He stared at me, waiting for a response. I didn't know what the hell to say. *Scared?* He asked softly. I nodded. *Ah I was also scared. Just imagine, there I was in Mespot to kill real living human beings who had families and loved ones. Oh I was scared silly. My legs wouldn't move, my hands wouldn't move. My mind was blank. Whoosh. Absolutely blank. Everywhere the bombs were falling and guns were chattering and the night sky was ablaze with flares and we were like rats crouched in the trenches. When silence fell I messed my pants. But things changed when I killed my first man. It was a fluke. A hundred yards, a crouched figure but I pinned him in my sights and let fly. He threw his arms up and fell backwards. I had killed a Muslim. I was now a Crusader. So that evening when we retreated for our first night rest to the tents I danced the Mespot Dance. Come along now little fellow, I'll show it to you.*

Saying this he grabbed both my hands and twirled and jigged and sang a garbled song that I didn't quite understand. Then came the chorus which he made me join,

Downing Turks like flies every day
Riddling their bellies full of lead,
Over the sandbags running out to play
Knock the beggars till they're dead...

Ho ho ho ho, doing the Mespot dance,
Hey, doing the Mespot Dance...

Big Mummy banged on the door. *Stop it, Alex! You're scaring Sean!*

I'm not scaring the little fellow. We're enjoying ourselves, that's all. Enjoying ourselves. What's wrong with that? Eh little fellow?

Open the door at once!

He ignored her and continued singing and dancing. Then he stopped. *Now then, let's look at family photographs,* he pointed to his large table which was covered with yellowed prints. Pictures of war-weary, shell shocked soldiers. You couldn't tell one from the other. *That's me there,* he pointed to a tall figure leaning against the crumbling wall of a trench among a bunch of sagging bodies. *See that bandage around my head? That's when I nearly got my block knocked off. Got away with just a scrape. And that's...* he paused then suddenly started sobbing. *He died just after that picture was taken. They all died. Every one of them. Dead. I remained. Why did I remain? They came out for us in swarms. We didn't stand a chance. There were bodies everywhere. Bodies on top of me.* He sat down and holding his face in his immense palms, sobbed.

With the door and windows shut, the room had become oppressive. The air was heavy with the smell of perspiration, old wood, dirty socks, old leather and paper. I felt as if I had been locked in a room somewhere in the past when the First Great War still raged and bombs blew the world outside into splinters. Fear grabbed hold of my throat and I could feel cold bony fingers tightening their grip. *Grandpa,* I shouted in my head because my mouth wouldn't open, *Grandpa, get me out of here, get me out of here. Get me out of here. I want to go back to Little Elliot Road. Aunt Katherine, can you hear me? Can you hear me?* I could feel the bombs shudder the room; I could hear the death rattle of the grievously wound and the squeak of rats. I wasn't in the room anymore but in the trenches of Mespot.

Big Daddy hugged me close, crying. *Sean, there's nothing more horrible than this. This is hell. Pure hell. Hold still, hold still, I'll protect you. Don't run wild, don't run wild, they'll shoot you dead. Stay calm, stay calm.*

I couldn't breathe and began choking and struggled to speak.

I could hear Mum and Big Mummy talking outside. There was

another bang on the door. *Open the door at once!* Big Mummy shouted, louder than ever.

He rose quietly, opened the door, let me out and then shut it behind me.

It took me nearly two days to recover from the shock. Phillip was hardly supportive and jumped on my bed and danced around it with an imaginary gun in his hands. When he tired of doing that, he marched up and down singing his version of Rule Britannia. Big Mummy came in, grabbed him by his arm and led him out. She returned a while later and sat on the bed. *I'm sorry Sean, sorry that Big Daddy frightened the daylights out of you. It's not his fault really, he didn't mean to do it to you. It's what happened to him in the trenches of Mespot that finished him off. He just can't get it out. Can't get rid of it. It haunts him. He wants to say sorry, may I call him in?*

I nodded.

She left the room and Big Daddy walked in quietly, his shoulders hunched. *I'm sorry Sean,* he said when he sat down on the bed. *I'm feeling really bad for having put you through that. I couldn't help it son. The war's done this to me.* He bent down and kissed me on the forehead. *Whenever you are ready to come out, you let me know, okay? And I'll take you somewhere special. Really special. Just you and me. But for now, you take it easy.*

Phillip popped his head in. *I'm coming too, I'm coming too.*

Big Daddy looked at him. *If you behave yourself, sure. But if you don't when we're out there, I'll...*

You'll do what Big Daddy?

I'll be angry.

Will you dance and sing when you are angry?

Mum pulled him away. *Big Daddy is talking to Sean in there. Don't disturb them.*

What's that idjit lying in bed for? He's not sick, he's not hurt. What's wrong with him? Why are you making a fuss over him? Why? He's a namby pamby chap, Phillip grumbled.

What gets into you Phillip? You're always pulling him to pieces.

Everyone makes such a fuss over that silly fellow. I should have drowned him in the tub. I should have!

Stop it. Where's all this evil coming from?

So he's the angel and I'm the devil.

That's your little brother, Phillip. Not some stranger.

To me he is a stranger.

That's enough, you hear me? That's enough!

Look at the way he is sucking up to Big Daddy. I don't want to go with them. I'll get bored. Big Daddy doesn't love me. He doesn't love me. He loves that sissy!

Big Mummy guided them both away from the room and called out to her husband. He left.

Lying there, I was confused. I didn't want Phillip to dislike me. He was my brother. But I was a thorn in his side, someone who was ruining his happiness. I wondered how he'd treat me if we had not shared the same family.

Drifting to sleep, I awoke to voices outside the room. It was Mum and her mother and sister and someone else too. *Probably the neighbour from two bungalows down the road. The skinny one with a large head balancing on a thin long neck*, I thought to myself. I think her name was Ida. Lying in bed, I could pick up snatches of the conversation, all of which revolved around what Big Daddy had gone through after he was wounded. Big Mummy spoke about it in a matter of fact manner and Ida interjected with little gasps. *He lay beneath corpses for two days before he was dug out and carried to the medics who didn't know what to do with him because he was in such a bad state. The makeshift first aid centre swarmed with rats that attacked inert bodies. So the trick he learnt was to keep moving various parts of his body. And that wasn't easy at all because either the body-part was numb and refused to respond or it was limp. But he stubbornly persisted and survived. They shifted him to base hospital and back to Bristol.*

What happened to him then?

And so Big Mummy unravelled his story in bits and pieces for the millionth time.

Years later Mum filled in the gaps for me to help me put the jigsaw puzzle of his life together.

When the war got over, young soldiers like Big Daddy couldn't easily find employment. The war pensions were meagre and the market in a mess. That's when a cousin of his who had made his wealth in India wrote to him and suggested that he make a trip across and seek his fortune among the natives. So the traumatised young war veteran sailed for Asian shores, setting up base in Trincomalee. They gave him a job in the railways and then shifted him to the post and telegraph service in South India.

The handsome young veteran who walked around with a slight limp quickly became a local legend. It wasn't long before Dolores Sanchez, the daughter of a Spanish silk and spice merchant met him outside church one Sunday and fell hopelessly in love with him. Of course, she first had to get the approval of her maternal grandmother before she could even think of plotting a strategy to get her man. Carlos Sanchez, a widower, was only too pleased to see his daughter marrying a fine young man who had fought for his country in the Great War. He was also relieved because the convent where she had lived and studied was pressing him to withdraw her as she was by then an adult. His daughter now taken care of in marriage, he could continue his business with renewed enthusiasm. Unfortunately, he died a year later. His ship went down in the Arabian Sea, caught in a storm.

Dolores took to marriage with enthusiasm and gave Alexander two beautiful and gifted daughters, Olivia and Imelda. The three women in the house were musicians. Dolores played the organ, Olivia the clarinet and Mum the violin.

When I asked Mum why she had given up playing the violin, she replied, *That was my past, Sean. I once gave my life to the violin now I give it to my four children. The three of you and your father. There's no time for the violin now. No time at all.*

A day or two later Big Daddy bundled Phillip and me into his Morris Minor, along with a picnic hamper, fishing tackle and an air rifle. *We're going into hills, boys. We're going to be wild.*

Wild, wild, that's what I like, wild, wild! Phillip bounced around on the back seat, slipped and banged his head on the door. The shock made him sit still for a while, but then he got fidgety again and started rolling the glass of the car door up and down several times until the handle came off in his hand. He got such a fright that he sat still for the rest of the ride into the hills.

The air became cooler as we started climbing the low hills after Mettupalayam and a whole new world opened as we moved through the wooded region, the sun streaming light with ribbons of mist. I breathed in the pure air and felt it spread inside me, cleansing me of all the anxiety that had filled me. Aunt Katherine's horrible death, Grandpa's death rattle and Big Daddy's Mespot dance were washed away for those moments and I had the chance to be myself. The day unfolded with a short walk into the woods, shooting and roasting a jungle fowl, angling without getting a bite, climbing trees, stealing fruits from orchards and picnicking in the shade of a giant old tree whose branches were a mass of twisted green and brown. Big Daddy wasn't Big Daddy anymore but a big boy, gambolling, shouting, singing and being himself.

Finally, he was so tired that he stretched out on a floor of leaves and slept for an hour. Phillip and I climbed up into the tree and sat there, looking out across the valley which had become blue in the haze. The fragrance of blue and red gum filled the air and in the distance curls of smoke rose from hamlets.

Big Daddy stretched his long, stout, arms and legs and yawned loudly. He sat up and stared at the land around him. *Now this is life,* he said. *But it's time to go. It's always time to go when life gets interesting. Come on boys, get the stuff down to the car. I'm taking you along to meet my old buddy Jason and his missus Celia. It's a bit of a drive but we'll pop in and see them, say hello and drive back.*

It took us nearly an hour to get there and when we reached it was dark. We drove up through an orchard and parked in the large quaint porch of the rambling bungalow. Jason came out, shouting a hello so loudly that one would have imagined that we were far away. Big Daddy responded equally enthusiastically, slapped the man on the back and then turned and pointed to us, *those are Imelda's two sons, Phillip and Sean.*

Pleased to meet you two, the man called out, *come on in.*

We followed them into the house and met his wife. *Oh hello,* she cooed. *What lovely boys, are these your grandchildren from Calcutta?*

Yes they are, replied Big Daddy, throwing himself into a large cushioned armchair. *That's Phillip and the little one's Sean.*

She took charge of us immediately, taking us into the dining room where she plied us with homemade brownies and cookies, topped off with hot chocolate. *So how long are you going to be with your grandparents?* asked the bird-like woman.

Until my Dad gets a job and finds a cheaper place for us to live in. Then we can go back, Phillip replied plainly and continued to munch on a cookie.

Oh, escaped from her lips and she shook her head as if she was trying to think of something sensible to say. But nothing else came from her direction. We sat in silence for a while then Big Daddy called out, *finish up boys, time we're headed home or the women down there will start getting worried.*

The tall gangly Jason couldn't resist taking us on a tour of the house and the menagerie he had at the back. It was a large house and by the time we had seen five warm, carpeted, rooms with prehistoric furniture and stag racks on the walls, Phillip asked, *how many more rooms to go?*

This is the just the beginning, announced the man.

When the tour inside was over we were taken around the enormous cages filled with exotic birds and some local species. *This is my private zoo,* Jason said proudly. *And there's more, much more. I've even got fighter cocks. Want to see them boys?*

Another time Jason, another time. We've got a long way back, Big Daddy aborted the tour.

Another time. But you boys must come up again. If your Big Daddy doesn't feel like it I can organise for someone to drive you two up. You're welcome to come and spend a weekend or more if you choose before you go back to Calcutta.

As we drove away I caught a glimpse of both of them standing in the dimly lit porch. She had her arm around his waist and her head tucked close to the side of his chest. They looked terribly lonely.

We drove a while in silence and then Big Daddy said, *Jason was once in the Army. Retired early quite a long time back. He was a Gunner. Damaged his ear drums...so there was no way they'd give him a promotion. That's why he left. He's one of my fishing buddies. Next time you fellows meet him, ask him to sing. He's got a great voice.*

What're they doing here in the jungle? Phillip wanted to know

They aren't staying in a jungle, Phillip, they have their own fruit orchard and farm. And on all sides of them other people have their orchards and farms.

Such a big farm, my brother went on, *where did he get all the money from?*

Some of it is his money, money that he earned, and some of it is what their parents left them when they passed on.

I keep wondering what my parents are going to leave me when they die, Phillip replied.

Sometimes, it's not money and property that parents leave behind for their kids, but values and right attitudes, Big Daddy said quietly.

I'm not sure what that means.

Well you have to grow up a bit more to understand what that means, Phillip.

And where are their children? Phillip continued.

Big Daddy was patient. *They don't have any children now. They had one daughter, a beautiful girl she was. She died in a car accident in Bombay.*

So what's the point of having such a big house and such a big farm if they don't have anyone to leave it for?

Good point my boy. They're trying to adopt a little girl. She's about your age, Sean. Her parents have too many children to support so they may just allow Jason and Celia to take care of their girl.

They've got such a big house they might as well allow the whole family to stay there.

If only life was that simple, Big Daddy sighed.

I slipped into sleep wondering what it would feel like living there, separated from my family and awoke in my bed back in Coimbatore. In the next room I could hear Big Mummy muttering away about how worried everyone was when we hadn't returned by seven. *You said you would be back by seven, what made you decide to go visiting? Come here, let me smell your breath, Alex.*

I just had coffee. Stop treating me like a child. I fought a war and came back alive. No one who has fought a war like I fought a war can come back a little boy...

Come on, Big Daddy, don't start that now. Put on your night clothes and go to bed. And no rushing around and tiring yourself. She'll be coming home from the hospital soon and we are all going to need all the energy in the world.

The Spanish Armada

Out in the garden the next morning, Big Daddy announced that Grand Mummy was returning from hospital.

Whose mummy is she? I asked.

She's Big Mummy's Granny.

But where's Big Mummy's mummy?

In Heaven I suppose. This one has refused to go. So she's still around with us. She was with Big Mummy ever since she was a little girl in the convent. She came from Spain with her. Make any sense to you?

I nodded. Then after a moment I asked, *Is she nice?*

She's okay. Problem is that most times she talks Spanish. She knows Tamil and English but she'll talk only Spanish. She'll talk in English if she likes the person or wants to get herself understood. And she hates black and brown or even yellow people. You're okay because you're pink. But she doesn't like your Dad. She thinks he's naughty because he's brown. Aw, but don't worry about all that. Just thought I'd tip you off about what's about to return to the house.

Does she have people coming from Spain to see her? I wanted to know.

She doesn't have anyone in Spain. They're all gone...so she feels all alone, no one to talk to her in Spanish. And she's fussy. There'll be a lot of this and that going on when the old lady returns. She's crazy. My advice? Never talk to her until she talks to you. Stay out of her way. One doesn't know when she's going to be good or bad. I never know what to do with her. So shall we go to the Grumpy Room? I want to show you something. No, no, don't be frightened. I'm not going to show you something dead but something alive.

So off we went to the Grumpy Room and he showed me the new nest that a magpie robin had built just outside the window of the room.

When we went back for lunch much later I mentioned it at the table and Big Mummy was quick to respond. *Shanti says that it's not good for a magpie robin to keep visiting this garden—it doesn't bring good news. Making a nest here means there's going to be a serious illness here. Laying eggs and hatching babies brings death. I don't believe this because I pray to the good Lord. But it's scary all the same.*

Ah, that's all baloney! Don't believe that silly maid. The poor creature has decided to build a nest and bring babies into the world here and you want us to throw it out? Rubbish! Big Daddy was emphatic. He ended that discussion by cracking loudly into a mutton bone. *By the way, where are Nora and Phillip? I haven't seen them all morning.*

They've gone for a few days to Olivia's place. There're lots of kids their age there. What will they do rattling around here? Anyway, Nora has decided to spend her time there since she seems to be getting bored here.

What about Sean? Has anyone bothered to ask him whether or not he's getting bored? he asked.

They'll bully him, said Mum quickly.

He has to learn to defend himself. I'm sure he can but you don't give him a chance to be with other kids. So what happens then? He's left to chit chat with us oldies. What do you want to do? Make him an oldie before his time, eh?

What are you trying to say? That you're bored with his company? Big Mummy asked.

As far as I'm concerned, I've got myself a new buddy. What say you? He looked at me and winked.

I winked back.

A couple of days later, Grand Mummy came home. The ambulance arrived at the gate and they brought her into the house in a wheel chair. She grumbled all the way from the gate to the front door and then smiled wryly, muttering in Spanish. She didn't seem to even notice me or Mum and focussed on throwing questions at her granddaughter instead.

I stood on the sidelines watching the antics of the small woman dressed in what appeared to be a cross between what a nun and a nurse would wear. All white...with a crucifix and rosary dangling from a cloth belt around her waist. Her round wrinkled face with its enormous liquid brown eyes was set in a shock of white hair. The small firm mouth let out words with the rapid action of an automatic pistol.

I caught Big Daddy's glance and he raised his eyebrows as if to say, *don't tell me I didn't warn you.*

In the days that followed, I tried my best to stay out of her way but my curiosity got the better of me. I crawled through the hedge that ran along the outside of her room and climbed up on a couple of bricks to peep in through the gap between the yellow curtains. There she sat propped up in her little bed, a dainty pair of spectacles balancing on her nose, trying to read a slim hardbound book. Ever so often, she'd start reading loudly in what must have been Spanish. Then she'd stop, put down the book and stare at the blank wall opposite, pick up the book again and look at the wall soon after that, saying in English, *the words are dancing on the page. Why don't they keep still so I can read them? Now they've jumped off the page and are on the wall. Come back here. Come back.* She babbled on for a while then stopped, eyes fixed on a spot on the wall. *I can hear someone breathing outside the window. I can hear someone looking at me. You! Who is staring at me through the curtains?*

I jumped off the bricks and scrambled through the hedge.

She can see things, Big Daddy told me later that day when I confessed to him about peeping into her room. *She can see all sorts of things. Real things and spirits. Just like your mum can. Your mum got it from her. Both she and your Mum have seen things in this garden, right here. I remember, just a month before she was taken to hospital, it was a moonlit night and she stood at her window looking out into the garden talking to someone. She claimed that there was a woman with a baby in her arms gliding up and down across the grass so she climbed out of the window and crawled through on to the grass. That's when I saw her on her hands and knees. Big Mummy told me not to stop her so I waited and watched. She stood up and seemed to be taking something from an invisible person then she turned and stumbled back to her room and climbed back through the window. We went in later and found her all muddied but fast asleep in bed. The next day she wouldn't let us go near her or the bed. Big Mummy found out from her that she had taken away the baby from the woman and hidden it in the big wooden box under her bed. 'Don't you take it away from me,' she kept saying, 'it's all I've got.'*

Even though it was broad daylight, the story scared me. *What happened to the baby in the box?*

There was no baby. It was a ghost.

And Mum has seen this ghost too?

This one and many others, so she says.

Have you seen ghosts?

I have seen things in the trenches that no one would believe could happen like dead men walking and talking and behaving as if they are alive. But I won't scare you, Sean.

You can tell me if you want.

Sean, look here son, you can't grow up on death alone, you must also experience life. I don't know why we adults are doing this to you, I don't know. But you seem to attract people like us.

Do you think I can see ghosts Big Daddy?

You'll know sooner or later. But why are we talking about all this? I'll tell you something more about Grand Mummy. Even though she says that she dislikes the black and brown children of this neighbourhood, she hides sweets and fruits in her room and puts them into a bag and leaves it at the front gate for them to pick up. Once she hid sweets under her pillow and forgot about them and the ants and other mites turned up in streams. We found her asleep covered in ants. He patted me on the head. *The reason I'm telling you this is so that you don't get a shock when you see it happening.*

One afternoon I heard her screech a string of words in Spanish. Since it concerned me, Big Mummy gave me a gist of what she had said. *You are making this into a hospital. This is no hospital. This is my room. Don't meddle with my space. You hear me, you prying people? I'm sure that rascal of a boy has been spying on me. Don't think I can't see him peeping through the window! Send him here at once or I'll come out there and get him. That's what I'll do, I'll come out there and get him and drag him in here and lock him up in my cupboard.*

She created such a fuss that I was sent in, shivering down to my ice cold little toes. I stood there at the open door. *Come in and shut the door behind you,* she croaked in English.

I did.

Now come and stand at the foot of my bed so I can see you better. Of course you must know that even if you were standing behind me I'd be able to see you because I've got eyes behind my head. That day you thought that I couldn't see you when you looked in through the window between the curtains? I saw you because I've even got eyes on the sides of my head too. You don't believe me? Come here and feel.

I went close and placed my fingertips on her temple. The skin was cool and smooth. She put her little wrinkled hands on mine.

Look at me child.

I did.

Yes, you have the family blood in you. I can see it in your eyes. Smile child, smile.

I did.

You are my great great grandson. I can see a quiet, wild animal in you. Let it loose, you hear me, let it loose and become yourself. Let me kiss your forehead and bless you. I leaned forward and she kissed my forehead.

Before you go, I have a job for you. I want you to come in here every morning and check if I am dead. If I am dead, close my eyes gently with your fingers and say a little prayer that my soul goes safely to paradise.

How will I know that you are dead?

It's easy. You'll know.

What if you are alive?

Say good morning.

And so I reported every morning faithfully to her room to check if she was dead or alive.

Sometimes she'd stick her tongue out from the side of her mouth and stare blankly at the wall in front of her and hold her breath. My heart would skip a beat and I'd reach forward to shut her eyes then she'd snap at my hand like a dog, frightening me. On other occasions, I'd find her in bed, eyes staring at the ceiling. Her arms hung limp beside her and she looked so peaceful that I was sure she was dead.

I sat there beside her for quite a while before I gently shut her eyes and said a prayer for her soul, shut my eyes and cried. But when I opened my eyes I discovered that her eyes were open. Afraid that I hadn't done it right, I tried again. This time she fluttered her eyelashes and I nearly fainted with shock.

Sorry for frightening you. This is our little game. I'll tell you what, tomorrow when you come to check and you think I am dead close shut my eyes and place one of these coins on each. Don't ask me why, just do it.

So the next morning when she looked like she was dead, I shut her eyelids and placed one coin on each then tiptoed out. Once out of the room I peeped in and discovered that the coins were shining. Wondering why, I returned to find that they had turned gold. She smiled. *These two gold coins are for you. They are very, very old. From the time of my great grandparents. Take them, they are yours. Even if you have no money and are starving, don't ever sell them because in them are family memories...family memories are very important, they remind us of where we have come from and who we are. You understand?* She held my hands in hers and drew me close and said softly, *I played this little game with you because I wanted you to learn that all this business of life and death is not really so serious, it's a game. Now you are alive, now you are not. I've made such a joke of death that it doesn't know what to do with me. I'm not going to die so easily. One day I'll be so old that I'll just vanish. Don't be afraid of all this. It's just a game.*

Three days later, Mum got the news that Dad had not only found a new apartment for us to shift into but he had also got himself a job. Train tickets were hurriedly booked and we started travelling north along the east coast again. Back to Calcutta to pick up the ends of the broken thread, tie it into a knot and continue life.

It took me a while though to adjust to the shift. Phillip and Nora resisted it. They wanted to remain in Coimbatore with their cousins. *Don't be silly now,* said Mum, *Dad will have me for breakfast if I leave you behind.*

A day before we left, I spent a lot of time with Big Daddy in his Grumpy Room. We said nothing. All he did was open the big trunk and show me his uniform. *Here, he said,* just before we parted company. *I want you to keep this so that you'll remember me.* It was a metal whistle. *It still has Mespot mud on it,* he said.

That night when everyone was asleep, I walked out on to the veranda to get a last look at the garden and the Grumpy Room. There was a nip in the air and an eerie stillness. Above, the sky was heavy with stars. There were so many up there that I got the feeling that the sky would not be able to hold them up and that they'd come crashing down, splinters flying in all directions. I was about to step on to the grass when something caught the corner of my eye. I stopped right there in my tracks and stared. It was a faint shadowy figure standing near the shrubbery at the far corner of the garden. *Is it Big Daddy unable to sleep?* I asked myself but didn't wait for a reply. *Big Daddy*, I called out in a stage whisper. Then the figure began to move, not walk or shuffle but glide. It headed across the lawn towards my right then stopped and seemed to look at me. I was so frightened that I couldn't move...then a calm washed over me. I wanted to say something, anything, but couldn't because I did not know who the person was. *Carlos*, I heard a loud whisper, *Carlos*.

I turned and walked away towards the Grumpy Room when the figure dissolved into the trees. Opening the door, I stepped in and sat down on a low stool. All around me hung memories of a past war in which people had perished senselessly. Tears blurred my eyes. I left, walking out across the lawn to the house. Big Daddy was at the door. *What are you doing awake?*

I couldn't sleep and I wanted to see the garden.

What else did you see?

Nothing.

I was watching you.

I think I saw something.

It's okay, you don't have to talk about it, you need to sleep now. You have a long journey ahead.

I lay in bed, eyes open, staring into the dark, alive, alert, accepting. My world had suddenly changed.

That was the last time I saw Big Daddy because he didn't come out to say goodbye but remained in his Grumpy Room. Four months later he was knocked down by a speeding express bus when he was out on his early morning walk. He had left home at six and about twenty minutes later Grand Mummy heard him singing his Mespot song outside her window. She shouted out to her granddaughter. *We've lost him. He's gone! He's gone!* Big Mummy told her to shut up and stop babbling nonsense. She replied, *Go to the gate, someone is coming to inform you. Go on, don't argue with me.*

Big Mummy walked out to the gate and a couple of people were standing there. She staggered towards them, knowing that she had lost her soldier boy.

Grand Mummy followed him a month later, passing quietly in her sleep.

Rooting and Uprooting

Memory keeps playing tricks with me. The more I think about that visit to Mum's family home, the more I remember. When a glass shatters. one manages to clear up all the pieces, all except tiny splinters that glint when they catch the light. That's what happens. I remember, for instance, that Big Daddy would start talking to his dead friends and then burst into tears and kick the big trunk in the Grumpy Room and punch his fist into the walls. Once he even broke the glass pane and slashed his knuckles. And there was something else. Both of us destroyed the magpie robin's nest and broke the eggs in it to prevent bad luck from visiting our home.

I have had to survive and sometimes this is the way I do it. And after a time all that remains are memories of specific times, people, happenings, feelings, the play of light and dark. Sequence becomes irrelevant. I must be brave now, I must push myself a little more. I must be brave and remember because by remembering I'll let go, I know that. *I know that.* The numbness in my body is giving way to pain, so deep, so endless that I want to give up. How do I bear with it? I don't know what has happened to me, why it has happened, why I am here... but what I do know is that I must gather up all that I remember about my life in one place, bless it and let it go. Whether there's meaning in it or not is not the point. The gathering is enough. That makes sense in itself.

The smell of blood has given way to the sickening stench of disinfectants. I prefer the smell of blood. It's real. I can't handle this anymore. I'm moving away, taking refuge in the past...

I remember the Royd Street apartment that our family shifted into after we returned from Coimbatore. It was a smaller one because rents had skyrocketed. Two cramped rooms and five of us. But we all managed because Dad had a job and there was food on the table and Easter eggs and hot cross buns at Easter and Diwali was a great affair. That was the time our Don Juan Uncle William got married again and I was old enough to go shooting with Dad and his buddies to the Salt Lake, just outside Calcutta where they'd blast early morning ducks out of the skies and bring back a dozen pillow cases packed with water birds smelling of wilderness. I learnt how to retrieve wounded birds and finish them off by hammering their heads on rocks. Strangely, that didn't disturb me. It seemed a natural thing to do. It was my way of feeling empowered, of establishing who I was, of being in control. There was a thrill in the experience of taking another life. I almost felt equal to Dad.

The important thing you must remember about finishing off feathered game is to make the whack or the jerk firm and hard. See, this way, he'd say, grabbing the injured pintail duck by its head and jerking it, snapping its neck. *This way. It has to be firm and hard. Use both your hands, make it sudden. Then put its head under its wing, squeeze it hard and drop the bird into the bag.* I'd often seen him swiftly pick up half a dozen birds at a time and do them in that way.

We'd turn up in a group when it was still dark and the Salt Lake smelled of the wild and the air was heavy with the morning calls of ducks and the honk of geese and crouching into position along the low bunds that divided the jheels would wait for first light and the burst of wings as ducks and geese took to the air. That's the time the guns would begin to speak, sometimes in unison and at other times one after another. Some birds fell like stones whilst others crashed into the wet mud and flapped helplessly. I once saw a row of three greylag geese come towards us with their enormous wingspans stretched to the limit and in a single moment when Dad's 12 bore volleyed into them they turned a twisted mass of feathers and nosedived earthwards. Blood-streaked, I found their twitching bodies in the slush. One of them seemed to look heavenwards at the morning sky alive with birds. Its wings flapped in an attempt to lift its body into the air. Unable to, it spread them out and rested on the earth, head flopping this way and that, a miserable choking gurgle oozed from its open mouth. They were heavy but I managed to haul them into the game bag and cart them to the car, my clothes spattered with red and sticky feathers.

At first, on shooting trips, I made every attempt to gain my father's respect. Then when I thought I had got that, I felt as if I had to excel to be admitted into the league of *shikari*s, even though I was too small to wield a gun. This happened when I was sitting with them around a fire at the end of the day and ate a piece of raw goose liver jokingly offered to me by one of the men. *Go on, let's see if you can eat that,* he had said. It tasted awful, like I was eating something that was still alive. Blood on my lips, blood trickling from the corners of my mouth, blood and liver turning over and over in my mouth, tongue struggling to guide the mash down my throat. I tried not to think of the taste and gulp the stuff down but it was very difficult. Finally I washed it down with warm water. It was nauseating but I was determined to survive the experience and not bring it back up. I had done it, I thought, now I was part of the society of hunters, the one in which its members were tuned to the act of killing—naturally, as a matter of course, like breathing. I felt I shared a secret code, a pact. After that, Dad often took me along, instead of Phillip. Finally, I became a permanent fixture.

I remember going with them after sambar, chital and black buck in the forests of Bihar. I participated in the hunt as a food and water carrier. A sambar was brought down with a 30 06 Springfield on the last day, taking the bullet on the run and carrying it two hundred yards before it keeled over, staggered drunkenly up, tottered a short distance, collided with the stout trunk of a mowra tree and collapsed in a broken heap. Before its life finally was extinguished, one of the group cut its throat.

Later, I watched two of the shikaris expertly skin the animal, neatly detaching the hide from the carcass and scraping it clean.

When we returned, I felt secretly superior to all those who hadn't been present at the killing.

That Christmas we had venison salted meat. Mum spent ages dressing the hindquarter of the sambar, then ages again preparing the meat and poking and prodding it with forks and knives and rubbing in seasoning. And when it was finally ready, relatives and friends came in droves and polished it all off. The last of it was eaten at a family dinner with uncles and aunts and cousins who laughed and joked and argued and it ended up in a free for all with Dad and his brothers calling each other names and swearing that they'd never speak again.

When they left, the apartment looked like it had been blasted by a basketful of grenades. It was always a delightful yet traumatic experience having so many relatives in one place. Our neighbours would turn up at the front door the next day with complaints. Often a local policeman would be brought to dispense a warning. But that made no difference because the pattern was repeated soon after.

Of course, this didn't happen only on family occasions. Dad had a way of picking fights wherever he went and often extended drunken brawls to our doorstep.

After one particularly close call where he had come very near being thrashed by a violent mob, Dad returned home and fell into a deep slumber. I thought about whether it was worth it after all to try and earn my father's respect. I couldn't possibly see myself beating up people. *What is the difference between injuring and killing birds and animals and injuring and killing people?* I wondered, thinking about Big Daddy's Mespot song and dance.

Somebody was peering in through the open window. I looked up; it was Big Daddy. I wasn't frightened but lay there staring out at him until he dissolved.

For quite a while after that, life at home pulsed at an even pace. This was mainly because the neighbours had informed the owner for the hundredth time and he had turned up and threatened to throw us out if there was any more trouble.

That year, the monsoons were particularly vicious. After the first few gentle showers, the blast began and the city saw incessant storms and rain. Finally, when the heavens seemed to relent we were allowed out to play rain ball—football in two feet of water. I had never had such fun in all my living years till then. Since the flood waters weren't so deep, I could safely splash my way through with the others using my head and hands to move the ball. A feeling of pure joy surged through my little body as I waded through the water, splashing it all around. Finally, everyone had retired from the game, everyone except Marylou, a tomboy of a girl with short cropped hair and a face that looked something like a bat's. When we were alone, she asked, *Am I ugly?*

No, I lied, wanting her to continue playing rain ball.

Okay, then prove it.

How can I prove it?

Kiss me.

Kiss you?

See, there you are. If I was pretty you would have kissed me. But I look like a bat that's why you don't want to kiss me.

That's not true, I said feebly.

Then prove it! I dare you.

I waded up to her and quickly gave her a little peck on the cheek.

That won't do. A proper kiss, come on!

So I tried again. When I got near her, she grabbed me and hugged me. She planted a wet kiss on my pursed lips.

Open your mouth, stupid!

What for?

Just open it!

So I did and she stuffed her tongue in.

Yuck, I gasped. *What are you pushing your tongue into my mouth for?*

That's what I've seen the grownups do, she said.

Who?

Your Dad and my Mum and they told me not to tell anyone.

You saw them? I asked in disbelief.

Yes, I did.

What else have you seen? I wanted to know.

Lots. You know that shed there in the corner?

You mean the servant's bathroom?

No the shed next to that. That's where the servants go and do things which they can't go and do in their own homes. One day I'll show you.

A couple of months later, when the rains had finally subsided, one Sunday afternoon, Marylou rattled on the balcony railings, *Sean, Sean, come on! Now's the time they go in there, come on.*

I sneaked out and we went over to the side of the shed and hid there. The sweeper with a limp turned up and looking around to make sure that no one was about, went in and shut the door. *He's waiting for a woman to come*, whispered Marylou knowledgeably.

But no woman came. *While we are waiting do you want to kiss me?* she asked.

No, I replied. *I don't like the way you stick your tongue into my mouth. It's okay if my Dad and your Mum do it like that, but I don't like it.*

Okay then, hug me.

Just then we heard the sound of sobbing coming from the shed. Marylou peeped through a hole in the metal sheeting and gasped. *He's trying to stab himself with a knife.* I pushed her aside and placed my eye at the hole. It was a horrible sight.

Marylou and I screamed. The man was so shocked that someone had been watching him trying to kill himself that he threw the knife over the metal sheeting and it landed right next to us. We screamed again. He ran out, blood dripping from his side, into the compound. By then, people were coming out of their homes and when they saw him in that state they started shouting. He stumbled around the place, wondering where to run. Then he staggered to the right of the building and ran along the side alleyway. A group of people followed him.

We remained hidden, wondering how we'd show ourselves without getting caught. Marylou and I hugged each other in fright.

The knife, the knife, what will we do with the knife? she kept sobbing.

Let's run, no one will see us.

The wait was endless. Voices approached and a group of neighbours opened the door of the shed. *Look, there's someone hiding behind that pile of wood and metal. Someone's hiding there. Maybe the killer. There, there.*

They moved aside the wood pile and found us crouched, clutching on to each other. It took our parents ages to get the truth out of us but the matter quickly settled down, the servant survived his self-inflicted injuries and life went back to an even keel only to trip again when I had my first attack of typhoid.

For the next few months, I remained in a cocoon of recovery, plied with Ferrodol and other nutrients. The days went by with Mum tending to me and the nights with the comings and goings of known and unknown visitors who moved through the apartment, stood around at the door, at the window and often sat by me before dissolving.

Dad promised to take us all out for a week-long holiday to his friend's farm in Gorakhpur when I was better. But that never happened. Instead, he lost his job and his nerve. It was surprising how he changed overnight. He turned violent, drank heavily and picked fights more easily. The neighbours began complaining to the owner and the entire locality was up in arms against us, forcing us out. We had nowhere to go. So in one desperate bid to get away from the mess, we shifted out to a suburb of Calcutta on the banks of the Hooghly to share the home of an old family friend. Nora was fifteen and Mum and Dad put her into a boarding school for her last years of secondary education. I didn't miss her presence very much.

The sordidness of our Calcutta existence was quickly behind us as we got increasingly accustomed to our new abode. Of course, the room the four of us had to share was a small cramped one but the generosity of the Handrahans, Mum and Dad's old friends from Kanpur, and the wide open expanses and the free flowing river outside was fitting compensation.

Not that Joe Handrahan was a very sociable fellow. He was a man of few words who'd be off every morning on his bicycle to work in the nearby factory and would return by seven, tired and hungry. When he did talk it was either about the corns on his feet, the hawks and jackals who ravaged his fowls and their chicks, the rising and falling of the river tides, the way the country was going to rot and ruin and the hallowed paradise of the 'UK' that awaited him. *I'm going home,* he'd often say after a drink or two. *Back home.*

How do you know you'll like it Joe? Dad would ask.

I can feel it in my bones.

Wait till you get there and feel the damp cold in your bones and you'll come rushing back.

That's my home, he'd reply, *Not this.*

He was always uneasy when Dad threw those questions at him. But Dad was smart. He didn't push his luck too far. After all, he didn't want to antagonise his host.

Zelda, his wife, was a live wire. She kept the air bristling with her sense of humour and her beauty. She exuded it from every pore. No one could ever understand why she had decided to marry Joe, skinny like a beanpole with his large nose, narrow set eyes and unusually large mouth with thin cruelly curled lips, whose only asset was his patience. There was a rumour that Dad and Aunt Zelda had once been lovers. It was said that she was his sort of woman—with her glowing cascade of black hair, large eyes and large breasts. Her walk appeared lazy but if one took a closer look it was quite obvious that she was swinging her hips gently.

Dwarf Among Phantoms

I was reluctant to set out on my own even though I was quite familiar with the area because I had been there on weekend picnics with my family. But it was one thing going to a place for the weekend and having a great time messing around with cousins and family friends and quite another living in a home that was not our own and feeling almost apologetic that we were refugees. That feeling was enough to deflate any urge for adventure that I may have nurtured.

Of course, my self-consciousness gradually wore away as I became increasingly aware of the electric green field that went halfway around the house, hedged on one side by tall lush shrubs that were heavy with bunches of small bright yellow berries and busy with butterflies of all shapes and sizes. Along the other side was an ageless frangipani tree, an enormous mango tree and a line of mast trees. Just outside the veranda stood two wild litchi trees. Outside the wrought iron front gate was the skeleton of a rain tree. Beyond that, the broad brown whirling Hooghly flowed on its way to the sea. I progressed to the steps that led down off the veranda and almost timidly I began my exploration. In a couple of days I was up and down the mango tree, lying in the shade of the hedge, watching birds eat the berries or flitting among the leaves. It didn't take me long after that to climb over the front gate and walk along the wall that hemmed the riverbank. I began to feel less and less a refugee and more a gypsy.

I wasn't like Phillip who could make friends quickly. When I bored of my own company, I tried trailing behind him but he didn't like it. *Shove off you little bugger,* he'd snap but I wouldn't listen. One day he kicked me on the shin and when I doubled up he turned me around and demanded that I face the wall and count one hundred or he'd kick me again. I didn't believe him so I counted up to fifty and turned around and he punched me in the stomach this time. I doubled up again and he spun me once more. *Count one to a hundred or I'll clip you one.* I did. When I turned around, he was gone. After that, every time I saw him leaving to go out to play with his new found friends, I'd quickly turn and face the wall and start counting one to a hundred.

Once Aunt Zelda caught me counting. *Who are you playing with?*

Friends. I lied.

Where are they?

Gone off to hide, I lied again.

Really? She asked. *Where do these friends live?*

Somewhere nearby.

As the conversation moved along I created two friends. I called the small one Chintu and the big one Bunty. After that day, I'd even push off by myself saying that I was going out to play with them. Everyone seemed to believe me and so I was encouraged to treat them as if they really existed. Chintu was like a little brother and Bunty was the one who protected me. Off on my explorations, I'd chat to them and they would even answer me. I'd dream of going off on adventures with them.

Of course the bubble burst when Phillip followed me after I had announced that I was going to meet my friends. When he saw me sitting on my own, there was no end to his taunting. *Ha ha, I knew it! Mad cap, making up invisible friends! Choo mantar choo. Agrum bagrum. Choo mantar choo. Chintu and Bunty. Boom!*

Why are you making fun of me? You are supposed to be my brother!

Your brother? You must be joking. You were picked up at a dhobi ghat. Your Mum and Dad washed clothes at the ghat in Kanpur. Someone brought you to our home. See that little hole in your ear? That's the hole dhobis make in their children's ears and later put earrings in them. Phillip knocked me down and sat on my back, pulling my hair.

For some time after that it seemed as if Chintu and Bunty had been wiped out. I was too ashamed to even think about them, forget about trying to imagine them. Then one day, I didn't have to even try to imagine them. They were there in front of me, in flesh and blood. I was sure that they were real. In fact they were so real that an uneasy feeling crept over me. I was too scared to even touch them in case it was true.

Have you ever been to the mango grove? asked Chintu.

Where? I wanted to know.

On the other side, Bunty said. *Come on, Let's go.*

He led the way along the narrow canal and I soon found myself on the edge of a beautiful grove of trees. They were not as tall and wide spreading as the old mango tree in the compound but many of them were actually pairs of trees with branches stretching out a foot high from the base of their trunks. Their leaves were unusually large and a rich green. The ground was covered with clumps of soft grass and tiny wild flowers. They were so small that I had to go down on my hands and knees to get a good look at them. Chintu climbed up a tree and Bunty busied himself with picking up stones and chucking them at the trunks of trees. Then the three of us set up a pile of stones with a single stone balancing on top and standing thirty paces away from it started throwing smaller stones at it as if it was a target.

I scored almost every time.

Here, said Bunty, giving me a catapult. *Try this. I made this specially for you.*

The vee was made of guava wood and the elastic straps were slim black vacuum rubbers and the *piddhi* (stone holder) was of thick but pliable leather. *Once you know how to use this,* he continued, *you'll become a crack shot. Go on, have a go.* He gave me a couple of smooth round clay marbles.

I aimed at the target and *whack* I hit it.

We played for a while and then I said that I had to go home and have lunch. I couldn't invite them because it was someone else's home. They almost instinctively understood and walked me to the back of the house then turned to leave. Aunt Zelda was at the back door. *You're just in time for lunch little fellow, and I've made your favourite—steamed rice, rasam, papads and mutton jhalfrezi.*

I didn't let her go on and interrupted her. *Aunty see, look there, those are my friends Chintu and Bunty.* I pointed in the direction that I had thought they had gone.

Sean dear, she ruffled my hair. *There is no one there.*

Of course there is. Two of them. They walked with me to the back, right out here near the patch of green chillies.

Sean, you were alone. I saw you walking along all by yourself, coming from where the canal is.

Aunty, I'm not fibbing. They were right here. I played with them. We went along the canal to the mango grove.

Where?

There, I said pointing out in the direction from where I had been.

There is no mango grove there. You've got a more fertile imagination than your Dad! Come along, lunch will get cold, where's that ragamuffin brother of yours?

I don't know.

Okay, come along. Your Mum's out with your Dad. They've gone to the post office. And they may go on to the market to do a little shopping for me. Come on.

And so, there was just the beautiful Aunt Zelda and I lunching by ourselves.

You must be getting very bored doing nothing the whole day, she said, pausing mid-meal.

No, aunty.

You have no one to play with. And you aren't like Phillip who can make friends easily. I wish we could send you to school, Sean.

Aunty, are you sure you are not pulling my leg?

About what?

That you saw me alone, that there is no mango grove.

No, I'm not pulling your leg.

I didn't believe it so I put my hand into my little cloth sling bag to take out the catapult that Bunty had given me. It wasn't there. I went cold.

What's the matter? Aunt Zelda looked at me. *Are you okay?* She placed her palm on my forehead to check if I had a temperature. Her touch was reassuring. She got up and came around the table to me and put her arms around my shoulders and drew me close, placing my face against her stomach. I felt safe. *You've seen something, experienced something. I know. I promise I won't tell anyone. This will remain between us.*

But when Aunt Zelda's gentle warmth and reassurance wore off, I began to think again about Chintu and Bunty. I was too frightened to walk along the canal by myself in the hope of meeting them or seeing the mango grove. So I sat quietly on the stone steps outside, looking at the open field, the hedge, the trees and the river.

I saw them coming up the road that ran along outside the fence and curved away to move along the river bank. They seemed to be picking up stones and trying to throw them into the river. When they turned the bend I got up and sprinted as fast as my legs could carry me, scrambled through the fence and headed down the road, hoping to catch up with them. But they had vanished. I went down the steps of the ghat to check if they were there. They weren't. On my way up the ghat steps I came across a large smooth black stone placed at the base of a banyan tree. There were bright red hibiscus flowers scattered around the stone. A couple of sticks of incense burned, sending up small swirls of perfumed smoke. Standing before it, made me feel strangely calm. Thoughts of my new found friends gently ebbed. I sat down and burst into tears.

Why are you crying little boy? a voice asked in Bengali. I didn't respond because I thought it would lead to another of my wild imaginings. *It's okay. Nothing bad can really happen to a nice boy like you.*

Who says so? I wanted to know.

I do.

I looked up and saw a little man, hardly four feet tall standing on the low wall of the ghat. *What are you doing here?* he wanted to know.

I'm sitting here.

He hopped off the wall like a chimpanzee and stood beside me. *There are snakes here, cobra, krait, bitchoos too. You be careful. Come.* He turned and trotted off ahead of me. I trailed him. Out of the satchel slung from his shoulder protruded the wing of a pigeon. A catapult in his left hand.

Is he real? I wondered, *or another Chintu-Bunty type?*

Where do you live? I asked.

He waved in the direction of Aunt Zelda's house.

That's where I live.

No, not there, far behind beyond that place. Along the Palta jungle, he explained.

You mean somewhere near the mango grove?

What mango grove?

The one where the trees are not so tall and the leaves are long and shiny.

He stopped dead in his tracks and looked at me surprised. *Why are you going on about the mango grove? There's no mango grove there.*

I saw one.

How can you see one when there's no mango grove there? Come on I'll show you what's there.

We walked along the low wall that ran beside the river and climbed up on to the bank of the canal. *This way,* he called out. *This way.*

After a short walk we reached his 'quarters' which stuck snugly into a row of outhouses attached to an exceptionally large estate.

Aarti, he called, standing at the doorway and pointing into his home. A moment later a woman emerged. She was small and delicate with a mouth red with pan and eyes that seemed to be able to see right into me. Then he pointed to himself, *Saathi.*

Sean.

If you wait some time, you can taste some of this pigeon. Yes?

I nodded.

Aarti took the bag with the bird and left.

Mango grove, eh? he suddenly asked. Then he called out, *This fellow says there is a mango grove here.*

Mango grove? Aarti called back. *What mango grove?*

He looked at me. *See, I told you there isn't any mango grove here. What makes you think there is one?*

I saw it. It was somewhere here.

Here? No, no.

The aroma of fried pigeon wafted out and even though I had had a full meal with Aunt Zelda, my mouth filled with saliva and I ran the tip of my tongue over my lips. Aarti brought out the meal that she had prepared and I relished a few morsels.

While we ate in silence I wondered why I had persisted with my queries about the existence of the mango grove since Aunt Zelda had said that one didn't exist and Saathi and Aarti had said so too. *What's wrong with me?* I asked myself and tried to push the matter to the back of my mind.

Do you go to school? asked Aarti.

No.

No? She was surprised and looked at her husband.

No school? Saathi asked.

No school, I repeated.

They continued eating.

On holiday? she looked at me for an answer.

No money.

Free Chrishin school here. Father Robinson, he'll give you admission.

I know him, he said reassuringly.

I said nothing.

Then I left, thanking them. *You come here anytime,* said Aarti, *you are my friend too. Come. Okay? Come. Saathi here, Saathi not here, no matter, you come Okay?*

Okay.

I walked back along the canal then entered the green field through a gap in the hedge. Back at the house, everyone had returned and Dad wanted to know where I had gone so I told him. *You shouldn't spend your time with servants,* was all he said. *Don't do it again. You'll catch all sorts of bad manners and sicknesses and whatnot, don't you have sense in that head of yours? Why can't you just be like Phillip? He now has a group of friends, decent ones, and has a good time.*

Phillip had a smug grin pasted across his face, *there's always space for a runt. You want to join?*

No, you'll all hit me. Like that day when you hit me.

Dad sat up and looked at Phillip. *Come here,* he barked.

No Gordon, said Aunt Zelda, *not in this house, there's going to be no beating here, you hear me?*

You come outside then, Dad looked at Phillip menacingly.

You shouldn't have had a drink, Aunt Zelda went on, *this is what it does to you. Imelda, tell him not to do this.*

Before anyone could stop him, Dad had grabbed Phillip by his torn collar and dragged him out squealing. We heard two smart slaps followed by a fit of sobbing.

The two women looked at each other, then Aunt Zelda looked at Uncle Joe who pretended to be reading his newspaper. *Do something!*

It's not my business; he knows best, it's his son. Anyway, what can we say, the man is drunk, tomorrow he'll say he is sorry. We all know Gordon, he's a nice guy at heart.

But he's drunk on country liquor, she replied.

So? He can't possibly drink scotch, he can't afford it.

And he can't afford even country liquor. He never drank with his own money but with mine. The market money.

I'll pay you back, Mum tried to reassure her.

It's not the money, it's the ethics.

Dad returned, dragging in Phillip with a cut lip. *We're friends, aren't we?* he asked. Phillip didn't respond. *You heard me? I want an answer. We're friends now, aren't we?*

The moment he let go of Phillip's collar, he shot out of the front door.

Run you little fuck, run, Dad called out after him.

That night when the rest of the house was asleep, I heard Aunt Zelda talking to Dad out on the veranda, telling him to control his drinking and his anger. There were long pauses in between the conversation; I wondered what could be happening. Later I heard her saying, *not here Gordon, not here, please Gordon, not here. I'm happy to go on to the roof...but not here, not here.*

Let's go, he replied.

I forced my eyes shut and pushed myself to sleep. It was tough going because I could hear their footsteps on the roof. Then there was silence. I slept.

Phillip returned the next day after Dad had left the house saying that he was going to Calcutta for an interview. I stayed out of everyone's way and when I got the opportunity I slipped off and went to Saathi and Aarti's place. Saathi was out but his wife was there, washing clothes by the canal. *Where's Saathi?* I wanted to know.

Gone to shoot birds and catch fish for today's meal.

I sat down on a boulder beside her.

You had asked about the mango grove, eh? she asked.

What about it?

There was one here. Right here. Ten years ago. The river flooded its banks and many homes were destroyed; some people died too. After that, the place was abandoned. Then the factory bought the land and cleared it and built this estate and these places to live. I found this out from the watchman last night.

So, there *was* a mango grove here. Then my friends may have been here too!

Come on, let's go in, I've got something for you.

When we were back indoors, she produced a packet of glucose biscuits. *There's milk too,* she said, smiling at me.

Whilst I ate the biscuits and sipped the milk, she stood watching over me like my guardian angel. *I wish I had a child like you. People who deserve to have children don't have them and those who don't deserve to have children have them by the dozen and they don't even realise how lucky they are. I feel like giving you a mustard oil massage,* she said. *Your skin looks dry and dirty.* I didn't stop her. She then heated water on a fire and bathed me.

Saathi returned home later with a bag of birds and four fish. It had been a good day for him. He bathed then flopped down and went to sleep. I left, resisting the temptation of remaining for a meal.

Walking slowly, I felt someone was tailing me, stopped and turned around but couldn't see anyone. Bursting into a sprint, I dived through the gap in the hedge and stumbled my way across the green. Storm clouds were gathered over the river which had become dark brown and choppy. A wind came in from the farther shore whining through the trees.

It rained heavily that night and I dreamed I was there when the great flood happened, floating on the front door that had been ripped from the house. Saathi and Aarti were on another door and the three of us floated around. And then from all around us we saw mango trees approaching us. It was as if they were gliding over the flood waters. They moved past us, collided with each other, took on another formation and started circling us this time. I started getting dizzy watching them go round and round us, lost my balance and toppled over into the turbulent river. The current carried me along into the dark night until the moon came out and the waters became calm. I slept on my back, floating like a log. When I opened my eyes, Saathi and Aarti were floating on the door next to me and I could hear Chintu and Bunty calling and crying.

The dream left me feeling as if I had slept a hundred years, and I awoke drowsy and disorientated. Outside, the rain beat down with such force that I was sure that the house and all around would get washed away. Would the river rise?

Fortunately, the river remained where it was and the force of the rain lessened, finally becoming so soft and gentle that it was blown in billows by the wind, transforming it into watery sails. The giant ship of earth was ready to set sail.

Days billowed into weeks and when the skies cleared and I got a chance to slip off and meet Aarti and Saathi. Their response to me and my presence became warmer and more protective. Saathi, even though he was old enough to be my father, behaved like an elder brother to me. Because of his diminutive size I found him unthreatening. Unlike Phillip who constantly made me feel bad about myself.

Aarti treated me like the child she never had. In her own way, she did her best to be protective and supportive, willing to give me the warmth of her silence when she realised that I didn't want to talk.

I got to learn that they had come down from Nepal three years earlier. She brought in the regular income by working as house-help on the estate of the Director of the Ordinance Factory. Saathi added birds and fish to their menu, did the shopping and sometimes cooked the food. I'd join him on occasions and spend a good part of the day out when Dad was on one of his trips to Calcutta, supposedly looking for a job. There were times when I'd even go back to their place and help him cook food. No one seemed to mind at home so long as I was doing my own thing and staying out of their hair. Sunset was the cut off time. I was expected to return before dark to roost at home.

And so the seasons moved on one into the other and nature altered her moods, teaching me that nothing remains the same. If you are alive, you will change. If you are dead, you will become dust and vanish in a gust of wind.

When the litchis began ripening on the trees outside the house, the flying fox catchers arrived with their nets which they strung up between trees. The giant fruit bats would fly into the nets and ensnare themselves, struggling all night to tear free. By morning, the nets would be heavy with trapped creatures. The catchers would lower the nets; taking out each creature carefully, they would crack it's skull with a wooden mallet. Then the furry skin would be stripped off the warm pulsing bodies before being tossed away in a bag. The violence fascinated me. I'd get up early in the morning and rush out on to the open ground to watch the trappers untangle the bats. I was surprised at how they suddenly became very still just before they were slammed with the wooden mallet. Did Aunt Katherine become still just before she died? I wondered. What were her last thoughts? And Grandpa? I shivered when I thought of Big Daddy being hit by a bus. He had no time to be still.

Soon the river got rougher and the tide higher, and I could smell the monsoon approaching. The skies darkened and the rains began all over again. Thundering blasts of water kept me indoors and gave Dad an excellent excuse to remain in Calcutta each time he went up for an interview. All of us knew that he was drinking himself silly but no one knew where he was getting money.

The Water Mansion

When winter approached, Terence, an uncle I had never seen before, popped up out of nowhere and insisted that we should share his mansion on the other side of the river. *I can't let you live in someone else's house like this,* he declared. *I am your brother, your flesh and blood, I owe it to you. It's a beautiful place, believe me. It's where the great poet Rabindranath Tagore once lived. You will love it there. Beautiful and secure.*

That line got Dad all sentimental and he agreed to share Uncle Terence's mansion. So one day we carted our bundles to a new residence. It all happened so suddenly that I didn't have time to see Saathi and Aarti and say goodbye. I wanted to thank them and let them know that I was very fond of them. They had become like my family.

However difficult it was to deal with, I was slowly getting accustomed to being uprooted, transplanted and dug up again, shifted and settled and shifted again. Even though I was still young, I had begun to accept the movement as natural. We were like nomads, moving from place to place in search of new pastures, new shelters, new hunting grounds. Dad was the only one who took all the decisions. No one else was allowed to do so. In fact, he never once consulted Mum. *What I say goes because I know what's best for you all. Imelda, you just get on with doing the cooking and cleaning and swabbing and the caring and the praying and all...and I'll do the rest, you understand?*

He exaggerated the benefits of shifting to Uncle Terence's house.

It's got space, class, style and it's in the family, our family. We couldn't have continued to stay with Zelda and Joe in that little room. Okay, you two boys could go running around the place and feel free but you'd always have to come back to the room. I was really uneasy there. Here, we've got everything and more, lots more.

Dad was right. It was a larger and more lavish set up—we occupied the entire ground floor of the mansion which had three bedrooms with attached baths, a spacious hall, a well equipped kitchen and a sprawling veranda. The first meal we ate there was a real feast and we stuffed ourselves till we could hardly walk. Dad couldn't stop belching and Uncle Terence kept assuring us that from then on, there would be no want.

Two days later, he went off on tour and left Aunt Jennifer, his wife, completely in charge. It turned out that she wasn't the generous sort at all because she announced, *I'm going to look after my own space upstairs, you now have the run of the place. Stock up and do your own cooking.*

Stock up from where? asked Dad

From the market, where else? She wasn't going to part with any stock for the kitchen. Initially she relented, but quickly hardened. *You have more than just a garden, grow your own vegetables. You are lucky Terence is not charging you rent. And anyway, Gordon, you should be out working. If you can't find a job, put your wife or children to work.*

She was an exceptionally large woman with a red face and a bulbous nose that had a way of poking itself where it had no right to. Carrying herself like a battleship from room to room she wheezed and muttered as she went along. If she sensed something was amiss she'd stop and whip her hands to her hips, take a deep breath and say, *What is going on for Christ's sake?* And if she didn't get a response, she'd ask, *What is this world coming to? I can't feel safe in my own home.*

Dad cursed and swore and raved and ranted and ended up sulking. Phillip and I started stealing vegetables from her kitchen garden then went out and flicked fish from baskets on the fish landing quay, trapped pigeons, doves and sparrows. The house help from upstairs provided the oil and spices. We survived—until Uncle Terrence returned and laid out lavish meals for us. We enjoyed the treat knowing it would stop the moment he left on tour.

Everything beautiful was stolen, was short lived, was desperate, was urgent. Living and dying were two sides of the same coin, the same experience. Often I couldn't tell whether I was alive or dead. Out on the staircase at the back of the mansion I'd sit and look out at the river flowing past the garden wall. It was the same river that flowed past Aunt Zelda's home and Palta jungle. But here there was no field between us; instead, there was a low lying garden and a wobbly boundary wall. The mansion was at the mercy of the river and its moods. When the bore tide came bouncing and crashing up its course, the river looked as if it would abandon its bed and swallow the house, at low tide it would lie there flat and lazy, asleep, resting on thick squelchy folds of clay. Water birds would glide up along its banks and land on the garden wall. The cormorants would spread their wings to dry and sun themselves, the herons would stand stock-still, beaks poised to strike; the pied kingfisher would shoot into the air, hang there for a split second then drop into the water and clip up a tiddler in its broad black beak. I would sit there looking out at the river and wonder if it was all real or was it just a memory and that nothing of it actually existed any more. Kids of my age were enjoying their childhood whilst I was already a jaded and helpless adult.

There were times when I was not in my body, I was sure of it. I was somewhere else. Looking down at myself, floating amongst other energies around me, moving away. I really wanted to move away. It wasn't worth being in that body anymore, every moment was a trial. When would it all end? Once I was beyond those thoughts and far over the river there was at first a feeling of freedom, a continuous state of being. Then fear that I would never be able to return. That would bring me back with a thump. My heart beat violently, I stood up and walked down to the river and climbing on to the wall watched its water whirl.

One day, when a bore tide had just passed by, I saw myself walking down the staircase over to the amra tree, climbing its stout branch that leaned across the boundary wall, stretching itself out towards the water. I climbed to the end till it dipped and dropped me into the churning currents. *Is it real? Is it real?* I kept asking myself. *Am I going to swallow so much muddy water that my stomach will swell like a balloon and I'll die? Is this it?*

By the time I was inside myself again, my heart was struggling to beat and slowing down. I sank, burbled beneath and rose again. The blueness of the sky hurt my eyes and I shut them. My legs thrashed in the water, my arms flip-flopped. I didn't want to die. I was scared. The current spun me along and I could not hear wild human cries. I tried to get out of my body because I could not handle the struggle anymore. *Get me out of this water, get me out!*

Then someone grabbed my arm, hauled me into a boat and began drawing the water out of me. Heaving, pressing, thumping, sucking. When I opened my eyes, I found myself in a lamp lit room with cow dung plastered walls. A young man leaned over. I looked into his eyes. They were warm, brown and gentle. *Shhh,* I heard him say, then closed my eyes and drifted into another world.

The next time I was aware of myself, I was sitting up at the doorway of the same room, looking out, blankly at the river bank strewn with piles of dead water hyacinths. He sat on his haunches in the small courtyard mending his nets, stopped and looked at me. *I am Sheebu. What's your name?*

I don't know.

You're still suffering from shock. I pulled you out of the river two miles from here. How did you fall into the river?

I don't know. I can't remember.

Where do you live? Can you remember? Barrackpur? Ichapur? Khardah?

I don't remember.

I saw myself saying all this but couldn't get into myself to really wake that body up. I knew that if I got into it I would be able to answer all those questions.

Sheebu placed a thali before me. On one side it had a small mound of steaming rice, a battered metal bowl which was filled to the brim with dal, some tomato chutney and a few pieces of crisply fried fish. *Eat*, he said then settled down near me and started mixing rice with chutney and dal and squeezing it into large balls which he stuffed into his mouth, following it with a chunk of fish.

I joined him, eating slowly until the thali was empty.

Do you want to stretch your legs? He asked. I nodded, so he held my hands and helped me to stand up. I started staggering around the place, unable to keep my balance. Then I fell. *You aren't ready yet.*

I slept on the mat in the room again, a deep dark sleep which was like falling into a whirlpool. When I surfaced from it, I was inside my body again but was now reluctant to tell him my name and where I lived. I pretended that I was still in a state of shock and could remember nothing because I didn't want to go home. There was nothing to return to.

But two days later, a local police constable turned up with Phillip in tow and picked me up. A case of abduction was filed against Sheebu and he was arrested. I was taken home wrapped in a tattered sail.

Apart from Mum, no one showed any signs of being pleased that I had returned. The next day I returned to my perch on the staircase at the back of the mansion.

Aunt Jennifer had started visiting our part of the house to inspect all her property. She maintained a regular inventory of all movable objects so as to keep track of them and ensure that we hadn't stolen and sold off anything.

Six months later, Uncle Terence informed us that they had sold the house and were moving out but he permitted us to stay there for another six months as the new owners would be taking over the place only after that.

A mansion all to ourselves! We had a vegetable patch, a few fruit trees and the occasional catch of fish from the river. That's the time when Dad got a temporary job as a door to door salesman. He was good at it. He could sell sand to the Arabs, as he put it. He drank half the money he earned and gave us the rest. But we got by on a wing and a prayer.

I stayed out of Phillip's way and spent my time rediscovering the gardens around the mansion. There were tall shady trees along the boundary wall then a line of fruit trees and flowering shrubs, an overgrown lawn in the middle and at the far end a well. And of course, behind the mansion, there was the battered garden that sloped down into the river. In one corner, a temple had once stood at the water's edge but it had long since toppled over and been washed away by flood waters. At the other corner there used to be a peepal tree that had a trunk which formed the face and hands of an old man. None of it remained.

During the day, there was a lot to explore but at night the house and the gardens took on a strange menacing character. It frightened me and I had no one to share my fear with. Mum slept like a log, Dad was sometimes there but often not. Phillip always had a gang of local boys visiting and they holed themselves up in a room upstairs. Nora, when she came down during her holidays would be either in a state of depression or a romantic phase and spent her time writing long passionate letters to distant young men. I would climb on to the roof and look down on everything below. It gave me a feeling of safety. To the east, lay the front garden and beyond the wall a community pond and farther still fields and homes fading into the blue blackness. To the north, groves of mango trees, bamboo and small squares of paddy fields, in the south were banana plantations. On the west, the river—dark and gurgling. Each time I turned to look at it I could feel the river inside me, churning somewhere in my belly, trying to set itself free and return. It was an odd feeling, something like wanting to vomit. I was scared. But from up there I felt a measure of safety. I knew for sure that the river couldn't reach me.

I spent nights lying on the flat of my back on the roof staring up at the dark sky crowded with stars, watching specks and sparkles appear and disappear in a wash of milky white and sometimes even dawn moving across the sky in trails of light. Far out somewhere, disembodied voices of fishermen floated up to me, hovered and then dissolved, drowned by the hoot of steamers as they made their way up river. I liked to imagine that the voices I heard belonged to the spirits of long dead fishermen, drowned in the river talking to those drowned on the high seas who had come visiting. I listened to the sound of the words as they floated along the waves of night air and sailed overhead, dissolving in the distance.

It was lonely up there. But I was free. Free from violence and the scrounging dinginess below. I knew of course that it wasn't going to last, that my days there were numbered, that the times ahead were unknown, that there was no visible hope or salvation of any kind. *Do I really have a guardian angel?* I asked myself but got no answer.

Towards the end of our stay the river flooded. Dad was away in Calcutta. It began one night when I was up on the roof. The swirling waters rose swiftly, spreading across the back garden and around the flight of steps, then climbed along the sides of the mansion till it filled the front lawn. I could hear Mum shouting below, Phillip and Nora joining her. My voice slipped in amongst theirs. Long lonely cries drowned by the angry voice of the river. The ground floor was awash with water and furniture floated around like wreckage of a sunken ship. Then the lights went off and it started raining. Afraid to move from the roof, I stood there shivering as cold water lashed me. When I could stand it no more, I walked dripping down the dark staircase to the floor below. Mum, Nora and Phillip were huddled around a lantern.

So there you are! they said in unison. I was stripped bare, towelled and given a spoonful of neat brandy which burned its way down my throat.

We were all overpowered by the feeling of being trapped.

How's Dad going to get here? asked Nora quietly.

What would he be able to do if he was here anyway? asked Phillip.

Be quiet, both of you! snapped Mum.

We spent the night huddled around the fading lantern, praying together till we fell asleep. The rain stopped the next morning, so we all stumbled up the stairs on to the roof to get a look at the waters below. The river had broken its course and flooded its banks, sending its waters out across the countryside. Only the tops of the mango trees were visible, the banana plantations were gone, rooftops in the distance seemed to struggle to keep their heads above water. Nothing was left of the garden. The raging waters had uprooted the trees and washed them flat.

Phillip insisted on checking out the state of the ground floor. Not long after he had gone, there was a shriek of delight. *Fish, fish! Plenty of them in the sitting room!*

We rushed down with buckets. As the flood had abated the water in the sitting room was ankle-deep and it was easy for us to move around with buckets and bed sheets, scooping up fish of all shapes and sizes. *Now don't be greedy, that's enough, that's enough,* yelled Mum excitedly.

The rest of them will anyway die, answered Phillip, *might as well catch them all. We can always make fish pickle.*

Oh yeah? Nora sniggered, *where are the spices and oil and all that stuff going to come from?*

Or we can sell them in the market. I'll go and sell them if you want.

How will you go there? she asked, *in a motor boat?*

We have such a useless family, he said finally, *that's why we are so poor.*

Be quiet! Mum said, *stop behaving like a mind doctor.*

What's a mind doctor? he wanted to know.

Someone who treats people who are sick in the head, she said.

There's a bigger word for that but you wouldn't be able to pronounce it.

A mind doctor? Do you think Dad needs to go to a mind doctor?

Mum stopped collecting fish and looked at him. *Don't talk like that about your father, Phillip. You don't even know what he is going through.*

I don't know for sure, he shot back, *but I know what we are going through because of him.*

Will you please stop it Phillip? I've had enough of your insults. Mum's voice had an edge to it.

Ok. But I've had enough of this family. Why am I calling it a family? This is no family. He threw down the wet sheet and stomped out of the room, tripping and falling into muddy water that was still standing outside. He waded out of it, wet and filthy and returned, looking a little foolish.

We ate fish for the next few days and threw away what remained because the flesh had started to rot. But a couple of days later came the next blessing: pigeons. A whole flock of them arrived to take shelter in the store room on the roof. We shut the door and went in with sticks. Later, Mum said grace with renewed fervour when we sat down to a meal of pigeons roasted on an open fire as both the gas supply and the kerosene was exhausted. Phillip enjoyed smashing chairs and other light furniture and feeding the pieces into the flames to keep the fire going.

When the waters finally settled, Dad turned up and behaved as if nothing had happened. He told us that we were to start packing because we were going to move. *Pack what?* asked Phillip.

Don't be funny, do as I say.

But Phillip didn't give up this time, he persisted. *I'm serious, Dad, what have we got to pack?*

Someone better tell this boy to stop arguing with me or I'll clip him one.

Phillip, that's enough, Mum warned.

Where were you when we needed you? Phillip demanded. He had begun to cry.

Dad slapped him so hard that he went flying across the room. He stumbled out of the house and was gone.

Let him go, Dad snapped, spitting out his words disgustedly. *He'll come back with his tail between his legs.*

How can you say that? Mum sobbed. *Where will the boy go?*

Now don't you mollycoddle him, you hear me? His voice was like a razor blade. First signs that he was about to go into a violent fit of rage.

Nora left the room. I cowered in the corner. Mum stood in front of him, alone, waiting. He slapped her across the face and she fell backwards.

The next day, Phillip returned and we packed our meagre belongings and left the mansion. Nora went back to school even though her holidays were not over and Mum was put on a train to Coimbatore. Dad hauled me along with Phillip from one friend's house to another. Many of the fair weather ones welcomed us in but in a couple of days started making all sorts of excuses about why we had to find somewhere else to stay, making it difficult for us to even appeal to their generosity. The so-called good friends made promises and assurances that they could not honour. Finally, we turned up at the house of Dr Das. He welcomed us in but was embarrassed that his apartment was so small. The three of us reassured him that we would be happy to stay anywhere. *We'll be out all day and only come back at night to this place,* Dad said confidently, *so we will sleep anywhere.*

No you won't, the man insisted. *You don't need to roam around the city if you don't have to. They are still children, Gordon, you go wherever you wish but please leave them here. We'll take care of them. You can come and go as you wish. There is food enough in the house, my wife and daughter will take care of you all. Don't worry.*

When I have sorted out my finances, lied Dad, *I'll pay for all that you have spent.*

Gordon, let's talk about that later.

Whenever we got chatting, Phillip would start getting restless. The poor fellow was used to being on the move all the time so being in the room with nowhere to go really irritated him. Initially he set up an obstacle course in the room and timed himself doing the round of jumping from the window ledge to the chair and on to the table and then to the bed and back to the window. Sometimes he'd topple onto me, scramble up and start again. When he wasn't doing that he'd sit at the window and look out on to the busy street, calling out to people as they passed. He even managed to charm a few vendors to give him a tasty morsel or two. The peanut seller was particularly generous and never failed to give him a handful of peanuts when he passed by the window.

Seeing his restlessness, the doctor's wife allowed him to go out on to pavement outside the apartment and play. He made friends easily and very soon had a gang of street kids gathered around him. They played marble games such as pill and hit, gaya paar and knockers and Phillip somehow managed to empty their pockets by winning quite a large collection of marbles.

When Anjali wasn't at school, I had company; otherwise, I'd lie there in the room staring at the ceiling. On those occasions, her mother would tend to my needs. Dad was rarely there and it seemed that he had almost relinquished his responsibility as a father. There was no word from Mum. She probably didn't have a clue where we were. Nora stayed away, preferring the security of the boarding school.

Phillip got into the habit of staying out until late at night and when he found that the doctor and his family couldn't control him, he sometimes returned only the next morning. Then the doctor sat him down one morning. *Listen here, Phillip my boy...*

I'm not your boy, he interrupted the doctor.

Your father has left you in my care. So I am responsible for your safety. You'll have to behave yourself. You hear me?

Phillip jumped up to leave the room.

You stay right here, the doctor was firm. *Stay right here and listen to what I have to say. You can very well play out on the pavement here or even down the road...but you come straight back for lunch, for tea, for dinner. And after dinner you are not to leave the house. Got it? Have you understood?*

Yes.

And another thing. I hear that you talk rudely to my wife and daughter. Stop it. You hear? Stop it.

Yes. Ok. Phillip walked out and stayed away for two days.

Anjali and her mother were worried. The doctor said, *Wait till Gordon comes back and deals with this. We have done our best. Anyway, when the boy is scared and hungry he'll come back.*

I had begun to recover and reached the stage where I had started to fantasize about all the sorts of food that I had not been allowed to eat until then. Aunt Katherine featured in a lot in these wild imaginings. I'd be there with her, eating her delicious kebabs and parathas, chatting with her. *Eat Sean, eat, I've made this specially for you. I soaked the pieces of mutton in dahi and cream and my special masala for an entire day, so that the juice of the meat and the masala and cream and dahi mingle and sink deep into each piece. It cooked fast. Juicy, isn't it?* She sat there at the table eating with me. *So tell me Sean, how has it been with you?*

Ok.

What is that supposed to mean? she wanted to know. *What's ok? You've just had typhoid and your insides are all worn and eaten up. It must be awful. And that stupid Terrence put you all through all that hell with his idle promises. And that fat nosed wife of his...actually I never liked her. She was always mean. But I can't blame her for being that way because she had such a difficult childhood. One of thirteen children. You are lucky because you are just one of three. But whenever I think of you I am scared about what you'll become. Who will ever want to know what you have gone through in order to understand you better? No one. Who knows what you'll become after you go through all this? 'What's the meaning of all of this?' I used to ask myself. It's different now.*

There was no food on the table and the room had changed. I was back in the room in which Grandpa lay dying. I sat there beside him looking into his eyes. *I am scared Grandpa, I don't know where I am going and what's going to happen.*

It's not what's going to finally happen somewhere in the future that you should be thinking about but what's happening now...

I'm scared.

He placed his hands on mine. *When I ran away from home as a boy I didn't know where I was going and what was finally going to happen to me. So I thought about the moment. You understand Sean? I know you are a boy and won't understand fully what I'm saying. Just remember the words, they'll mean something to you later. Stay in the moment.*

But I don't know why I was born, Grandpa.

Who knows why they were born? That you are alive, that's important. Stay alive, Sean. You are hungry now, there on the table there, your mother has put a bowl of chicken stew for me. Go and have some of it before she comes, go on.

I went to the table, sat down and started eating. It was my mother's stew, a complete meal in itself: peas, carrots, French beans, potatoes, onions, pieces of succulent chicken all immersed in a thick gravy. It was everyone's favourite. All the grown-ups called it Imelda's Stew, food for devils and angels alike. I had often watched her making it. In good times she went veggie and chicken shopping in the New Market, a coolie trailing her with a basket in which he carried her groceries; in difficult times she'd shop from street corner stalls or cart vendors and return to cook the stew on a small kerosene stove. I was her official taster. *Magic piece*, she'd call out when she wanted me to check if the chicken was ready. She'd pop the tiny piece into my mouth and wait for the verdict. *Mmm*, I'd lick my lips and she'd smile.

When it was cleaning up time, she'd wipe the last of the gravy from the pot with a slice of bread and call out, *lion's share* and I'd return to her side and take the slice from her.

Her stew lost its character when we couldn't afford butter. Margarine was an awful substitute. It didn't have the same wholesome flavour. So she tried replacing stew with pot roasted beef but that wasn't really welcome because the inferior quality meat was most often stale.

I was alone in the room in the company of one long dead visitor replacing the other. It was an uneasy feeling—I realised that they were not in my head but physically present in front of me. *I always liked bacon and eggs and sausages,* said Big Daddy, standing at the window and looking out on to the night street, *and crisp hot toast with a fine layer of butter spread over it, helped down by piping hot Darjeeling tea with a spot of milk in it. Too much milk spoils the flavour of the tea. That's for breakfast. For lunch, a plate of rice with rasam and crisply fried spicy prawns. You should try it. For dinner, a bowl of thick chicken soup. Back in the trenches we got beans and boiled meat. If we got lucky, we'd get a chunk of cheese and canned corned meat. Washed down with hot ditch water. There's nothing like a good meal in your stomach; it washes away the blues and makes you feel that life's worth living after all.* He turned and faced me, *Come here Sean, I'll show you something.* But I couldn't move. When I finally looked up, he wasn't there but the room was filled with the aroma of kathi kebabs.

Nausea washed through me and it felt as if my insides were going to start pouring out of me because there was nothing there to hold them in. I lay in bed on the flat of my back, staring into the dark. The night was filled with whispers but I couldn't understand what they were saying. I closed my eyes and when I opened them someone was leaning over me. It was the night nurse.

It was confusing moving from time zone to time zone, the past mutating to the present and then falling backwards like the face-shot victim of a sniper. Lying there in that hospital bed with the smell of disinfectant suffusing the air, I wondered where I was. *Is something the matter?* she asked.

Nothing. Why do you ask?

You've been very restless, talking and shouting in your sleep. I have to give you an injection.

Am I badly hurt? Can I sit up? Will I be able to walk?

You're lucky. They're moving you into a private room, a single room. You can shout your head off there. You can be yourself.

I don't remember what happened.

That's not important just now. I'll give you this shot. It'll knock you out. It'll save you the memory and pain, the confusion.

A while later I was like a feather floating into a bottomless well. The dark wafted up to receive me, making way for me as I travelled downwards. My past spun around me like threads of silk and enclosed me in its delicate but firm bind. When I finally floated to the surface I found myself in a sunlit room in the upper floors of the hospital, a wide window opening out on to a view of the sea visible over the roofs of buildings. The sky was a clear blue, streaked with shreds of clouds that formed dramatic patterns which kept shifting and changing.

You're mending faster than we had expected and we hope you'll be ready to go in ten days. Till then you'll have to be patient, said the small graceful fellow in white with the face of an owl, drawing his chair nearer to the bed.

Will I be able to walk?

You have been walking, every day for a while. Didn't you realise that?

No. I've been so confused. I don't know what's real and what's unreal, what's past and what's present. My head's a muddle.

Listen he said, leaning forward, *mending yourself physically is what you first need to do. Get your body together. Get it healed. You do want to live, don't you?*

Yes. But honestly, am I going to live or are you just leading me on?

Listen, just get your body working properly first and then you can take the next step.

That doesn't answer my question.

Of course you are going to live. You need rest, though.

Who has put me here?

He'll come and tell you himself. I'm not allowed to talk about this. He's a close friend of your family. He's writing off your bills. Actually, he got you shifted from the Municipal Hospital and booked you in here. You spent a few nights in the general ward and then you got this room. Thanks to him.

When I shut my eyes, he left the room.

Opening my eyes, I found myself lying in the dark room in Dr Das' house. I listened to sounds of the milk van rumbling past and the clink and grind and rattle of the trams as they made their way down Circular Road past the cemetery and up towards Park Circus, gradually the street came alive with early morning vendors and babus hurrying off to work. Calcutta was up and stumbling into the day. Phillip returned at breakfast time and no one said a word to him. The doctor and his wife had given up trying to tame him.

Later that day, the doctor went off to get Dad from the 'station'. When they returned, Dad looked like he had neither shaved nor slept for days. He looked as if he had gone through some difficult experience. *They locked him up,* said Phillip with a smirk when we were alone.

Dad announced that we were leaving Calcutta, heading to his cousin's home in Mathura. *Space enough there,* he said briskly, *we can take up half the place if we want.* I had heard that one before and was already scared.

Of course we weren't headed straight from Calcutta to Mathura but to Kanpur first. There we visited three of Dad's brothers, uncles I had only vaguely heard of. At every house we visited, the reunion began warmly, gradually transformed into cordiality, then old disagreements began surfacing and finally altercations and fights would break out. We'd leave hastily. The shifting around became so complicated and emotionally draining that we decided to stay with Dad's old friend from his shikar days. Uncle Gurpreet was a giant of a man with an enormous stomach and a laugh that was infectious. When he saw us get down from the cycle rickshaw outside his gun shop just off Mall Road, he rushed out to greet his old buddy. *Gaardan, big boy!* Dad was engulfed in a bear hug. *It is fantastic to see you! It's a dream come true!* he bellowed.

Dad looked genuinely delighted to see his old chum. For a moment, we got a glimpse of the clear-eyed young man he must have been. *Guru, look at you! You're looking so healthy and wealthy.* He lightly patted the man on his big belly. *Well fed for sure! And as handsome as ever. Lovely must still keep you on a leash.*

Uncle Gurpreet laughed and his belly shook like jelly. *No no yaar, now I'm a good boy.*

And a big boy.

So yaar, where are you putting up? Not with the brothers I'm sure. But which hotel? Lotus? Lotus is the best. And if you are staying in a hotel check out at once. I'll drive you there right now and get your luggage and you'll shift into my house. Don't say no, Gaardan.

Only if it isn't too much trouble, replied Dad, trying to sound reluctant.

Trouble! What nonsense! Good, then it's settled! You all stay with me! the man slapped Dad on his back. He laughed again and I watched his belly wobble and bounce. Then he passed wind. *Oops, I thought I was on the firing range.*

He turned his attention to us. *I saw both of you when you were just born. Beauties yaar, beauties. And look at you now, oh so handsome.* He picked us both up in his arms and kissed us on the cheek and then put us down, *Sorry yaar, handshake, let's shake hands. You should see my Bubbles, she's now a very lovely girl and she says she wants to be a doctor, already she knows what she wants to be. And my Happy, aarey he sings so well. My adorable Neelu, my beloved, is still like a fresh rose bud. But they're all in Gorakhpur for the holidays. And you two must be on holiday too. What fun you must be having. Ok Gaardan, let's check you out from Lotus.*

It took Dad a little lying to slip out of the awkward situation and avoid telling his friend that we had no where to stay and all that we possessed was in the cycle rickshaw with us.

Okay, let's put your day travel stuff in the car then, he insisted. We did just that and Uncle Gurpreet barked his last instructions to his assistant in the shop and we shot off down the Mall as if we were about to miss our train.

The house looked more like an outsized, colourfully painted barn with turrets on four corners, surrounded by multiple gardens and a small orchard. At the back, towards the far end, was an extensive field where Uncle Gurpreet and his battalion of a family took turns growing various sorts of seasonal vegetables. They had a tractor called Jolly and seven helpers whom they called the seven dwarfs.

A couple of days rolled into weeks and gradually Uncle Gurpreet figured out our condition. He insisted that Dad return with all of us to settle down in Kanpur and he said that he was happy to build a small place for us in one corner of his property. *We are better than brothers yaar,* he kept repeating. But Dad turned the offer down. Then came an offer to settle us in Gorakhpur where Uncle had a large automobile recycling factory. *You can take care of that,* he said. *My whole family trusts you, Gaardan. You are like our own. You shouldn't have left Kanpur. All of us really missed you. Come on. Say yes, and we'll get Nora and Imelda here and you can start all over again. One place to stay here and a place in Gorakhpur.* Dad said that he'd think about the offer.

Being in Kanpur didn't seem to suit Dad. He was uneasy wherever we went almost as if his past was waiting to catch up with him and drag him into times that he was trying to forget. His childhood, his youth and his early married years lurked around corners. Though much had changed in the city of bicycles and factories, much remained.

The place where Grandpa's house once stood now had a training college for nurses occupying most of the space. The rest was taken up by a polyclinic. Uncle said nothing as we drove past the property. *Shall we go to the cemetery?*

Dad said, *We'll need to get flowers.*

We pulled up at the gate of the cemetery and stood outside looking at the dump that it had become. There were no tombstones or gravestones left and wild shrubs were everywhere. A pile of brick and plaster rubble lay there, offloaded by a builder working on some nearby site. And there was a large pool of water that had formed. It was stagnant and bred a cloud of insects. *This is more like a garbage dump*, Dad whispered to himself. Uncle said nothing and we headed across the ruins towards where the line of family graves once lay. A mongoose shot out of its hole in the ground and ran off into the thicket. Huge rats emerged, looked at us and retreated. Empty liquor and soda water bottles lay broken all around. *Here's where they all lie—your grandpa, grandma and so many more. All gone. And all that's here is this garbage heap.* Dad looked like he was about to start crying.

Uncle stood there awkwardly, wondering what to do with the bunch of freshly cut flowers he had picked from the garden before coming here. *Sorry brother, we don't come this side of town. If I knew someone had to look after this, I would have.*

It's not your fault Guru. It's mine. Ours.

Before we left, Uncle did the strangest thing. He walked to one end of the graveyard and started placing flowers side by side in a long line, dropping the last few on the surface of the stagnant pool of water. I watched them float away.

When we got home, we discovered that Dad's brothers had tracked him down. They wanted to know why he wasn't staying with any of them. He listened to them and when they were through burst into a rage, raving and ranting about how they had neglected the graves of the family. The mother of all fights broke out and Uncle used his diplomatic skills and bottles of liquor to calm raw nerves. They drank each other under the table then dragged themselves to their cars and left.

We left for Mathura a few days later. Huge tears rolled down Uncle Gurpreet's cheeks as he peered in through the window of the compartment.

Travelling with Dad was quite different from travelling with Mum. Phillip didn't mess around very much and he was a little more civil. Besides that, the compartment wasn't as crowded as the one I had travelled in southwards. The holiday rush was over and there was a lot more room to breathe. That, I must say, was a big relief for me. Even though Dad was an unreliable fellow and couldn't really be trusted I did feel a little more protected when travelling with him.

What made the journey somewhat enjoyable was that there was a nip in the air and a haze softened the countryside that we travelled through.

We arrived early morning when a fine mist hung over the holy city of Mathura and the river Yamuna. The temple bells were clanging madly and every living creature seemed to be celebrating the new day. A pleasing warmth crept over me as we drove from the railway station to our new lodgings in a jeep.

Abandoned

The house sat on the outskirts of the city on an immense stretch of land which included a private woodland, a roughly cleared playground, a bamboo grove, an old fashioned open air 'royal bath', three gardens and two rows of quarters for household attendants. The successful civil engineer Prem Shastri's wealth was evident, from the posh interiors of his house in polished wood and brass and bronze to his fleet of cars, his wardrobe, his collection of pipes and aromatic tobacco, his well stocked bar and his retinue of liveried house-help. Sheila, Dad's supposed long lost cousin, Prem Shastri's wife, was a bird-like woman with a small but stubborn voice that had a way of piercing the thickest of heads. All she had to do was wag her little finger and she'd have the entire household on their knees in front of her. She had everything she could wish for, except a child. From the moment we entered the house, she was all over us. It was obvious right from the start that I was the favourite because I seemed to get a little extra of everything. Phillip didn't mind in the least because he hated being fussed over. I must admit, I rather liked it. A quantum leap from stealing vegetables from a kitchen garden for supper to being asked what sort of menu I'd prefer. The speed at which everything happened was overwhelming and I was literally swept off my feet with little time to think.

Dad faded into the background as he went back and forth between Gwalior and Mathura getting interviewed for a possible job. Phillip found something or the other to occupy himself with and I was left to be pampered.

For the first month or so, I hadn't really been out of the house and started getting claustrophobic and breaking out in cold sweats and hyperventilating. One afternoon I escaped out of the back door of the bathroom into the fresh air outside and set off to explore the estate. The sheer openness of the place was exhilarating. Wild hares, partridges, jungle fowls and peacocks were everywhere and the air smelled of freedom. I ran across the playground, rolled on the soft grass of the lawns, inspected the 'royal bath' and introduced myself to the two resident dogs. Somehow it all felt so familiar.

Prem Shastri stood at the edge of the woods, shooting at cans with his twelve bore. *Ah ha, there you are Sean, lots of space to run around, eh?*

Yes, I said, out of breath.

Come on, let me show you around the place.

I've seen a lot of it already, Uncle, I replied.

Ah, but you haven't seen the woods. There's a lot in there. Come along...

I followed him into the first grove of trees. The deeper we went, the cooler it got. *These woods are old,* he said, *and the trees have spread their roots everywhere. Careful you don't trip over them. Here, hold my hand.* His grip was firm as we walked along. When we emerged into a clearing, he released my hand, and turned to me with a smile. *You have the softest fingers I have ever touched,* he said. Then he ran his fingers over the back of my neck. *So soft here too.*

When we returned, Khyal Singh, his man Friday relieved him of the gun and we walked back to the house, Uncle Prem ahead of me. I followed him unthinkingly. Once inside the house I heard Aunt Sheila's raised voice. *You didn't take him into the woods Prem, did you? Just the two of you? Listen, I don't want any hanky panky. If he's going to be with us I want it to be normal. You hear me? Normal.*

I heard Uncle Prem's steps shuffling towards me so I fled. My foot slipped on the polished wood flooring and I went sliding along on my face. I crawled up and scrambled out without turning to check if I had been spotted.

That night I asked Dad, *Why are we here?*

Because Uncle Prem and Aunt Sheila are happy to share their house with us.

Why would they want to share their house with us? I asked. *They're so rich and we have nothing.*

Because we are related and they want to help us.

How are we related?

From Grandpa's side.

How?

Go to sleep now Sean, we'll talk about this in the morning.

But that morning never came and life on the estate slipped into an easy rhythm of unbridled luxury. Days fell into days filled with exploration and discovery. To the east of the property I found a deep ravine which ended in a small rocky cave. That became my secret place.

Then one day Dad announced that Phillip was being sent to a boarding school in Agra and that I was going to be admitted to a local school run by nuns.

The very idea of school was alien to me. All of my short life till then had been filled with staying alive and living from moment to moment. School rarely featured in the scheme of things. Yes, I did remember going to school when we had first moved to Calcutta from Kanpur. It was one run by Jesuits where I had a class teacher who would to fix her hair in a net and dress in white and looked like a nurse in a hospital. Some of the older boys called her Jection (short for injection) Ma'am. The fellow sitting next to me was so scared of her that once when he wanted to go to the loo he couldn't ask her so he did it right there on the bench. A perfectly formed sausage of turd. Everyone was amazed by his skill.

A hazy memory of a playground teaming with rowdy children, lunch times of steaming rice mounds dripping with dal and topped with a fried egg; walking home through the rain under a little blue umbrella wearing matching gumboots; Sports Day and the grand Christmas Party. And after all that...school became the place where other kids spent their day. There were often times when I really wanted to go to school, to wear a uniform like other kids, to carry a school bag on my back packed with books, to have my own geometry box, to cheer my school in a match, to say I belonged where other kids belonged, to be in a class where I could put up my hand and answer a question and the teacher say *right*, to march in a school parade, to be like other children, not to be scrounging around from hand to mouth, wondering where my next meal was going to come from and being with grownups who often treated me like an adult giving me no chance to be myself. And now, after all this time, I was being sent to a school, again.

The first day was intimidating. It was almost as if I had landed on another planet. Nuns in habits floated around the place and neatly dressed little boys and girls chimed *good morning* in unison. There was a pen where a couple of geese honked and a group of kids sat under a neem tree obediently singing nursery rhymes. The ones that couldn't keep up were occasionally whacked by a fierce looking nun.

But I surprised myself by slipping into the routine. In fact I quickly became Sister Bridgette's pet. *You are my little bulbul,* she'd coo, every time she caught me alone. I swore to myself that when I grew up I'd carry her off to some far away place and marry her. She was small and plump with bright curious eyes, a button nose and a smile that had a way of easing embarrassing situations. Her little fingers either pinched my cheeks or drew me close to her. And her fragrance was spicy and warm.

She became one of my reasons for going to school. The other was beautiful Marian. Peaches and cream with a mouth like cherries, deep green eyes, black hair and a voice like bells. The daughter of a Kashmiri father and an Irish mother, she was just about an inch or two taller than me, in the same class and lived down the road.

When the other kids saw us walking around together on the playground they started teasing me, *girlie, girlie, always with a girlie.* I didn't fight back. But one day when it got too much Marian punched a fellow in the face. He lurched backwards and covering his nose with his hands went away wailing like a siren. When Sister Bridgette asked to see his nose, he showed her the blood on his hands.

That's from my nose, Sister, he wailed. Then he pointed to me accusingly. *He hit me!*

The next day his parents turned up and complained that I had punched him. My father was called and given a dressing down. It took him just half an hour to charm Mother Superior off her feet and the next moment he had nuns asking his advice on the construction of an open air performance stage. Dad knew very little about construction but there he was offering expert advice. Luckily, thanks to some minor carpentry jobs he had done when he was younger, he supervised getting the stage built along with several small additional classrooms at rock bottom rates and became their knight in shining armour.

When some saint or the other's feast came around, Mother Superior would hand me a small note for Dad. The next day a wild hare would be delivered, or a few wild fowl, all bagged with a gun borrowed from Uncle Prem. At Christmas, they wanted a turkey. Since that wasn't possible, the nearest was a peafowl. So Dad borrowed the gun again and bagged a peafowl from behind the bamboo grove on the estate and sent it to them. They offered mass for him.

Meanwhile, Marian and I had become buddies. We knew each other's minds and hearts inside out. Soon school time wasn't enough and I started going over to her place and feeding the pets her father had kept in cages. There was a jackal, a flying fox, a mouse deer and a dozen parakeets. Her parents didn't mind me hanging around the house. In fact her father would often walk with us through mustard fields down to the riverside to watch flocks of wild birds rise and settle on the water. Through his binoculars we'd observe large turtles trail out on to the opposite bank, sun themselves and then return. And as the sun fell low over the fields, we'd return when cries of grey partridges and lapwings filled the air. In summer, the banks of the river became water melon beds and we were treated to a juicy pink slice of the fruit.

Even though Dad didn't have a problem, Aunt Sheila decided that she was going to put her foot down. *There's no need for you to go to other people's homes,* she chirped, *no reason at all Sean. Call them here if you want.* Dad did not intervene. It looked like he was there for the free board and lodge and had relinquished all responsibility.

Marian would often visit me. She'd come over early evening and we'd spend an hour or two rambling about the place. Then came our First Holy Communion. She wore white and I was allowed to wear a dark blue suit which Uncle Prem had specially got tailor-made for me. Everyone in the little chapel smiled broadly when they saw us and I felt blessed to be eating the flesh of Christ with my friend.

We became inseparable.

On one occasion when both Uncle Prem and Aunt Sheila were away in Delhi and Dad was on the estate, he helped himself to a .22 from the gun rack and was out in the wood after hare. *Come along you two, join me if you want.*

Marian came along because she whispered to me that she had powers that could heal hurt creatures. *My mother gave me those powers,* she said.

When Dad knocked a hare off its feet a few minutes later, she rushed up to it and cradling its bleeding body in her arms, sang a song to it. But it remained dead as a doornail. She insisted on carrying the dead animal in her arms, staining her pale blue frock with splashes of blood. Her mother was furious and didn't let her visit for a month.

That's the time when Dad got a job in Gwalior. He promised to visit me on weekends but never did.

I was alone.

Aunt Sheila insisted that I sleep with her at night because she didn't want me to be alone. It was a scary experience because she'd get up in the middle of the night and walk around the room chanting prayers then sit down in her rocking chair which creaked eerily as she rocked it...and as I slipped into sleep the sound travelled with me and conjured up bizarre beings.

I felt abandoned. Granted, the Shastris were kind to me and gave me the very best but I didn't really belong there. I belonged somewhere else. I didn't know where. Not belonging anywhere was like being in a limbo. I needed help so when I met Father Joachim, the parish priest of the little church standing in the premises of the school, I got chatting with him. *Waiting for the jeep to pick you up, eh?* he asked.

Yes Father.

Come on, you can wait in the veranda here. Sit on the steps. I'll get us some hot chocolate. You'd fancy some wouldn't you?

Yes.

Sipping hot chocolate a while later he asked, *How is everything at home?*

Fine, Father.

The Shastris are such kind people. Taking you in and caring for you and all that. Not Catholics, not even Christians, but such kind people. You should consider yourself lucky. It's the hand of God in all his mercy and bounty at work here.

Yes Father, I responded, the words sticking in my throat.

Which child with your sort of background gets a chance like this?

I said nothing.

He was closed. I wouldn't be able to talk to him. I thought he would understand, but I was mistaken.

Is something worrying you? he asked after a pause.

I remained quiet.

I know adjusting to a new environment can be difficult. Say your prayers on time and Jesus will stay by you. He continued his advice as he stood up quietly and creeping along to the wall behind him unhooked a leather whip that was hanging there. Then he stalked towards the farther end of the balcony, whip in hand. His eyes were focussed on a squirrel on the wooden railings at the end of the veranda. As he neared, something happened to the animal. It stopped nibbling and sat there very still as if it knew that its time had come. The whip cracked and the creature flew off the railings and lay kicking on the floor.

Got the devil! Nice coat. It'll make a lovely purse. He turned to me. *Want to see a squirrel being skinned?*

The jeep arrived and I left. The world was going crazy around me and I was out there trying to make sense of it all.

It was a relief when Marian started visiting me again. The monsoons were approaching and one evening when she was there the sky was overcast and it looked like it was going to rain heavily. *I can stay a while more*, said Marian. *Do you want to explore the woods? There's still enough light.*

It will start raining, I was reluctant.

So what? My mum doesn't mind me getting a little wet.

But Aunt Sheila gets...

She cut me short. *Don't worry about her. She's not your Mum. Let's go.*

I followed her into the wood, creeping along between shrubs until we hit a narrow path and reached the place where the hare had been killed. She drew a circle in the mud with a twig, threw a little dust over her left shoulder and then her right and shutting her eyes, whispered to me, *now its soul can rest in peace.*

A fluttering ahead of us attracted our attention. A turtle dove had just been frightened from its nest. We crept forward and leaning into the bush saw three gleaming eggs in a mass of twigs. I lunged forward to touch them. *Don't, she said. Don't do that. You'll be cursed.*

She had hardly spoken when a rumble of thunder rolled high above us and it started raining. I turned to run but she stopped me. *Let's get wet*, she whispered.

We walked back slowly in the rain and as we reached the edge of the wood she turned and hugged me close. *Will you always be my friend?*

I was so overwhelmed that I didn't know what to say.

Back at the house, Aunt Sheila was going crazy.

She's behaving as if she's your Mum, said Marian.

Yes, that's what had started getting oppressive. The Shastris were now behaving as if they were my parents. My father wasn't even mentioned and his absence didn't help one bit. In fact it made things worse. I missed the river and the fresh breeze that blew along its banks, kicking up whirls of fine sand. I missed the great flocks of wild birds rising and falling. I missed the quiet water licking my feet. I missed the river so much that I ended up confiding in Uncle Prem and asking him to help to make it possible.

You are a very special fellow, Sean, and we are special friends. I'll find a way out. And he kept his word. Early every evening I was allowed to take a walk with Bhaloo and the two dogs, Badshah the German Shepherd and Faltu the Lhasa Apso. We'd head out of the gate, turn right, walk along one length of the boundary wall of the estate and then cross over to the other side of the road where a dusty path led away between farmlands. Badshah and I quickly made friends and we'd take off on our own ahead of the other two. Sometimes, he'd get it into his canine head to rush off into the fields after some wild animal or the other and I'd go charging after him. When we finally caught up with each other, he'd bark loudly and trot back with me.

Once Badshah downed a hare and shook the life out of it. Bhaloo took the dead animal away from him and carried it to his quarters to skin and cook. Having once tasted wild blood, Badshah got into the habit of hunting. It was our secret. When he became a bit bolder, he turned his attention to the wood on the estate and hunted hare, wild fowl and other small creatures. When he considerably reduced their numbers, he started stealing fowl at night from their cages. He polished off a number of Aunt Sheila's Black Minorcas, Rhode Island Reds and Leghorns. *It's a wolf,* she insisted. *Jackals don't do this.*

You talk with such authority as if you know the difference between a wolf and a jackal, Uncle Prem reacted.

Of course I know the difference, she was adamant.

What is it, what's the difference?

A wolf has a bushy tail and a jackal has a thin long curly tail.

Uncle Prem laughed then went into his store room and came out a while later with two pelts. He spread them out on the floor. *So now, that's the difference.*

She took a good look, *there's hardly any difference.*

Well, that's your opinion. A lone animal has been operating here, picking up fowl. I suspect it's a lone jackal. Or, you just may be right. I'm not going to use my .22 on him, nor my 12 bore. I'll try out the 275 magnum.

When we went out for our evening walk I sat down by the Jamuna with Badshah and patting his head said, *Stay away from the fowl, Badhshah or Uncle with shoot you.* He wagged his tail and looked at me as if to say, *try and stop me.* Bhaloo suggested that I speak to Uncle Prem and tell him the truth.

He'll be angry that I never told him earlier...I'm sure he'll tell Aunt Sheila.

So what? She'll make a little noise and after that she'll forget about it. That's the way she is. She never remembers anything because half the time she's talking to spirits and doesn't pay much attention to living people any more.

When we got back to the estate, Uncle Prem was busy setting up a machaan in the tamarind tree near the fowl cages. I waited for him be alone then I quickly told him everything. He looked at me and smiled. *Thank you for being honest about this Sean. This will be our secret. Only our secret. But I'll have to frighten Badhshah tonight or else he'll keep killing the fowls. He has to be stopped. The bang should scare him off.*

That night, he shot the animal in the head. Bhaloo told me later that the impact of the 275 magnum bullet spun Badshah around and he dropped a few feet away with his brains blown out. When Aunt Sheila heard about what had happened, she became hysterical, screaming at Uncle Prem and worked herself up into such a state that she blacked out. She had loved Badshah like her own child. She fasted for three days and had to be force-fed to bring her back to her normal state.

She set about enquiring into how and why it had all happened. Even though I was somewhat sure that Uncle Prem wouldn't squeal on me, I was terrified that she might find out through Bhaloo. *No, I won't say anything,* he reassured me. *I'd be stupid to do that. If I say anything, I myself will be in trouble. I'll lose my job and she'll even put a police case against me. More than that, she'll cast a black spell on me.*

She will never do something like that.

Who says so? You don't know what she is like. She cast a black spell on a watchman who wasn't doing his duty and he shrivelled up in two months and was dead. When they took the fellow to the burning ghat he was as light as a feather and no one recognised him. She's dangerous.

The Hive of Bees

One evening Uncle Prem joined me where I stood on the edge of the wood. *You must miss your evening walk with Badshah.*

Yes, I do.

If you had told me what was happening earlier than you did, maybe you would have saved Badshah.

I'm really sorry, I said.

Sorry won't make him alive again. He's dead now.

You won't tell anyone will you? Please don't. You promised you wouldn't!

I didn't promise, Sean. I wouldn't say something I didn't mean.

Are you going to tell her?

Maybe. Unless we can find a way out.

I'm willing to do anything Uncle, anything. Please don't tell Aunty.

See Sean, I've been doing so many things for you and you show no gratitude. I take care of you like my own son, I send you to school, I bought you that suit for your first Holy Communion, I organised for you to go for evening walks...and there's a lot else too...and this is what I get in return? Since you've shown no gratitude, no simple thank you even, I'm afraid I have to tell you what I expect from you.

I'll do anything you want, give you anything you want. I am grateful for everything. Please don't tell Aunt Sheila about Badshah.

Okay, I'll take your word for it. We'll go up to the roof tomorrow afternoon, when Aunty is asleep. You understood that?

Yes.

I've never seen you go up to the roof.

I've never been there because it's always locked. And there's nothing to do there.

There's lots to do there. I'll show you. You'll enjoy every moment of it. I've got the keys.

The next afternoon, I met him outside the shut door. He unlocked it quickly, his hands shaking slightly and we climbed a narrow flight of stairs which reached an equally narrow corridor. *This way, Sean,* he whispered urgently. The corridor went in a sort of spiral upwards and reached a small room at the top. There was a chair there and a small cot. *I come here when I am lonely, Sean,* he sighed. *And I'm lonely now. Are you lonely?*

I nodded, not really knowing what else to do. He put his arms around me and drew me close in an embrace and started kissing me all over my face and neck and his hands moved all over my body. I didn't know what to do.

Take off your pants Sean.

No. I don't want to. I started to feel uneasy.

I want to teach you something that you will learn to enjoy. All lonely people do this. You are lonely and I am lonely and that's why we are doing this, he whispered.

What are we going to do?

Take off your pants, Sean, I'm saying this for the last time. If you don't, I'll take them off and if you stop me I'm going to tell Aunty about why Badshah died. You understand me?

I was so frightened that I couldn't move.

He yanked down my pants and I heard the buttons pop off and go rolling across the floor covered with pigeon droppings. His hands were all over, touching me in places I had never been touched by other hands, making my body feel warm and strange. Then he dropped his pants and showed himself to me. I struggled to get free but he held me close and kissed me all over. *Now you kiss me,* he commanded, grabbing me by the hair and lowering my head. I bit him hard and he struggled to push my head away. I bit again and he slapped me hard on my back and sent me reeling. I scrambled up and started running down the corridor without my pants, sobbing. The run was endless. Finally when I reached the door, it was locked. Uncle Prem stood there behind me. He pushed my face against the door and slammed his body against me. Something burst inside me.

The smell of his body was sickening.

Later, he said, *here are your pants. Put them on. And not a word about this to anyone, okay? Not a word. It's our little secret,* he said, stroking my hair. I staggered out, retching.

I lived in terror in the weeks that followed. I was frightened, alone, sick, sore, bleeding. I was living in Uncle Prem's house. He was sending me to school, feeding me, clothing me, giving me all that space to do what I pleased in. He was taking his due, his payment. It was his right. But even then, I knew what was happening to me was wrong. I was trapped.

I was in a mess. I had become attached to life on the estate and yet I was allowing myself to be broken and used. Was that the price of happiness? Was that better than being dragged from hovel to hovel by a drunken irresponsible father? Which was better? Which was worse?

I spent late afternoons in my cave, crying and talking to imaginary people, asking them to come and help me. But no one came. Finally, I decided to tell Marian. Telling her wasn't as difficult as I thought it would be. I took her to my cave for the first time, climbed in with her, sat her down near me and told her everything.

After that day, Marian avoided me in school. She didn't come home to play. When I tried to speak to her, she would make an excuse to leave. She began spending time with other groups of children and soon after that, she transferred to another school. I never saw her again.

For me, it didn't end with that encounter on the roof. It went on and on. Uncle Prem grabbed me whenever he got the opportunity. I had become his pet. He bought me toys and gifts and new clothes and took me on outings with Aunt Sheila so she wouldn't suspect anything. It made me sick to play with the toys he got me, wear the clothes he bought for me and eat the chocolates I was forced to eat in his presence.

I was helpless. I was angry. I was hurt. I hated the way he looked and smiled. The way he touched me. The way he made me feel so strange. The way his body smelled. My stomach turned every time I got a whiff of that scented tobacco of his. I wanted to hurt him, to kill him. Sometimes I wondered whether people looking at me could tell how I had changed. Other times I was sure that people got to know the moment they looked at my face. I know it wasn't the same face any more. I would lock myself in the bathroom and climb up on a stool and look at my face in the mirror. That was not my face staring at me. Those were not my eyes.

I felt so desperate that I wanted to kill myself so that I'd be so far away from everyone that no one would be able to touch me anymore. But I knew that it wasn't easy to drown myself in the river because the Yamuna was shallow that time of the year. The 'royal bath' was filled to the brim. The water was green and slimy and there were all sorts of creatures swimming inside. The very thought of them filling up my body sickened me. I vomited. I steadied myself and walked to the edge, paused to jump and then turned and ran as fast as I could away from the place. I went back to my cave and sat there till I heard Aunt Sheila calling.

I hated every moment of my life.

Sometimes I would lie awake at night, my eyes shut, going through all that I had experienced in my life till then. All I saw were a swarm of nightmares, like bees buzzing around me. And now this. This was like the hive that attracted them. They quickly settled on to it. Yes, I now had a hive of bees inside me. I wanted to disturb it and set free the swarm in rage but I couldn't, so it remained inside me.

Things started looking more scary when they began discussing my future as if they had adopted me and I was now part of their family.

One night at dinner, I stopped the discussion. *I want to go home.*

Aunt Sheila looked at Uncle Prem. Then she looked at me. *Home? What home are you talking about?*

My home.

Where's your home?

My mind went blank.

Go on, I asked you a question.

Where my family is, I replied.

Where is your family, Sean? It's where your security is. Where you get fed and clothed and educated and cared for. That's where your family is. And that's here. Right here.

I want to go home! I burst into tears and left the table.

The next day when Uncle Prem caught me alone he said, *If you open your mouth, you are done for.*

I am going to tell Aunt Sheila what you've done to me. I am going to tell her.

Then you'll see what I'll do to you.

Let me go and I won't tell. Let me go home. I won't say anything, I promise!

But you don't have a home.

Call my father and tell him I want to be with him.

Ha! Your drunken father? He has a job now, but soon he won't even have that and then what are you going to do? Tell me, what?

I want to go to my Dad. He'll take me to my Mum. Let me go or I'll tell on you.

If I could, I'd wring your little neck, he said, dragging me to the room on the roof.

My father turned up a few days later, furious with me for insisting on leaving. The Shastris treated him shabbily and made him wait out in the veranda, finally handing me over with a small suitcase of clothes. Aunt Sheila didn't even look at me as I left. I could feel Uncle Prem's eyes burning a hole into my back as I walked away.

Trust you to mess things up, he said as we made our way to railway station in a cycle rickshaw. *Now I'll have to take care of you in Gwalior. How am I going to do that if I go to work every day? You had it so good here and you threw it all away.* After a brief silence, he said, *And I'm the one who has been made a fool in all this.*

I wondered how.

Living with Cat Aunty

A few months later, Dad got a job in Calcutta and we were all reunited. Mum returned from Coimbatore and Nora from the hostel. Phillip who was still in a boarding school in Agra visited us only for his holidays. I tried to block out the horrors I had experienced in Uncle Prem's house. With a hint of security creeping in, our family life seemed to take on the veneer of normalcy. We tried our best to brush the past under the carpet, but the damage had already been done. It was evident that Mum had changed. Though she did all that she could possibly do to take care of us, her enthusiasm had ebbed and she had begun to merely act like the person she used to be. Dad bumbled along, trying to pretend that everything was fine and life had treated us well. Away from us for so long, Nora had already drifted from attachment and constantly talked about what she would like to do with her life. Phillip was distant and used the 'family' for his own convenience. I suppose it was his way of coping and surviving.

As for me—I was relieved to be with 'my family' again even though it was like being part of a charade. Confusion, hurt and loss lay like feral creatures, waiting to surface and break free. I kept them subdued by the feeling of wanting to be 'normal'.

Since finding an apartment with a reasonable rent was difficult, we settled for sharing a place with a woman by the name of Elaine Marquise. She was a generous soul and did her best to make us feel at home, cooking our food and maintaining the house. We didn't have to do a thing, except wash our clothes. The flat was quite spacious and we occupied a large bedroom which we partitioned into two with curtains strung on spring wires resting on poles. The sitting and dining rooms were the common areas which were comfortably furnished. They opened on to a small garden with a rockery, a patch of lawn and numerous little flowerbeds.

It would have been more than just pleasant living there if it hadn't been for her cats. They were everywhere, fourteen residents and a hoard of visitors. We couldn't tell one from the other. They all seemed so scruffy and stinky. Each had a name—there was Fester Neck, Poo Poo, Gentleman, Grinner, Big Butt, Gnasher, Pudgy and others with names like Daakoo, Ding Ding, Elvis and Pee Pot. Fester Neck sat curled up on the mantelpiece, close to the fruit bowl, Gentleman sat in the armchair, Grinner in a chair at the head of the dining table...and the others were everywhere, reclining, arching their backs, rubbing themselves against unwilling legs, stretching out in the doorway, scattered in the garden. The more I took a little note of them the more I began to distinguish one from the other.

Occasionally, I took a swipe at them or gave them a swift kick when they started bothering me. *Don't you dare hurt any of them,* said the lady of the house to me, a few days after we had shifted in. *They are my children. They make up for my sister Annie. The river took her away. She loved cats. I keep them because they remind me of her. Every morning and night when I pray I say, "this is for you Annie". If you don't know how to love cats, I can teach you,* she offered.

I didn't reply.

Elaine prattled on. *I'm all alone. My parents went to Heaven a long time back and my sis followed them.*

How do you know they went to Heaven?

I dreamed of them some time back. They looked very happy and they were all in white and their bodies were glowing.

I've seen people after they're dead and their bodies aren't glowing.

What did you just say? You mean in your dreams?

No. I've seen dead people.

Have you told anyone about this?

No.

If you see anyone in this house, will you tell me?

I didn't reply. But a month or so later when I got up at night to get myself a glass of water I saw a woman sitting in the armchair in the sitting room. She had a rosary in her hand and it looked like she was praying. I wasn't sure what to do—put the glass on the table and quietly walk back to bed, or remain standing till she decided to leave.

I sit here every night, I love this chair. It was my grandmother's chair.

Your sister says she saw you in Heaven. Are you in Heaven? I asked.

Does it look like I'm in Heaven?

I don't know.

I'm waiting boy, I'm waiting for my time.

I suddenly noticed that there were no cats in the room. Not a single one.

So you're wondering where all the cats have gone?

It was scary, she could read my mind.

No, I lied.

She laughed softly. *You're a very clever boy. Cleverer than you realise. I'm going to tell you something, something you won't believe. It's about my sister. Now don't be frightened when you hear this, ok? Don't be frightened. Come here boy, come a little closer.*

I stepped closer.

Closer, closer.

When I was near the overpowering aroma of jasmine enveloped me.

My sister, she's a liar. A dangerous liar. I didn't drown in the river. She pushed me off the roof of this house. No one suspected her because they thought that she loved me very much. She killed me to lay her hands on all this after my parents died. Now she has to live with her shame and her guilt. Follow me boy, follow me, she said and I did. The front door opened and we stood outside. *Look, there's the body. On the pavement.*

I peered out at the body lying with its head smashed on the sidewalk. I was alone. I sat down on the front steps staring at the body. *What are you doing out here?* It was Mum. She grabbed me by my arm and yanked me into the house and shut the front door. *What were you doing out there?*

She showed me her body lying out there on the pavement.

What body are you talking about?

The body on the pavement, she showed it to me.

Who showed you the body? What are you talking about Sean? You've had a nightmare. You're sleep walking.

I'm not.

Come along. She led me back to bed.

What's happening? mumbled Dad

Mum didn't reply.

The next day I noticed that Gentleman didn't sit in the armchair. He stayed outside in the garden and didn't come in.

Is there breakfast this morning? Dad asked, ready for work.*Nora, you better take a look, maybe the woman has kicked the bucket,* he said jokingly.

Don't say that. Mum didn't think it funny. She knocked on the bedroom door and a weak voice answered. She pushed it open and went in.

Dad sat at the table waiting for breakfast. *Sean, what are they up to in there?*

Should I go and see?

Don't you go in now! Nora? Nora! Come here at once!

Yes, Dad, Nora emerged, still heavy with sleep.

Check what's happening in there. He pointed in the direction of Elaine Marquise's bedroom. She staggered off in that direction, returning a little later with Mum in tow. Their faces were pale.

There's something wrong with the woman, Mum said. *She's lying there in bed and shivering. She doesn't have temperature, doesn't appear to be ill but seems to be frightened silly.*

And she's drooling. Like she has fits or something, added Nora.

Must have epilepsy. Just leave her and she'll be up and about sooner or later, Dad concluded. *Now is anyone going to get me some breakfast or do I pick up something at work?* Mum went into the kitchen and rustled up some eggs. Dad continued to mumble impatiently. He left hurriedly after what he called his 'meagre' breakfast. Mum and Nora went back into Elaine Marquise's bedroom and stayed there till the afternoon.

I'll take you kids out for a Chinese lunch and we'll leave her to recover. She's had some kind of shock.

That night, I emerged from our bedroom, reluctantly, on the pretext of getting myself a glass of water. Someone was sitting in the armchair. I pretended not to look in that direction...but when I did I discovered that it was Elaine Marquise. She sat there quite still, without saying a word. And then when I was about to leave she said, *I want to talk to you, son. I need to talk to you.*

I didn't know what to say.

That's ok, not now. I can wait till tomorrow. Tomorrow.

Yes, tomorrow. I went back to bed and lay there all night with my eyes tightly shut but refusing to sleep. I was scared of what I might see if I opened my eyes and didn't want to sleep because I was scared of the dreams that might visit me.

I open my eyes and look out of the window at the sky which is overcast by a pale grey haze, gusts of cool breeze come in from the sea and I can taste the salt on my lips and inhale the fragrance of seaweed.

This room feels more like I'm in a hotel than a hospital. Am I really in a hospital? I can't tell whether I'm awake or asleep. Is this real or unreal? My memory keeps playing tricks with me. A nurse walks in and says something that I do not understand. She raises the

head-end of the bed so that I am half sitting up. I watch her uncover the lower part of my body and sponge me down.

They still aren't sure what your relationship with that woman was. So they are coming in again later today to ask you questions. Why don't you tell them what you know so that they'll go away. What secret are you hiding brother? I've been taking care of you all this while and wondering to myself why you have had to suffer this way. I know you are good man. I know. I can feel it. There's something good and honest about you.

I cut in on her ramble. *What are you talking about?*

She looks at me with her deep set dark eyes. *You, brother.*

What's this 'brother' you keep calling me?

It's my way of drawing a line between myself and men I feel something for. So I don't get involved.

You don't even know me.

Alright. I won't speak anymore. Sorry. She finishes tending to me and heads for the door. Then stops and says, *By the way, you have security guards outside your door twenty-four hours.*

That's the joke of the day.

If you don't believe me why don't you get up and have a look for yourself.

You know I can't do that.

Of course you can. She leaves.

Thank you, I call out after her. *Thank you...sister.*

Dad's voice skips from another time warp and flows in. *We better find another place to live in. This woman and her cats give me the willies.*

I'm sure it's just loneliness that makes her behave strangely. Mum says.

You sound like one of those mind doctors, Imelda. I don't think it's just loneliness. I think she's a crank who gets affected by the moon. This is full moon time.

I lay there on the other side of the curtains listening to them. It was early in the morning and Dad was about to get out of bed.

That was just the time when both of them would say anything of any consequence to each other.

That afternoon when Nora was out and Mum was having one of her naps, Elaine Marquise called me into her room. *Sit down boy, there on that comfortable chair. Yes, that one. Now then, you know why I've called you here? You know what I want to talk to you about? No?*

No.

About this voice in my head. I keep hearing it in my head. It sounds like my sister's voice. Annie's. I try to answer her but she ignores what I am saying. Just keeps saying what she wants to say. I know you are just a boy and this is none of your business but I'm asking you to help me to contact her because you can see things.

How can I do that?

I don't know, she replied. *Please help me.*

That night I slipped out of bed and went into her room. *Come, sit. Now then how do we go from here? You tell me. Please.*

I don't know. It was at that moment that I felt the presence of someone else in the room. I looked up, over her shoulder, and discovered her sister standing behind her.

Please help me son, please.

What do you want to ask your sister?

Just tell her that I am sorry. I am sorry, I am sorry for what I did. Tell her I'll do anything that she wants me to do if she stops talking in my head. I can't stand it anymore. My sister never drowned, son, my sister never drowned. I am so sorry. I am so sorry Annie, Annie please forgive me!

Annie still stood there behind her and the room was filled with the fragrance of jasmine.

In the name of Jesus, Mary and Joseph, Annie set me free, Annie set me free. Son tell her to stop, she's shouting in my head. My head's going to burst. It's going to burst any moment now. Save me, son! She grabbed hold of me and squeezed me hard, dropping us both to the ground. She held me with her entire body, pinning me down with her arms, torso

and legs, shivering violently and dribbling from the side of her mouth. Annie stood and watched us. Then she disappeared. Elaine's body relaxed. I scrambled to my feet and left her lying there, whimpering.

A few days passed before the lady of the house made the request again. Something inside compelled me to agree and I went to her room again. With each visit, she became increasingly strange until the last encounter when she admitted that she had pushed her sister off the roof down onto the pavement and her death. She sobbed loudly and passed out. *And I made everyone believe that it was suicide.* Annie remained, watching us, obviously waiting for something to happen. And it did. Dad burst into the room and was horrified when he saw us lying on the floor, Elaine clutching on to me.

He let loose a string of the foulest words he could muster up and dragged me out of her arms and into our bedroom. Once in he picked me up and threw me on the bed with such force that I banged my head on the wooden boards through the mattress. *What's going on? What's going on?* he snarled. *What were you doing in there? What was she doing with you?*

Lying there, stunned and defenceless on the bed, looking up at him, I wondered what he would have done if he had witnessed what Uncle Prem did to me. Would he have turned and walked away because it suited him at that moment? I'd never know.

We're shifting out of here, he told her the next morning. *We're shifting out of here in the next few days. And if you dare touch my son again you will be dead and your body parts fed to the cats.*

It's not what you think happened. Your boy saved me! she said softly. *He saved me. He's very special, that boy.*

A day later, Fester Neck disappeared, quickly followed by Grinner and Big Butt. Then two more. The others followed. Vanished into thin air. Elaine sat up all night waiting for them to return but they didn't. She became inconsolable; her wobbly wrinkled body trembled with her continuous sobbing. Mum took over the cooking and cleaning of the house and we helped her with clearing out the garbage.

When we left for our newly rented apartment, she had just one cat left. The last I remember of her was our brief conversation in the hall. It was evening and she sat clutching a cat, seated in the armchair. Light streamed in from the little garden outside. She looked so old and lost. *This is my punishment. Annie took them all.*

Don't worry Aunty, they'll come back, I said.

Oh you little wisher, you dreamer, they'll come back you say. They won't come back. How can they come back?

Wait and see, was all I could say.

Miracles don't happen child, don't ever pray for them to happen because they don't. When you are supposed to be alone, you will be alone and no one will be able to do anything about that, you hear me? They can do nothing.

I backed away.

Later I heard Dad say with a grin, *I drowned the wretches.*

Mum and I bumped into Elaine in the vegetable wing of New Market when we were out shopping some time after that. She hugged Mum and they exchanged pleasantries but she didn't look at me. It was as if I wasn't even there. When I got home I found a hundred rupee note in my shirt pocket and wondered how it had got there. It was a windfall for me and I added it to the Diwali cracker pocket money that had been given to me.

Outside, the city was alive with pre Diwali crackers. We had the money to enjoy ourselves but it wasn't the same anymore for me. I wasn't normal. I wasn't myself. I didn't know who that 'myself' was. I was play acting, pretending to be a boy, pretending to be excited, pretending to be happy. I knew it would be short lived.

The Growing Years

I pretended to enjoy myself in our new home which took up the entire upper floor of an old bungalow. There was a large courtyard with a mango tree in the front, a substantial lawn lined with fruit trees and a service lane behind the building. At the back, in the corner, were two cement water tanks. The space available for us to live in and play in was lavish compared to the other homes we had inhabited in Calcutta.

The Fletchers occupied the ground floor section of the bungalow. Sub Inspector Geronimo Fletcher had moved in there with his wife Philomena after their eldest son Bernard was born and over the years struck such deep roots that they didn't see themselves as tenants anymore. By the time Lolita and Felix were born, they had acquired the undisputed use of the courtyard, the lawn and all the spaces around the building. Geronimo even had a painted sign saying 'Fletcher House', put up on the pillar of the gate. Any other family shifting in would have to be satisfied with using their own floor space and the roof above.

The cop was a big fellow who had a face that looked something like John Wayne, at least that's what he thought. In fact, he even turned up at a costume party dressed like the *True Grit* star. According to Dad, that was his only claim to fame. As a cop he was a bit of a disaster—he was indecisive, physically unfit, lazy and displayed very few signs of intelligent initiative. Dad was great at analysing everyone else. Anyway, Geronimo didn't have much of an opinion of Dad either.

But Geronimo was a good father and husband. He spent as much time as he could with his wife and kids. Breakfast and dinner was a family commitment every day of the week. On Saturday afternoons, he would take his sons angling to one of the lakes in the city and bring back more than enough fish for dinner. Once a year, the entire family went off with friends to forested areas in Bihar where they would pitch camp and spend two weeks hunting and angling. John Ashton, his brother-in-law, would record the trip's highlights with his Super 8 camera.

The cop had developed a whole library of such films and after one of his kids' birthday parties, he'd set up a rickety projector and treat everyone to an hour's viewing. That would always be the highlight of the occasion. Dad claimed that it was all fabricated. None of that really happened, they had play-acted it all.

The Fletcher home was the hub of action during those years and kids would start streaming in by four in the evening, ready to play any of the games in vogue at that time—badminton on the lawn, tops and marbles on the large mud patch near the mango tree, kite flying on the farther end of the lawn and hula hoop in the cleared area near the front gate. When it got dark, the entire gang of kids and young people would play 'relievers'...a great opportunity for pair-offs, kissing and fondling in the bushes and behind the storage shed with some even cuddling in the trees.

The ten-year olds, a gang I soon became part of, included colourful characters like the twins Derek and Ian who never seemed to agree and ended an argument with their fists, Pat Salters and his younger brother Gregory, Pip Paul the guy who couldn't hold his pee, Sally the blonde, dark eyed Rachel and the pale and delicate Angel who finally ended up drowning in her bathtub.

The teenagers had Bernard, Lolita and Felix amongst them, along with Phillip, Daphne, Jen, Celestine, Christina and Margaret. They were more preoccupied with music, movies and the chances that they could get to feel each other up. Whenever Phillip returned from his holidays, he managed to create quite a sensation with his boarding school adventure stories, ghost stories and tales of mystery. So effective were his engrossing tales that both Lolita and Daphne fell for him at the same time. They commissioned me to ask him which one of them he preferred.

What'll you give me if I ask him? I wanted to know.

A bar of chocolate, said Lolita the freckle-faced, mousy-haired one with the legs of a runner.

Two bars of chocolate, said Daphne, the dark-eyed, dark-haired, dusky complexioned one.

That means I get three bars of chocolate.

They nodded.

So off I went and presented the question to Phillip.

What are you getting to ask this question? He wanted to know.

Three bars of chocolate.

Give me two and I'll answer.

I had no choice.

He picked Lolita because she had nice legs, light eyes, light hair and liked Cliff Richards. Daphne accepted defeat and gave me three bars of chocolate because I had been so helpful and brave. *If you were older Sean, I'd have chosen you.*

I blushed.

And anyway, just for your ears, your brother and I kissed in the bushes...not just once but many times. That's why I was so sure he'd choose me. That means he's kissed others too.

Sorry.

Why are you saying sorry?

Even though I was considered to be part of the ten year old gang, the older boys and girls were happy to include me. The only one who showed apparent hostility was Felix. *No place for pansies here. What're you doing here? Go play with the babies, pansy.*

What's a pansy? I asked Daphne.

Why do you want to know?

Felix called me a pansy.

A girly boy.

So he thinks I'm like a girl?

Yes, he thinks you behave like a girl.

Do you think I'm a pansy, Daphne?

No, not at all.

Then why would he call me a pansy?

That's his problem. Not yours.

Whatever Daphne said to try and convince me didn't help at all. I started getting really worried. *I am a pansy. A girlie boy. That's why Uncle Prem did what he did to me—because he saw me as a girl. There's something wrong with me. There's something wrong with me.*

I started becoming sensitive to the way people looked at me. Not just Felix but all the other boys and girls too. I became paranoid. Had they seen something?

What's gotten into you, Sean? Daphne asked one evening. *I don't see you playing with all the others. Did someone say something? Was it Felix again? Want me to settle him? Or it's something else? Something that happened at home?*

I didn't know what to say.

Before Daphne left, she said, *If that Felix ever calls you a pansy again called him a rosie.*

What's a rosie?

Just a flower. It'll irritate him. Do it. Challenge him. Don't be afraid. Then she left, leaving me alone on the steps outside the bungalow.

Felix came out with an air gun. *See what my pop got me. A Diane Model 25. Now I can shoot whatever I want.* He loaded it and fired into the tree. *Bet you haven't even seen the backside of one of these,* he sneered.

I've seen bigger guns than this. I've even been shooting with my Dad and uncle. I've seen them shooting ducks and geese and even hare and a big sambar.

That doesn't mean you know how to use one of these. Bet you don't know.

I do.

You do? Yeah? You do? Okay then I'll put this can there on the wall. Here's the gun, shoot. Hit that can. If you don't, you'll have to walk around without your pants.

And if I hit the can? Will you walk around without your pants?

You won't be able to hit the can.

I asked him again. *If I can, will you walk around without your pants?*

Don't challenge me pansy-boy.

The bees started buzzing around inside my head. *Yes,* I said suddenly, *yes, I'm challenging you, I'm challenging you, rosie.*

What did you call me?

Rosie.

He snatched the gun back from me. *You don't deserve a chance, you pipsqueak.*

So you are scared that I might hit the can and you'll have to take off your pants! I laughed.

I had tied him up in knots. He didn't know whether he had to be angry about being called rosie or have the guts to challenge me to hit the can. Finally he settled for the latter. *Ok, if you miss the can I will not call you Sean but pansy in front of everyone and you'll have to take off your pants and run around the lawn.*

What if I hit the can?

You won't.

Are you scared I will?

Okay, I take the challenge. Hit the can and you can call me rosie and I'll run around the lawn without my pants.

I took back the gun from him, aimed and fired, knocking the can off the wall.

That was a fluke! A fluke! said Felix, sounding a bit panicked.

But I hit the can so take off your pants rosie, take off your pants. When he refused I started shouting, *Take off your pants rosie, take off your pants!*

The gang of ten year olds gathered around joining me, chanting *take off your pants rosie, take off your pants* in unison. That's when Bernard turned up. He snatched the gun out of my hand and grabbing his brother by the arm took him into the house.

I stood there feeling pleased with myself. I wasn't going to take Felix's bullying ways any more. I was ready to fight for myself.

I was brought back to earth by my mother with a reminder of an entrance test the next day.

It turned out to be a disaster.

All the boy has done is copy down the sums and played around with the figures. Pages of it. It's like he's trying to make a fool of all of us. Father Grisham was a round, bald headed, red faced priest who stood with his legs apart and his hands behind his back when he spoke. His piggy eyes bored holes through and through me. *Sorry,* he said finally, *no place for this boy here. We like winners. If not winners, at least ones with common sense. He doesn't have that in him either. And also from what you've told me, he's hardly been to school. How in God's name is he going to fit in? Nowadays, you need either brilliance or at least common sense. With neither of the two, you are surely lost. Teach him at home and when he is old enough, teach him a skill or a trade.*

Mum's biggest worry was not that I hadn't got through the entrance test but that she'd have to tell Dad that his son had failed. Not wanting to prolong the agony she cornered him after dinner that day and told him what had happened. *Sean failed the entrance test. He's not getting in.*

Good news, he muttered, *because if he had passed and got in, we wouldn't have been able to pay his fees and foot all the other expenditure.*

I don't understand why you're saying this Gordon.

It takes you so long to understand anything. I just lost my job.

Oh.

Oh. That's all you have to say?

For quite some time Dad's moods had been fairly well settled because he had a job and was earning his livelihood and supporting his family. But the moment he couldn't do that he panicked and went around the bend.

Before he could really lose control, Mum came up with the idea that we should sub-let one of the rooms in the house. The one which was self-contained, had its own bathroom and separate entrance. He thought that it was a good idea and they set about spreading the word. Within a week a young couple shifted in. The rent that came in from them was just about enough to keep us going, without any frills and life moved along on a somewhat even keel. Except of course, our rent was always in arrears.

Felix and I sank our differences and started roaming around a lot together. We usually kept our adventures for Sunday afternoons. Sometimes we'd slip off with a couple of other boys to poach fish in the Loudon Park pond, casting our line from among the bushes by the waterside, hiding from the watchman. On other occasions we'd walk along Park Street, cross Chowringhee Road and have a great time roaming the wide expanses of green that the maidaan offered.

Once when Felix and I went to poach fish in Loudon Park, he got caught by the watchman. The fellow locked him inside a small store room among gardening tools. *Let me out. My Pop's a cop and he'll lock you up, you son of a pig.*

The watchman was furious because he was a Muslim. *What did you call me?* he shouted.

Son of a pig, taunted Felix.

The man started throwing stones on to the tin roof of the shed. The sound was deafening. *Stop, stop,* shouted the prisoner, *stop, I'll go deaf.*

Go deaf, said the fellow, *go blind too for all I care.*

I was afraid to come out of the bush where I was hiding for fear that the man would catch me and shove me in with Felix. But then I heard him yell, *Sean, go tell my Pop!*

I burst out of hiding and broke into a run. The man chased after me, tripping over a stray dog sleeping on the path. That was just the lead I needed and I was away...down Loudon Street till I reached Park Street, crossed over and took a short cut through Park Lane and headed home. John Wayne had hung up his holsters and boots and was asleep when I got there and was upset when his wife shook him awake and told him the story. He rang up the Park Street Police Station and ordered a Black Mariah to come and pick him up along with two armed guards. I sat up front with him in the police van which blared its siren and rattled down Loudon Street.

To his misfortune the watchman was still throwing stones onto the tin roof of the shed when we got there and was thumped down with lathis till he was out for the count. The captive was released and we drove home with John Wayne whistling a tune to himself and the handcuffed watchman begging to be released.

When we got back, Felix exaggerated the story beyond recognition. In one version of his story, both of us took on the watchman in hand to hand combat and in another we even wrestled him to the ground, only to be attacked by several of his goons.

Felix had a fertile imagination and I began to admire the way he could produce stories from thin air. I learnt quickly from him how to make up stories and we got on well together. Being accepted by him was very important to me. I felt I was a real boy. And it was good to feel that I had someone to share secrets with...not that I was ever going to reveal my dark secret to him. He'd surely call me a pansy then.

One of the many secrets we shared was about the time when we watched a bullock being slaughtered in a neighbour's backyard. That was the time when we went off exploring the service lane behind the house that wound its way between buildings. Felix carried his air gun on his shoulder hoping to spot a pigeon he could take a shot at. When we turned the second corner we saw a small gathering of people around a bullock tied to a post in the courtyard beside one of the apartment blocks. *Shh,* said Felix, *they're going to slaughter the animal.*

Right there?

Yes, right there. And they'll share the meat amongst all the families in the building. I heard my Pop saying that the cops are trying to stop people from doing this.

We stood outside, peering in between the bars in the fence, waiting for something to happen.

Two of people in the group carried large knives and a third had a massive meat chopper, butchers use to chop through flesh and bone with a single slam. It was evident that they were going to kill the animal.

The bullock began making strange moaning sounds when they washed it down with buckets of water. Then they dropped it down on its side and tied its legs. It struggled to get up but they kept holding it down. Finally, the group moved back and one of the fellows with a knife knelt down and cut the animal's throat. The others joined in and then the man with the chopper asked them all to move aside and beheaded the animal.

It was a very messy affair with blood splattering on everyone's clothes.

What are you looking at? asked a voice behind us. We nearly jumped out of our pants in fright. The owner of the voice was an old man wrapped in a shawl. *Want to get a closer look? Come on.* He guided us in and introduced us to the group. *These two young men want to see what an animal without its head looks like, move aside.*

I've seen what an animal without its head looks like. I corrected him.

But you haven't seen an animal of this size killed with knives, have you?

No.

So now you've seen this too.

We stood there amongst the group with red splashed all over their clothes. I wanted to turn and run for my life but was too scared to even move. Felix stared fascinated as they set to work to skin and cut the animal. We were each given a cloth bag with a chunk of meat in it and sent away.

My Pop will shoot me if he knows where this comes from, Felix said.

Then give it to your Mum, I suggested, *maybe she won't tell him.*

When we got back I rushed upstairs and handed over the bag to Mum in the kitchen, giving her only a brief background. She took the hunk of meat out of the bag and placed it in a large metal bowl. It seemed to still be twitching with a life of its own. Mum looked pleased. *We can make a good roast out of it and still have some left over for a stew.*

I had lost my appetite and couldn't bear the sight of the meat, even when it had been turned into pot roast and stew. *Where did all this meat come from?* Dad asked.

I saved a little for a treat, lied Mum

Clever woman, said Dad, chewing purposefully.

I struggled to get a few morsels into my mouth and down my throat. Later I could feel the meat twitching in my stomach.

Felix spun one of his yarns and managed to avoid telling his parents the truth. His mother turned the meat into a couple of delicacies and even sent a bowl of kofta curry up for us to taste.

We didn't speak about the experience for some time and Felix stopped carrying his air gun around. Something had snapped in us and it would be a while before we could get on with our lives in the normal way...whatever normal meant. And when that happened we decided not to stray out of bounds again and settled for mooching around in the compound. That's the time Phillip returned for the last time from school. He had finished his final examinations and would have to wait for his results. Girls were obviously on his mind more than ever before because he set about behaving like a man, smoking cheap cigarettes on the roof with the others, drinking an occasional beer and whistling at pretty girls in short skirts.

Nora was already in her second year in college and had a string of boys wooing her. Dad would insist that she returned home straight from college and didn't allow her to attend any function after sunset. *As if I can't be up to tricks during the day,* she once commented.

I don't think that's funny, he snapped. *If you want to meet them, let them come home.* But when they came visiting he'd become hostile and only let them into the house on a Sunday evening. Once in, they weren't allowed into her room and had to sit around the dining table chatting. That scared them off. Only the hard-nosed persistent ones survived.

But Nora's classmates from the convent were allowed in whenever they wished to visit. They'd lock themselves in the room and play Chubby Checker numbers and do the twist.

How boring, Phillip would say, *aren't there more exciting things to do than twist around and jump up and down?* His idea of excitement was to have a few puffs, a swig and then kiss and squeeze a girl behind the water tank at the back of the bungalow. Felix and I were once spying on them when Jen took her pants off in front of him and he shut his eyes tight. *What's wrong with you?* she asked.

Nothing, was all Phillip could say.

Then give me your hand.

Oh no, he whispered and pushing her aside, ran off.

Jen saw us watching and waved. I didn't shut my eyes. I smiled and waved back.

Around that time Dad got a part time job and started picking up some decent money. That's when he threw a party at home. It started at seven in the evening, went on through the night into the morning and limped all the way to the next afternoon. One of his new-found friends brought along a cabaret dancer. She did her act in snatches till midnight then she suddenly vanished with my father. They returned at five the next morning. I know because I noticed the time.

After that party, Dad was another person. He started returning home very late from work and sometimes he'd even disappear for days on end.

One day the tenants moved out and Dad lost his job. The double blow was too much for him to manage. With nothing put away for a rainy day, the downward spin was rapid. Violence began again. Every time he found another woman, he would stay away from home. When she'd dump him, he'd come back like a bear with a sore nose, growling and gnashing.

During that time I had repeated attacks of typhoid and Dr Das declared that mine was an extraordinary case. *He should have been dead a long time ago,* he said solemnly.

Sure, I said to myself, *I should have been dead a long time ago. I don't know how and why I am alive.*

Nora and Mum took the brunt of his violence and we all lived in fear of the next outburst. That's around the time when Mum was so desperate that she tried to jump from the roof. When she didn't succeed, she slashed her wrists, but not deeply enough. And when that didn't do the trick, she turned to prayer and penance. Nora took the other way out. She eloped with the slightly built, soft spoken son of a funeral parlour owner. The fellow's name was Hector. *Can't even say shoo to a fly,* said Dad, *and he's gone and performed this heroic act. But they won't run far. They'll be back.*

Days stretched to weeks and months. Everyone stopped talking about Nora. The big issue before us was how to cope with Dad's constant disappearances. Phillip took the easy way out by vanishing. Rumour had it that he had joined a gang. Someone even claimed that he had been picked up by the Agra cops and clinked.

Finally, exasperated, Mum packed our belongings, unearthed the meagre savings she had hidden in a tin can at the back of the cupboard and she and I made our way to the railway station to travel unreserved to Coimbatore. Dad somehow seemed to have gotten wind of the plan and caught up with us before the train left, and grabbed hold of me and Mum before we had even boarded the train. He created an embarrassing scene on the platform and made off with me before the Railway Police arrived. *You go wherever you please but he stays with me,* he called out to Mum.

On the way back to the bungalow from the railway station, we travelled in complete silence and I wondered what fate awaited me.

Then There Were Three

We returned to the bungalow, gathered our belongings and left.

Where are you off to? asked Felix.

I don't know.

What do you mean you don't know? You mean you don't know where you're going to live?

I nodded.

When you do know, let me know. We can meet. You can always come here or I could come there wherever that is. We had good fun.

Come on Sean, Dad called out, *the taxi's waiting.*

That means you're going pretty far from here, Felix said, almost sadly.

Yes.

See you. See you soon, I hope. And I'm sorry I called you pansy.

That was so long ago, I've forgotten about it, I lied. The world of friends I had struggled to build around me vanished like sand castles on the beach. With each wave the shore mutated.

Sean, we don't have all day, Dad was impatient.

We walked down the crooked lane with our belongings to the main road.

Where's the taxi? I asked.

There's no taxi waiting. We're taking a rick. Why would I waste money on a taxi?

Our destination was Kanani Mansions on Free School Street. Third floor, flat 306. The door was opened by a young woman who must have been around Nora's age. Slim, tanned, a small oval face, wide eyes, wholesome lips and hair that fell about her shoulders like satin.

This is Sean, my son Sean. And Sean this is Caroline. You can call her Aunty.

Hello, Sean, she said. *Welcome.*

Hello...

Call me Carol.

Absolutely not! You'll call her Aunty. There was an edge to Dad's voice.

Call me Carol, she repeated and wrapped her arms around me. *What are you still standing at the door for? Come on in. Here's where you'll be staying.*

You'll call her Aunty, you hear me? Dad whispered, loud enough for her to hear.

Carol, darling. Call me Carol, she smiled, taking the case from me and leading me to the corner of the room. There she had set out a small divan, a desk and chair and a wooden cupboard. *This is your space. Do whatever you want here when you're at home.*

You two get to know each other, Dad said breezily, *and I'll nip out for a while.* He was gone, leaving me with a total stranger. I was secretly indignant that he hadn't even had the decency to tell me in advance what he had planned. It was obvious that had been his second home...a place none of us were aware existed. Everything was happening too fast. Again.

Carol sat on a small cane stool. *Can we have a little chat now that your Dad's not here?*

I flopped down on the divan and looked at her straight in the face.

I know this must be a bit of a shock for you but I suggested that we do it this way so that we get over with the first steps quickly. Listen Sean, I'm not trying to replace your Mum. I'm just your Dad's special friend and we live together, he and I. You are his son so when I take care of him I also take care of you because you belong to him. This is getting messy, she smiled. *It's not at all easy for me.*

Why didn't you let me stay with my Mum?

Because then your Dad would have no family left. He'd be alone.

So it's because of him that I'm here. Because you want him to have a family, because it's good for him. What about me? Did anyone ask me what I'd like?

I know, I know, you must be very upset. But you are still too young to know what's good for you. Grow up a little more and you'll be able to decide for yourself. She was visibly uneasy.

But I was not going to slow down the momentum. *I am thirteen. I know what I want and what makes me happy.*

She side-stepped the confrontation. *That's a nice age. Now we have to get you fitted out with some new clothes and then straight into school. Boys like you should be in school with other boys your own age. Your Dad says you're a bright fellow. I can see it in your eyes.* She continued to talk to me but I had stopped listening. The tone of condescension in her voice irritated me.

Don't you want to have my Dad all to yourself? Why do you want me here?

I just told you, Sean. What more do you want me to say?

So you are bearing with me even if you don't like me.

Who says I don't like you? Why are you putting words into me mouth?

You don't like me. I can see it on your face and hear it in your voice. You are looking down on me.

I am not looking down on you, will you stop doing this to me please Sean? I am trying very hard. Give me a chance. Maybe we can become good friends. Please.

Where do I go for a pee? I asked, looking around the room.

That way.

I went in, shut the door behind me and sobbed my heart out, washed my face and putting on a brave front walked out into the room again, resigned to the fact that three people were going to share that space and that I'd have to live with that reality.

It was rather awkward for both of us because we were strangers and shared the same room. My father didn't seem in the least bit perturbed by the arrangement.

What on earth does she find in Dad? I wondered. *He is old enough to be her father, doesn't have a job, drinks, he's irresponsible.*

But the ways of love are strange. She doted on him. Hung on to every word he spoke. Laughed at his stupid jokes. Pampered him. Went out and bought him clothes. Cooked for him. And had even agreed to take care of his son. Something was wrong somewhere. She was far too nice and warm and kind and considerate and accepting. It was too good to be true. Experience had taught me not to trust.

However Carol never gave up and hard as I had become inside, I began to create a little space for her in my life, acknowledging her gestures of kindness and affection. After a round of clothes shopping in New Market one day, she took me for a treat to Flury's and I had hardly put two spoons of chocolate cake into my mouth when she said, *You haven't asked me what sort of work I do. So that means you know.*

No, I don't know.

I'm a crooner. I sing in a nightclub just down the road from here. It's called the Blue Fox.

A crooner.

Yes, a crooner. That means a singer.

You get paid to sing?

Yes. Something wrong with that?

And you make records too?

Not a chance. I'm not in the big league, Sean. I wanted to be a star but then I realised it's not going to happen. I don't have the best voice, but I look good up there with the spotlight on me and guys when they see me get all excited. They don't even notice my voice just me, moving around.

I've never heard you sing. Can I hear you sometime?

Not in Blue Fox. They don't allow kids in there. Only on a family occasion at lunch time. When that comes around I'll tell you. But I'd be happy to sing for you at home one of these days. Back in Allahabad, we'd all get together and sing. My Dad, Mum, my big brother Oliver and sister Jessica. We didn't need any entertainment. We entertained ourselves singing jazz, blues, pop, country and all sorts of stuff, anything that we felt like. Yes, those were great times. The problem was that my Dad used to get depressed all the time. He worked in a gun shop and one day loaded a gun and shot himself. That left four of us. I really doted on Oliver. He was a boxer with a solid body. He was a boxing champ in college. He had medals hanging along one wall in his room. And we all had a lot of hope that he'd become some sort of champion. I mean big time. But he ended up a journalist. Can you believe that? A journalist! And then one night on late shift he was leaving in a hurry and walked straight into a closed door. He came home, lay down to sleep and never woke up again. That's how we lost him—to a concussion.

*So, I said to myself, there's just three of us left and if I hang around here any longer, who knows, I may be the next to go. I fled. I came to Calcutta to try my luck as a singer. I've got an okay voice and look pretty good. What do you think? Do I look pretty good? You don't have to be polite...*Carol smiled. *So I thought I could make it. Well I have. Not very successful but okay-okay successful and Blue Fox pays me fine.*

I hope I'm not boring you stiff. I needed to tell you a little about myself so you can see me for what I am, not just your Dad's special friend. I know lots about you from your Dad. But it's all in bits and piece. I hope you can help me put the pieces together. But I promise Sean, I'll try not to ask you difficult questions.

I was silent.

Maybe I'm going too fast into all this, she whispered. *Guys anyway don't open up so easily. And I'm sure you've had one helluva time. Sorry. Another time maybe. There's still time.*

When I got to know her, living with Carol was a pleasant experience. There was something gentle and homely about her as she moved around the room, singing to herself and going about boring everyday tasks with a light heartedness that was surprising. *It's good fun playing "family family"* she'd say with a laugh. *Nice when three of us sit down to a meal and you clear the table and I wash the dishes and your Dad sits there like the man of the house with his feet up.*

Two significant developments took place. After a lot of effort and string pulling, Carol got me into a school down the road from where we lived and Dad landed a job in a cotton mill that was in Howrah district, a couple of hours from the city. They made him their Store Manager and agreed to pay him a reasonably good salary and a decent travel allowance. To celebrate our good fortune we had a sumptuous Chinese dinner at Waldorf's on Park Street, a peach melba dessert at Mags and a drive down the Strand. All the way home, Carol treated us to a medley of her favourite songs.

That night I dreamed of Mum. It was a strangely sad dream. I was walking down a crowded pavement that ran along Free School Street and suddenly she walked past me. It took me a moment to realise it was her. Then I turned and started back, pushing my way through the crowd. I could see her stooped shoulders way ahead of me and quickened my pace to reach her but the distance remained between us. I woke up choking, looked around me in the dark, still frantic from the dream. Carol was having sex with my father on the mattress spread on the floor. I shut my eyes, feeling sick listening to her tender endearments. When she was quiet and everything was still and calm, an overwhelming feeling of guilt enveloped me. I felt Mum's presence in the room. I remembered the last time we spoke.

Sean, there's nothing more for me here, I think I should leave. I'm going back to Big Mummy in Coimbatore. That's where I should be. I'm not of any help to Dad or to you and we're just together out of habit. I'm sorry you didn't have another sort of mother. I tried my best and nothing worked. So it's not going to make a difference whether I am here or not. But I feel bad to walk out like this, son, I feel as if I will be abandoning you, unless you want to come along.

I chose to 'escape' with her to Coimbatore because the security of Big Mummy's home would be a safer option. I lay there that night wondering whether I'd have missed Dad if I had managed to get away.

There had been no news from my Mum ever since her dramatic departure and it was very unlikely that Dad was in touch with her. Did she miss me? Was she trying to get in touch with me? Why was her presence so overpowering?

Moving between waking and sleeping, living and dying, I am not sure anymore if all that has been happening has actually happened or merely figments of my imagination.

They sit around me picking at pieces of information like vultures, gobbling, thrusting, tearing. There doesn't seem to be anything left and still they persist. I was taken a while ago to the morgue to identify the body of the woman. I couldn't. Often death changes features to such an extent that the body you see belongs to some other being and not the one you knew. It's a stranger. They show me her personal belongings and I can relate to nothing. There's no identity card of any kind, no driving license, nothing. Nothing at all.

They insist that I know who she is and that I am hiding her identity.

So what about this pistol? Your fingerprints are all over it. You can't say that you don't remember using it. One of them, the guy with a lisp and an egg shaped head sporting a few stiff patches of hair, holds it up and brings it over to me. It is in a transparent plastic packet. He leans over and looks into my face. *What do you have to say?*

Nothing. I have nothing to say. I don't remember what the hell I was doing with that pistol.

It's clear what you were doing. You were shooting at people. You dropped three, the lisper says. *Two fellows who deserved to be shot and one policeman.*

They sit and watch me, waiting for a response.

You can't blame me if I don't remember.

We'll be back. It doesn't end here.

They leave.

I feel defenceless and vulnerable lying here. When will all this end? Will it end or trail behind me like all my other nightmares have?

The small graceful fellow in white comes in and sits down beside me. *Listen,* he says, *you need to build up all the strength you can before you get out of here. Then go away, leave Mumbai, go far away from here, somewhere beautiful, calm, you deserve it after what you did.* He leans closer to me as if to share a secret and whispers, *You're a celebrity. You've been on the front page of every newspaper and magazine, on television too. They've got their vans parked outside the hospital.*

When will I be discharged?

It's a legal mess at the moment, he says conspiratorially, *but you'll be cleared. It's obvious that it was an accident, I mean killing the policeman. It's obvious he just came in the way. But no one can figure why you did all that shooting and risked your own life.* He sits back and wipes his face with a tissue and sighs. *Where did you learn to shoot like that? There's CCTV footage showing you in action. That's what's confusing them.*

What?

That you were so good with weapons. They're wondering where you got your training. Listen I'm telling you all this Mr Varma because I want to help you remember…

What's in it for you?

Nothing, nothing at all. I want to help you remember.

Have they sent you in to try where they have failed?

No. He sighs and goes to the window. *Do you see things?*

What sort of things are you talking about?

I mean people. Do you see dead people? Imaginary people?

No, I lie.

Think about it. You might need help.

Now you're messing with my mind.

I'm trying to help, he says.

The more you say that you are trying to help, the more I get suspicious of your motives.

Sorry, I don't want to add to your distress. If you want to talk to me. I am Dr Dilip Desai. Ask any of the nurses. I'm on the floor above you. I'm on call.

I lie here, wondering what is going to happen next, who will walk in, what memory will visit me. I close my eyes and begin gently floating backwards.

Greenwood and Beyond

Greenwood on Park Street, a day school that boasted of a hundred percent results in the state board exams, was run by an enormous cigar-smoking gent with a crew cut and the loudest voice I had ever heard. The school occupied the same space as the Silverwood Recreation Club. After four in the afternoon, the school furniture would be stacked away and the club would swing into action. The classes were small and the teachers inexperienced. But the good thing about the place was that it had a cheerful air about it. Even the giant, who went by the name of Bartholomew Johnson MA, exuded a light heartedness that was refreshing. *Sagging spirits today?* he'd cheerily ask a new kid looking morose. *Come along, I'll show you something interesting.* Then he'd lead the fellow into his enormous office. *You like fish? Take a look at my aquarium. Here, sit right here.* Placing a stool in front of the glass case swarming with fish, he'd leave the boy fish-watching with a small mug of hot milk and continue his rounds of the school.

A seated Johnson wasn't a common sight. He was everywhere, walking down the corridor, inspecting the water tank, discussing maintenance work with plumbers, teaching the senior class book keeping, pottering around the accounts department, doing surprise checks of classrooms, observing teachers. I'm pretty sure that when he got home, he'd fall asleep standing. His wife would handle the front office and receive visitors and meet parents, patiently sorting out their problems. Apart from these two individuals, the rest of the school worked at its own pace. There was Sharma Sir, the paan chewing Hindi teacher who had the habit of saying *don't worry yaar, the most is you'll fail, so what?* And Sen Sir the Bengali teacher who loved talking about his wife's cooking and the genius of his Pishi Mashi. Others too—Das Sir the History teacher who had an Emperor Ashoka fixation, Vimal Sir the science wizard who gave our entire class private tuitions for a fee at home in his spacious covered veranda. *You need to sharpen your wits and polish your intelligence so well that you can see your reflection in it,* he'd say. The Moral Science guru was an evangelical big mouth who claimed that for a student to become truly enlightened he had to keep his eyes and ears open and mouth shut.

These fellows were the permanent fixtures. They had been there from the time the school had started. The others flowed in and out aimlessly. We had a string of English teachers. There was the amateur poet Mirza Sir who taught us for exactly a month, another who broke a leg on his first day in school, yet another who was a Dickens freak and after him came Lama Sir. He was a peaceful chap who went around with a benign smile on his face. He loved my essays and often read them aloud in class. *Lovely essay, Sean Varma, good job. Well done.* I wanted to tell him to go tell Carol, since it was her work. I hated doing homework and she loved to help so it was a convenient arrangement.

Lewis Sir was a perfectionist. He didn't seem to give a damn about what we had to say in our essays, so long as we wrote neatly.

Where's the loop to your 'l' Varma?'

It's right there, Sir.

You think I'm blind?'

No, Sir.

Then why's it that I can't see the loop of the 'l'?

I don't know.

A ripple of giggles swept through the class.

Lewis Sir swung around and glared. A few snorts remained. *What's so funny?*

Silence.

He turned to me again. *How did the loop suddenly appear?* He asked. *You did it just now right here as I turned to look at the class. You're a shifty character Varma, let me tell you straight, I don't think it's going to get you far in my class. Now you write me two pages of 'I' before the bell rings. You hear me?*

So before the bell rang I turned out two pages of 'I'. He walked out.

It was evident right from the start that he didn't like me and I didn't like him. At almost every twist and turn I gave him a run for his money and he would have wrung my neck if he had managed to pin me down. Actually I'm not sure why he didn't like me. Was it because I was the sort of fellow who refused to toe his line and did whatever I felt like doing? I wasn't sure. But what I was sure of was why I didn't like him. He reminded me of Uncle Prem. He had the same sleazy way of looking at boys in the class from the corner of his eye. And that most peculiar slimy smile which he reserved for boys like Sunil Kapur, the effeminate boy who would come to school with talcum powder on his face, smelling a little like his mother or sister. Lewis Sir couldn't resist patting him on the head each time he passed him in class. Sometimes he'd even rest his hand on the boy's shoulder and run it along his back. No one seemed to notice but me. I could spot fellows like him from a mile. The eyes, the smile, the language of the body, those straying fingers, all telltale signs. I watched him handle unsuspecting classmates. Every time he came near me, I froze. My defences went up and I was ready for a fight.

It happened one day.

He had given us a couple of opening sentences and told us to develop them into a short story. I went home, ready to request Carol to help me out. But something stopped me. I was determined to take Lewis Sir on by writing the story myself.

I was alone at home that evening. Dad was going to be late at work and it was Carol's evening out at Blue Fox.

My notebook lay open on the dining table. I stared at the lines on the page. They lay there waiting to be written on, defying me with their blankness, telling me, *write, write with everything that's in you, teach him a lesson, show him you can write, show him that you aren't some little twit but special, show him that you Sean, that you are special, that you know.*

I developed a headache staring at the lines with my pen poised reluctantly over them. And then they started becoming wavy and jiggled and danced and floated and swam across the page and with a vengeance I jabbed at them with words, pinning them down. Slowly they started settling down as strings of words stretched out on them. I wrote page after page after page. The headache eased. The story was happening right there in front of my eyes. It seemed to be happening by itself. My hand was holding the pen that was writing. Each 't' got crossed, each 'I' dotted, the 'l' was looped and the 'g' was shapely.

When Carol returned, she found me asleep at the table.

The next day I got up late and found myself waiting for ten minutes outside the shut gate of the school as punishment. When I finally got in, I settled down in class, expectantly waiting for my adversary to arrive in the fourth period. I felt empowered. I was ready to take him on.

Lewis Sir stepped into the ring for combat. *Sean Varma, read your story,* he barked.

I'll show you, you shit, I said silently, *I'll show you what I can do.* I opened my bag and rummaged around for my book. It wasn't there. I had obviously left it behind. He watched hawk-like as I fumbled. *I'm not down as yet,* I repeated to myself, *I'm not down as yet.* I controlled myself and calmly took out my English Class Work Book (all of them were covered with the same sort of brown paper so from a distance you couldn't tell one from the other) and flipped open a page casually and started pretending to read out a story. I remembered what I had written so well that I dramatically narrated the story that I had created the night before. My narrative was obviously very effective because the class giggled at the jokes, murmured in approval at the description and even gasped at the high drama. When it was over I got three rounds of applause and a whistle of delight. Then came the slap.

Lewis Sir had been standing behind me once I had got into my story. He had watched me read from a blank notebook. *You think, I'm an idiot or what? You think you can make a fool of me? I'm going to make you bleed for this.* He slapped me again.

I felt the two stinging slaps knock my head back but I remained on my feet. *You are a liar. You didn't do your homework. Liars burn in hell. Liars lose in life. Liars are rotten.* He grabbed hold of my shoulder and shook me up. His spectacles flew off and when he bent down to pick them up I was sorely tempted to kick him in the face.

Mr Lewis, control yourself, Bartholomew Johnson entered the class. *You are a teacher and not a slave driver. Please see me in my office at lunch break.*

The bell rang and Lewis Sir left the class.

Nobody knew what happened in Johnson's office but when Lewis Sir came out of there he was shaking with rage. He stormed through a group of kids, pushing them aside and headed straight for me. *Run,* I heard someone call out, *he's coming for you!*

But I wasn't going to run. I waited for him. When he reached me, he stopped and looked at me straight in the face, his hands almost clenched into a fist. *I was told to apologise to you. So I'm apologising to you for having slapped you even though you deserved it. In my ten years as a teacher, I have never apologised to a student. Never. Look at my face properly once and for all and remember I will have my day, outside school. I'm leaving.*

His backhanded apology had made no impression on me. My feelings hadn't changed. I felt humiliated. The beehive inside began to stir. On the way home I kept imagining what it would have been like if I had kicked him in the face and he reeled backwards and crashed among the desks and chairs, his nose bleeding, a stunned look on his face.

I reached home to find a small chocolate cake on the table. *That's for the magnificent story you wrote Sean. I read it. You had left your book behind. You didn't get into trouble did you? What're these marks on the side of your face?*

A friendly wrestling match in school, I lied.

Be careful you don't hurt yourself doing that one of these days. Come here, let me take a look. Sean, seems like someone has slapped you. I know a slap mark when I see one. Now sit down here and tell me who hit you. How did this happen?

Nothing happened, I insisted.

Have it your way, she smiled and sliced the cake to celebrate my story.

But the beehive inside was stirring. A rage was growing. I had decided that it was my rage, mine alone. Only I knew where it had started from. No one, absolutely no one, had the right to share it with me. I didn't want anyone's pity or sympathy or support or any such thing. This was mine and mine alone. I was going to deal with it myself.

Carol was worried, I knew she was, I could see it on her face. Her hand trembled slightly.

A few days later, she took me out shopping and we ended up in Flury's once again. *Sean,* she said quietly, *I think you need to talk about what happened in school. Sorry to tell you this but I went to school and found out for myself. Why didn't you tell me? Is it because you don't trust me? I know I am no one to you, I'm just your Dad's 'girlfriend'. I'm not your mother or sister or aunt or anything but where I'm concerned you are special to me, believe it or not. That means I care for you. I know I don't know your whole story but I do know a bit of what you and your family have gone through. You are still a boy you know, who needs to be protected, who needs someone to stop other people from taking advantage of you. I think both you and I are quite similar. I mean it. We need each other. If there was another life before this one then I'm sure we knew each other, well.*

I said nothing.

So, why didn't you tell me what had happened in school? Say something Sean, please. She had tears in her eyes and her lower lip trembled. *You don't trust me?*

How could I explain to her that it was my business, my life, my humiliation, my rage? How could I tell her that it wasn't easy to talk because no one had ever really wanted to know what was going on inside me? No one had ever wanted to protect me. Who really cared a fig when I was left to the Shastris? Where was everyone when Uncle Prem touched me the way he did? Where was everyone when he destroyed me? Who asked me after that about what I had gone through? There was no explanation. Everyone had just pretended that it hadn't happened. It was just brushed under the carpet and forgotten and I was expected to go on and pretend the same. Mum was a kind, gentle and supportive woman who wasn't capable of hurting a fly, great, but what I couldn't understand was why she didn't even want to know what had happened to me when she knew that I had been left there alone. She was my mother after all, wasn't she? Was she too afraid to ask? Was she so gutless?

Sean, Carol lightly touched my hand, *where are you? Are you listening to me?*

Yes, I replied, smiling.

You want to know something? she asked, changing the direction of the conversation, *you have a beautiful way with words. That story is so moving. It reads like a poem. A song. Listen Sean, I have no expectations of you...only that you be honest with me because I am here for you.*

What's the point? I asked

You're too young to ask that question.

What's got into both of you? asked Dad later. *Is something the matter?*

Must be the weather, quipped Carol.

That happens with women, sure. Weather affects women because they are so sensitive. Not men. Men are supposed to be thick skinned. So what's got into our little man here?

I'm a boy, I corrected him.

Same thing, man or boy. We're all male, right? He finished his drink, we had dinner and they went off to see a film.

An hour later I found myself in bed filled with a restless hive of bees. I didn't know what to do with them.

I didn't dream that night.

Lewis Sir returned to school from his suspension a quieter man, walking with a slight stoop. He didn't teach our class English anymore. A rumour went around that he was on drugs because he was slightly crazy and it was those drugs that made him look and act the way he did.

Gradually, he faded out of our conversations. Instead, a new primary teacher took his place, in a different sort of way. Slender, tender, delicious Florence Bhattacharaya quickly became the reigning sensation. All the senior boys fell desperately in love with her. Even though it became a little embarrassing for the other teachers, Florrie (as she was affectionately referred to) relished the attention. She had a huge mop of black curls that highlighted her delicate face and a spectacular body to go with it. Even Bartholomew Johnson seemed unsettled by her presence. His tours of the primary section became more frequent and word had it that he was crazy about her.

Florrie was quickly replaced by other beauties. The tennis ladies. Silverwood Club opened its courts to ladies from three every afternoon. That meant that they'd be playing through the last hour of school. It suited all of us immensely. For one solid hour standards seven, eight and nine, would be treated to tennis played by scantily clad women. Oh the joy, the sheer, undiluted joy that overcame us when we watched those beauties whack balls across the nets. The teachers had a tough time holding our attention and often threw a few sly glances in that direction too.

Johnson tried to put an end to the disturbance by setting up small movable screens to block the view. But that shut out the natural light and ventilation so the idea was abandoned and the treat continued.

It was also about this time that I started becoming aware of Carol's physical presence. Sometimes it was a little unsettling when we were alone at home and she moved around the place in her shorts and skimpy t-shirt. I'd find my mouth going dry.

But then, the nearness and intimacy of three people living in one room was about to change. The Managing Director of the cotton mill that Dad worked in was so pleased with his performance that he promoted him to a senior position, gave him a fat pay check and a host of perks, including a bungalow allotment which was in the Mill premises.

Carol was pleased with the news and immediately set about planning for our new abode. Dad dashed her hopes. *I suggest I take a look at the place first before making plans for its interiors.*

'I' ? She asked. *I'd prefer if you said we.*

I meant 'I', Dad stressed.

But we are going to live there aren't we?

Yes, sometimes there and sometimes here.

You mean we are not shifting there? She looked at him quizzically.

No, I'm shifting there because I work there. And I'll keep coming and going from here. You have a job here, your life and your friends. You don't have to disturb that. This is your life too. And Sean has school here. You two can come to me for Sean's holidays or when you have a break.

My life is with you Gordon and with Sean. This is a relationship. This is a commitment. Am I right or wrong? Tell me.

Yes.

Then we should take decisions together.

We'll talk about it some other time.

But that time never came. Dad shifted to the new place and organised for us to visit on weekends. Carol didn't make an issue of it and got on with helping Dad to feel good about his new position. *Let's celebrate, give ourselves a gift. Let's go out. And we're not leaving Sean behind...*

And so each of us got a gift. Dad bought himself a second hand Ambassador car, Carol got a barbecue set and I got an air rifle. I had caused a bit of a flutter when I said that I wanted one. Carol was noticeably disturbed by the request but Dad laughed it off saying, *a chip off the old block.* I could well understand why Carol was so uncomfortable with guns and wondered whether Dad knew the background.

The very next evening I was taken to a gun shop and bought an air rifle, a Diana Model 35. *This is one weapon you'll always cherish,* he said expansively.True, it was a beautiful weapon. The butt and stock was of fine grained wood. Excellently balanced. I could throw it to my shoulder and steady it in a jiffy. I couldn't do much with it in Kanani Mansions though. There were buildings everywhere so I would take it out to the maidaan and shoot at targets there. The temptation to start shooting doves and pigeons that grazed in the green expanse of the maidaan was overpowering. So one day I asked Carol, *do you know how to make a pigeon grill or roast?*

I do. That's all we did when I was young. My Dad would bring a couple of birds every day. He'd use an air pistol he bought from the shop in instalments to shoot them. Carried the damned weapon with him all the time. I grew up with dead birds lying in the kitchen, waiting to be cooked. If you want to kill birds Sean, do as you please, but don't bring them home. Clean them, cook them and eat them somewhere else.

From that day on, I never used the air gun in Calcutta. Instead, I spent time cleaning it and polishing its wooden case whenever I was alone. When Carol was home, we spent time playing board games and word games and listening to the radio and I almost felt happier than when Dad was with us. *I think,* she suggested one day, *we should start doing a bit of running, I'm putting on weight and that's not good and you could do with some exercise, too.*

So every evening we walked down to the maidaan and jogged for a while and walked back in the dark, hand in hand. For the first time in my life I didn't feel alone. The unhappiness of the past seemed to recede and fall into some sort of abyss and I went to bed at night with a feeling of belonging. Mum, Nora and Phillip were part of another life that I had once lived and died in. Mathura never existed. Dad started becoming an intrusion and the sounds of sex at night disturbed me and made me unusually jealous. Carol noticed this but nevertheless gave him the attention that she owed him and when he was gone she focussed completely on me.

Our first visit to the bungalow that Dad had been alloted was exciting. It was located in the residential section of the Mill known as the Western Staff Quarters. *In earlier times,* he said with pride, *only the whites stayed in this part so you can see why each bungalow is specially designed. Now we are in the same class as them. We really deserve to be living here.*

Carol went from room to room, taking a look at the furniture, the fixtures, the curtains, the finish of the walls. *So this must be the master bedroom,* she said opening a door and peering in, only to be hit by a blast of ice cold air.

Specially air conditioned, Dad waved his hands like a magician. *Cool and comfortable. You can sleep for a day without realising it. And the giant double bed is pure teak. Look at the cupboards.* He opened the doors with a flourish, *so much of space inside. Sean you can play cricket inside one of them. Hah ha, this is life.* He strutted ahead of us opening the bathroom door. *Go in and take a look, the latest fittings. And pure marble tiles and a brand new bath tub.*

Looks good, Carol looked at me, *don't you think?*

I nodded, smiling. It was good to see a happy person and not one who was desperate, savage and violent.

The entrance of the bungalow faced a small garden which rolled up to a fence. Beyond that was a lake surrounded by rain trees, dense with nests of water birds. There were cormorants, egrets, storks, herons, dabchicks and a host of others squabbling and chattering and calling restlessly at night and rising early with the mist to set out to feed in the jheels far away. Catfish and murrel leapt and splashed, crinkling the surface of the water.

Our first dinner was a delight. Kamaluddin, the cook who Dad kept referring to as Kitchen Master, turned up in a white jacket with white gloves. He dished out roast duck and apple sauce with all kinds of fancy side dishes. Later Dad called out, *Kitchen Master, dessert!* And in came the lemon meringue pie.

After dinner, Carol insisted that we go for a walk to get a glimpse of all the other bungalows. Dad was discouraging, but she insisted so he let us go. We walked past stately homes, manicured gardens, a mini golf course, tennis and badminton courts and a club. Beyond that was a small bridge which spanned a narrow arm of the river and the road led on to the Mill. Initially, I was quite overwhelmed by the opulence but by the end of the walk I felt quite proud to be part of Dad's success. By the time I was in bed, even that feeling had past and I lay there listening to the squawks of water birds. In Calcutta, I had got used to sharing a room with another person, comforted by her presence. But here in this luxury, I was alone. The master bedroom was on the other side of the veranda, whirring and humming with the sound of the air conditioner.

At some point in the night when I was still half asleep, Carol climbed into bed next to me, kissed me on the head, stayed for quite some time and left when I was asleep. Her fragrance still lingered on the pillow the next morning when I opened my eyes.

All through that Sunday, she did a balancing act between Dad and me until it became so apparent that Dad almost looked jealous. That evening, we had a visitor, one of his colleagues, and Carol was referred to as a family friend. *What's going on here?* she asked Dad later. *What's this family friend thing all about?*

I had to say that because he wouldn't understand.

What do you mean by 'he wouldn't understand'? It's none of his bloody business to understand or not understand. You and I are in a relationship. That's got nothing to do with him or anyone else in this place.

It has, Dad interrupted her.

What has? she wanted to know.

Our relationship.

So you're not supposed to be in a relationship here?

I'm supposed to be married. But I can't lie and say that you're my wife.

What the hell are you talking about? Carol was trembling with rage.

I am married, am I not? And you aren't my wife. I can't possibly tell them that we are in an extra marital relationship. I don't want to give them the impression that I'm some sort of unreliable fellow.

Jesus Gordon, you take the bloody cake. Now I understand why you didn't want to let me come here. You don't want them to know. I'm leaving, right now. And I'm taking Sean with me! Carol stormed off.

We got on to the last suburban train back to Calcutta. Carol cried all the way as the dark landscape slipped past, fragrant with paddy fields, date palms and bamboo groves. When we got back, she slept with me all night and didn't bother to leave before dawn.

I know, she said a couple of days later, *your father's going to try and make up and if he can't make that happen, he'll take you away. I don't know how I'll manage then.*

Those were prophetic words. A month later, Dad moved me out of Kanani Mansions and Greenwood, and put me into Martins Public School as a boarder. The shift was so insensitive that I felt as if something had been torn out of me. An emptiness remained that left me feeling incomplete.

Rolling Up My Sleeves

Brigadier J.W.J Williams didn't walk, he marched. A retired big shot from the Gurkha Rifles, he had taken to running Martins Public School as if it was the training ground for future officers His predecessor was a Rhodes Scholar who tried to turn it into a school for academic excellence. And two or three school heads before that, there was an ex-Olympian who had tried to make Martins into a sports academy. Throwing back his shoulders, the Brigadier went ahead of us, waving his arms and drawing our attention to the amazing facilities that the school offered. There was a massive playground, indoor swimming pool, tennis and basketball courts, a table tennis room, an indoor boxing ring and well equipped classrooms and laboratories.

We were introduced to Mrs Salters, the Matron of the Senior dormitory, Mrs Beane the Matron of the Junior dormitory and Mrs Tuttle, the Matron of the Mini dormitory. *Though Mrs S is the one who you should be concerned with,* the Brigadier said to us, *I thought it appropriate for you to meet Mrs B and Mrs T. You don't know when they'll come in handy. Particularly Mrs T. She is also the Hospital in charge. The Hospi, that's what we all call it, is right on the top. And Mrs B bakes the best cakes this side of the Hooghly.*

Brigadier Williams waffled on and lost our attention. We headed back with him to the Bursers Office where Dad paid the deposit and the year's fees in advance and we left to fetch my large black metal trunk which was neatly packed with all I needed. By evening I was back and knocked on the Matron's door. *Who is breaking down my door?* she bellowed.

It's Sean Varma.

Roll Number 114, she barked. *Come back later!*

Just then a big fellow walked up to me. *I'm Saul, Saul Abraham. Are you Roll Number 114?*

How do you know?

I don't. I'm asking you.

Why?

Why are you so stuffy? I just asked you a simple question and you can give me a simple answer.

Yes.

Good. Your bed is next to mine. I'm going to enjoy ragging you tonight.

Before I could throw a response at him, the Matron opened her door. *Abraham, I hope you aren't bullying him.*

No Ma'am, not at all. He grinned wickedly and walked off.

Come on, bring your trunk to the store room. I'll give you your bed linen and other things you need to take to the dorm.

When we were done, I found myself sitting on my bed wondering how I'd last the night.

114, said Saul, *you better catch some sleep before the action starts. Those fellows are waiting for midnight to begin. So sleep.*

Yeah, so you can rag me first. I'm a sitting duck here.

No, I was joking. I'm also new. I joined a week ago.

So we're both sitting ducks.

The lights went off at ten but I didn't lie down. I was far too scared.

Go to sleep before it's too late, Saul whispered.

Shut up, I found myself snapping.

Suit yourself.

I eventually drifted off. Saul was right—it must have been around midnight when I was rudely awoken with the slap of a wet towel.

Come on, it's time for a bath! the leader of the gang said. My wrists and ankles were tied and I was carried off to the bathroom where they put me under a cold shower. A few minutes later I was carried back and untied, only to be whacked over and over again with a stinging wet towel. *Sleep well, baby,* someone sang. It seems Saul had received the same treatment

In the early hours of the morning, they repeated the shower treatment but this time they gave me a towel to dry myself. After three nights of shower treatment I was handed over to the boot polish wallahs who smeared me with black and brown polish. They in turn passed me to on to the swimming instructors who made me spit on the floor and then 'swim' in the puddle of my own saliva.

In Martins, ragging had been polished to a fine art with a long line of specialists who initiated each treatment. No one ever reported what was happening to the Matron, the Principal or any of the teachers. It was an accepted code of conduct. Bear it with a smile because one day you too will get a shot at it.

After ten days of persistent ragging I couldn't stand it anymore and climbed out of the window and sat down on the broad ledge in only my thin cotton pyjamas. It was four in the morning and Ghora Srivastava (nicknamed because he walked like a horse) was out on his morning jog. *Oey! What are you doing out there? Gone crazy or what? Go on back in, idiot. You'll fall down!*

When he didn't get a response he ran off and got hold of a collapsible metal ladder and convinced me to come down. I was in a daze, walking with him to his apartment. *Shanti! Shanti!* he yelled. *Get me a shawl.*

His wife popped her head into the sitting room. *What happened?* I looked at her and didn't say a word.

He's one of the new ones... probably got ragged.

How did he get out?

Get the shawl will you, the boy is going blue.

She wrapped me in a shawl and made me lie down on the sofa.

Now stay calm, I'll get you something hot to drink.

Before Ghora went off to complete his jog, I could hear him and Shanti talking about me in the other room. I shut my eyes letting the warmth of the shawl spread over me. I felt secure. She returned with a steaming mug. *Here you are. This should warm you up.*

She watched me sip the hot tea. *What were you doing out on the ledge? If you were trying to kill yourself by jumping from there, it was a stupid plan. You'd have probably broken a leg or your arm or something.*

I shook my head.

I know, I know, that's what they all say. No. But I know you must have felt really lonely and the ragging pushed you to the edge. That's why you wanted to jump.

I didn't want to kill myself. I just wanted to be alone. I was hiding.

That's a rather odd place to hide, don't you think? Shanti looked sceptical.

She had begun to irritate me. I was grateful that she had allowed me into her house and warmed me up...but why was she trying to make me admit that I was planning to jump?

Rest now. When you are up, I'll be happy to listen to you.

I have nothing to say.

That's what they all say. And finally most of them try again and again till they succeed. Try and sleep, I'll talk to the Matron.

No, please don't! Everyone will come to know and they'll laugh.

Trying to take your own life is no laughing matter. She left the room without even listening to my reply.

A while later the morning bell rang. The Matron would be opening the dormitory and waking up everyone with her foghorn voice. I threw off the shawl and swinging the door open, bolted down the garden path, streaking across the tarmac and up the flight of stairs. Mrs S had just opened the dormitory door and had gone in to switch on the lights so as to wake everyone up and I zipped in past her. *What was that?* She was startled.

Saul saw me dive for cover two beds ahead. He burst out laughing.

What are you laughing at? the Matron asked annoyed that she didn't know what was happening.

Nothing.

There must be some reason, out with it! Up everyone, this isn't sleep time. It's time for waking and...

Oh shut up, a voice from a distant corner shot out.

What did you say?

Shut up.

Who said that?

I did.

Who? She headed in the direction from which the voice had risen.

Me, another voice chipped in.

Then another and another voice joined the fray and the poor woman stood there in the midst of the noise and waved her cane. *Shut up, up, shut up, up.*

Finally, she managed to quieten everyone and get us out of bed, all except Saul who had decided to push his luck a bit more by pretending to sleep. *You there, up.* She tapped his covered body with her cane. *Up.* When he didn't respond, she yanked off the cover, and he sat up, naked. *Shame!* she yelled and fled to her room.

Later, when we were down in the dining hall for tea, Saul asked, *Where did you go, man? All the guys were searching for you.*

Outside the window.

Where outside the window? You jumped out?

I was on the ledge.

But how did you come in from the door?

Just then Ghora tapped me on the shoulder. *Just come here a moment, boy.*

I moved away from the table, feeling inquisitive eyes burning into my back.

Why did you run off?

I didn't want everyone to know. Please thank Ma'am but I'm fine.

Please tell her I wasn't trying to jump. Really.

I'll tell her, he smiled, patted me on the shoulder and sent me back to the dining hall.

What did he want? Saul was curious when I got back.

He helped me.

But he's the one who needs help, whispered Tony Biswas, overhearing our conversation. *He's got a crazy wife and madcap son. That fellow there. The one who is looking at you, man.*

The fellow sat at the end of the table. When I caught his eye he spat into his palms and rubbed them together.

That's what he does before he puts on his boxing gloves, Tony muttered. *He's a killer in the ring. Don't ever agree to fight him in the ring.*

When we were trooping out on to the field for the morning run and exercise, Ghora's son swaggered up to me. *Want a round in the ring?*

I kept walking.

Hey, I asked you a question. Do want a round in the ring with me? You don't have to try and kill yourself, I'll be happy to do it for you.

What's he talking about? Saul wanted to know.

He didn't tell you? The fellow asked Saul.

Tell me what?

That he tried to kill himself this morning? My Dad saved him.

Saul looked at me in surprise.

I ran on to the field.

Later in the day, after lunch, he asked, *You really tried to kill yourself?*

No, I told you what happened, I was so fed up with the ragging that I climbed out of the window to hide. Ghora saw me there and got me down with a ladder and took me to his house...

And you met his wife, the crazy woman?

Yes, she kept thinking that I had tried to kill myself, that's where the story started.

So that's how her son got to know...now he's spreading it everywhere in school.

He wants me to do a round with him in the ring.

Don't even think about it.

Anyway, I don't know how to box, I said finally.

Ask Christ Almighty, he'll teach you, Saul suggested.

Who's that?

The boxing coach. Christ Almighty, the man with the feather foot and a tap that will lay you flat. He's a genius in the ring. Ask him. He's coming in tomorrow. I want to meet him too. I never learnt boxing the right way in the army.

You were in the army?

Special training. In Israel...

You're from Israel? From the Israeli Army? What are you doing here?

Fellows like me come here for a few years of education. It's common. Didn't you know that? You really are in your own world, Sean! I did a training stint in the army, we all do that there. My sister is still in the army. I'll show you her picture. He flipped open his wallet and took out a small black and white photograph of a hefty person dressed for combat. *That's her, she's a paratrooper. I'm going back and straight into the army. I came here to learn English. I want action man, action. I want medals.*

That means you have no family here.

I've got an uncle here, he has a pastry shop in New Market. That's where I go on weekends. What about you?

I told him the better parts of my story, spicing it up on the way.

Lucky fellow, was all he could say.

The next day when Christ Almighty turned up, Saul did the talking. *This guy wants to learn how to box.*

Not as easy as all that, Christ Almighty declared. *I have to be convinced you mean it. So here's the stop watch. Keep the time whilst they spar.* He stuck the stopwatch in my hand, *Time three minutes. Just three minutes.*

So I kept time as boxers belted the life out of each other. About a week or so later, Ghora's son turned up and put on his gloves and walked over to me and asked, *So when's the day pipsqueak? I'm waiting for you to pluck up the courage.* But his sparring partner arrived and they slugged it out instead. There was blood on his gloves when he swaggered out of the ring, hissing, *I could have killed him.*

Chirst Almighty heard the comment and he tapped him on the shoulder, *listen here sonny boy, boxing is a sport not combat. I'll have to speak to your father about you. The next time you come in here and start hammering fellows you'll be in for a lot of trouble, you hear me.*

I can take you on too, coachy dear.

My dear little boy, said coach said, *I was the Indo-Burma boxing champion four years running. Seventeen knockouts, twelve TKOs and countless on points. Do NOT challenge me.*

I am challenging you.

The coach turned and blew his whistle. *Will someone kindly call Srivastava Sir?*

The altercation finally ended with Ghora grabbing his son by the arm and dragging him home. Christ Almighty turned to me. *We'll start today. Run around that field five times with your fists up in front of you as if on guard, like this. And get back here fast.* I followed his instructions. When I got back, he taught me how to shadow box. *Okay, this way, your right fist half open guarding your face and your left leading, jab like this, left left, right, left left, right. Keep your feet moving so you use the swing of your body to carry your punch.*

He was amazingly swift on his feet and made circles around me, when we sparred. *You need a couple of weeks more and then you'll be ready to spar with other fellows.*

I worked hard at it till one day he asked me to spar with Abdul Aziz but stopped the session midway because I had dropped the fellow twice. *You are supposed to be sparring, not turning this into a fight. Sparring is as much practising footwork. Sure there's a lot of glove work but don't get carried away. You hear me, Sean? Don't get carried away. You'll become a fighter not a boxer. Always remember, a boxer is a dancer in disguise, one who is in control of every single muscle and nerve and joint in his body, one who understands every beat of his own heart, one who is so tuned to his mental, emotional and physical self that he is in control. A fighter is like a wild bull, a wild animal, a rabid dog. So decide once and for all what you want to be and follow your dream. If you want to be a boxer, you are in the right place Sean. If you want to be a fighter, take off those gloves and leave the ring.*

I saw the sense in what he was saying. He was dedicated to the old tradition of boxing. *So why do you let Chota Ghora into the ring? He's a fighter not a boxer. Why do you let him in, eh Sir?*

Because his Pop is the Sports Teacher and he got me this job. I owe it to him.

At dinner, Saul delivered the message. *Chota Ghora wants to fight you. Yes or no?*

I looked down along the table and caught the fighter's eye. When I had fixed him with a stare, I spat on my palms and rub them vigorously together. Saul clinked his enamel soup bowl with his spoon, Tony followed suit and very soon the whole hall echoed with clinks. *What's all the noise about?* I asked.

That's when everyone knows there's going to be a fight in the ring.

By four in the evening the next day two groups had formed. One consisted of a handful of boys who had bet on me and the other consisted of my opponent's supporters. He had a mob out there, all shouting for him to knock me out.

Christ Almighty stepped into the empty ring and quietened everyone. *Good evening boys. Sorry I'm holding up the action but I have to tell you a few things...*

Chota Ghora's supporters yelled, trying to drown out his voice, *knock out, knock out, knock out. Bang, bang, bang, bang, boom. Sean gone. Sean gone. Sean gone. Sean gone.*

But the coach continued and amidst the din, I heard him say, *This is not a street fight, it's a boxing match...so use your skill not your anger.*

No hitting below the belt or the back of the head, no kicking, elbowing and heading. I will disqualify you if I catch you doing any of that. When the bell rings you'll start and when it rings again you'll stop. I will stop the action if I find any one of you is hurt or liable to get very hurt. One round, three minutes. That's it.

When he stopped talking Chota Ghora's supporters yelled, *knock him out, knock him out, knock him out.* Then the bell rang and he came charging across the ring like a crazed beast. *Knock out, knock out,* they shouted.

His leading left glove smashed through my defence and landed on my nose, snapping my head back, almost knocking it off my shoulders. I stumbled back and dodged his curving right follow through. He lost his balance and hit the ropes, face first. I quickly stepped out to the centre of the ring and waited for him. My nose was bleeding and my head buzzed. Slower and more careful this time, he circled me, waiting for an opening to rush in. And then he came in, and the mob howled, *knock out, knock out.*

He threw a few left-right combinations, missing every time and in the flurry, he exposed himself. My gloves flew into him, hitting him in the face and chest and then when he staggered I let him have a clean swift right hook on the chin which laid him on the canvas, out cold. The spectators were so surprised by what they saw that they couldn't even utter a sound.

I left the ring and joined my supporters who hugged me and patted me on the back. *Never seen anything like that before,* said Saul. *How did you manage that?*

That's what happens when you have to save yourself.

Back in the dormitory, admirers mushroomed around me and that Sunday Saul visited his Uncle's pastry shop in New Market and brought back a couple of chocolate cakes.

The experience in the ring was the first big turning point in my life. I began to feel more self-assured, more outspoken and more assertive. I didn't bully, I didn't brag but felt that I could take care of myself and help others to do the same for themselves. The other turning point was when I volunteered to run in the cross country house team because our House was short of a runner. I was never a runner but I lied that I had run such a distance before. Since my reputation for being a determined and focussed person had travelled swiftly ahead of me and had made a splash, the Sports Captain of the House accepted me into the team.

The eleven mile race started on a cool December morning, kicking off from the riverside of Red Road, across a vast green field in front of Fort William, down the Strand and up around the memorial to Queen Victoria, then back again, followed by four vast loops around the green. After the first couple of miles I was ready to die—because my breath was out of my body and refused to return. With much coaxing, it returned reluctantly and I limped along, pushing the limits of my body. Instead of resisting, it responded and magically my lungs pumped air and my head cleared. I saw nothing else but the path before me, pulling me on. I heard nothing but the sound of my heart beat. I tasted nothing but sweat and saliva. I smelt nothing but the animal fragrance of my skin. I touched nothing but the morning breeze that blew into my face to remind me that this was indeed the moment when I was truly with myself. No one else existed at that moment but me. Nothing else was important at that moment but the race. And even though our team did not win that year's cross country event, I had discovered my own true worth.

Dad was not there to cheer me on or appreciate my effort at the end of the race because he had more important engagements. A company meeting in East Pakistan had kept him away. I had stopped going back to Dad's bungalow on weekends because there was an emptiness about it that was unnerving. Long holidays were spent in other boy's homes or out on camps.

Then one day, a letter arrived from Mum. I recognised her handwriting instantly—small, neat and near perfectly formed words. The envelope was small and white and the flap had been carefully glued down. So like Mum, precise and proper. I walked over to the stone bench in the shade of the enormous tamarind tree on the other side of the sports field and opened the letter.

My darling son Sean,

I am sure you'll be surprised when you get this letter because by now you would have given me up as a lost cause. Well, here I am—your mother, still alive. Still in Coimbatore, caring for Big Mummy who hasn't been keeping well. We've had a lot of tests done and we are still trying to find out what exactly is wrong with her.

I've taken up a job with an NGO down the road from the house and put in four hours of work a day. That brings in a bit of income for me to spend on little things for myself and also buy a few things for the house and Big Mummy. Aunt Olivia and her family have left for Australia. What a tough time they had getting away, the paperwork was a messy affair and they even got duped by a travel agent. But that's all too complicated to explain here. If you were here or I was there and we were both face to face I'd be able to tell you about all that happened in a jiffy. Writing it all down is too much for me, it would be like living through it all. Besides that, I also have some problems with the joints in my right hand.

How have you been? Martins is a topnotch school, so I'm sure you must be enjoying it there. I'm told they offer students a lot of facilities and they've got a beautiful playground. I am so happy for you.

I know you won't believe it but I tried very hard to track you down and finally got through quite unexpectedly to your Dad's ex, Caroline. Actually she got through to me and gave me your address. She's a good woman and I'm sure she would have been good for your Dad. But then it wasn't the Lord's will. She says that you are turning out to be a real looker and you're kind and gentle. I honestly don't know how you managed to survive and become what you've become.

Every night when I pray I remember you all and bless you. Please forgive me son, forgive me for all I couldn't do for you.

Write if you want to.

God bless,

Your Mum

I put the letter back in its envelope and sat there looking at the world around me, wondering how I had survived and moved on. The person who had written the letter seemed to belong to another life—one that I had left behind. I was not sure what to feel. Those old feelings of guilt had faded and I was now living for the moment, in the moment, rediscovering what it meant to be alive.

Other letters followed, much shorter ones. One of them mentioned that Nora had two kids and she was living with her family in Bangalore. *She has promised to visit, let's hope she keeps her word,* she wrote. But no word of Phillip and no suggestion that I should visit. Was she waiting for me to say that I wanted to see her?

Waves of nostalgia would wash over me and deep seated feelings of guilt surfaced. But life in school carried me along with all its intensity and I was drawn into the moment again.

Finally, the last year in school arrived, the year when I was part of the Battle of Senior Dorm when Tony lifted a bed all by himself and threw it at the invading forces from the East Wing; when Tam Bam (or so we called him) the Chinese immigrant was expelled because he spiked Jay Morris's meal with a potent sedative and the bully Ralph the Ripper's underwear with itching powder; when I congratulated Chota Ghora for winning the Sportsman of The Year award and we hugged each other; when lovely Loretta walked into my life and turned me upside down and inside out.

I was ready to kill for her.

Turning My Life Around

I first saw her with a group of girls who had come from the school across the road for swimming practice to our indoor pool. She was the quiet one who took her time as she walked with the group from the main gate, along the field to the pool. *Hurry up Lorrie!* her teacher would shout, *We don't have all the time in the world!*

This happened so often that groups of boys perched on the wall started calling, *Hurry up Lorrie!* Instead of getting upset, she'd wave back. For a new girl, she had scored magnificently.

When the Company van came to pick me up to take me home for the Diwali holidays, I was more than surprised to see Lorrie seated at the window. By the time we reached the Western Staff Quarters, she had told me her entire story. Rasmick Priantz, her Armenian father had disappeared one night when she was seven and his body turned up in a dustbin not far from their home in Madras. Someone had murdered him, no one knew why. Simone, her French Mum went on to marry Rama Srinivasan, a brilliant engineer from Coimbatore. *And he's just signed a contract to work here,* she added.

The magnetic poles in my life had suddenly shifted and for the first time, I enjoyed being home even though Dad was rarely there. Loretta was the belle of the Western Staff Quarters, out on the tennis courts in her delectable little shorts walloping the ball across the net, her endless legs carrying her from one end to the other; on the mini golf course swinging her lithe body; at the table tennis table, hopping about; at the snooker table, poised in perfect concentration; on the sun bed, flipping through pages of a magazine.

I don't like reading and studying and sitting around, she'd say, *I like doing. Going places and doing, that's why I don't get on with this lot here. I don't get on at all with them because they are so stuck up. All they do is prance around all dressed up or flex their muscles.*

She wanted to know about my life, my family, where Mum was, did I have brothers and sisters but I didn't give her any definite answers so she stepped back from her questioning.

I have a secret, she said one morning when we were sitting on the sidelines of the tennis court, waiting for our turn to play. *A secret wish. Want to know?*

If you want to tell.

I've never fired a gun. I want to. Any sort of gun. I want to know what it feels like.

So what'll you give me if I help that wish come true?

Anything you want.

Anything?

Yes.

Okay then, this afternoon. Come over to my place, I'll show you something.

Are you trying to make a pass at me?

You want to see a gun? Then come over. I'm not making a pass at you. And I don't intend making a pass at you unless we're both happy about that. We're friends, aren't we?

I've a problem with trusting people.

Okay then, there was an edge of irritation to my voice. *Let's forget about your wish then. I was just trying to help it come true. And by the way, you told me a while ago that you'd give me anything I want if I helped your dream come true. Right? Why did you make that offer? Say if I had wanted to kiss you or touch you or something like that, what would you have done?*

Do you want to do that, Sean?

That's not the point.

It is. Think about what you've said.

You too.

We sat there quietly, then she broke the silence. *Will anybody be at home at that time?*

Maybe, maybe not, I don't know. Anyway, if you don't want to come into the house you can go around the side of the bungalow and meet me outside in the garden, near the lake.

So that's what she did.

I brought out my air rifle and showed her how to use it. She learnt fast and after a few shots managed to knock the small can off the fence. *This is really interesting,* she kept saying.

What is?

The feeling I get when I use the gun. I feel warm all over.

It's the excitement.

What do you mean by that?

I mean the power. Using a weapon. Then I slowly unravelled the story of Big Daddy who fought in the First Great War and of my own Dad and his shikar outings. I went on opening up other related stories like I was opening up old dusty boxes in an attic. The dust of memory rose in clouds and silenced me.

We sat on the steps, looking at evening throw long shadows on the lake as water birds returned in flocks and settled squawking on the rain trees.

She broke the silence. *Well then, what do you want?*

Teach me how to serve top spin, I lied.

Liar. But then, thank you for being patient. She rested her head on my shoulder and we watched the face of the lake suddenly darken and vanish from view. Late evening brought out a pair of spotted owlets who chattered from the hollow of a nearby tree then fell silent.

It happened when I was seven, Uncle Sid, my father's cousin touched me and made me feel what little girls are not meant to feel. And then one night when he was driving me to my grandmother's place he turned the car off the road and parked it in a small grove of trees. Then he unzipped himself and showed me what he had. I was so frightened and helpless that I closed my eyes and took a deep breath and did whatever he asked, hoping that it would end there. It went on. Sorry, I'm so sorry, I'm telling you this. I'm so sorry. Please forgive me for telling you all this but I can't keep it in any longer. I could feel Loretta trembling beside me.

For that brief moment I was almost ready to tell her about Uncle Prem. I knew exactly what she had been through and a wave of relief swept through me when I realised I was not alone. But I held back because it was clear that at that moment she needed to confess, to unload, to someone who she felt she could trust, someone who hadn't gone through what she had. I was sure that she didn't want to share her darkness with a bruised soul. That wouldn't give her any sort of strength or comfort. I was sure that if I had told her about myself she'd surely have walked out on me. I didn't want that to happen.

Dad was out in Calcutta that night so Kamaluddin pampered me with a Mughlai spread which he topped off with *shahi tukra*, my favourite Indian-style bread pudding. To make sure I would digest all of it, I set off on a long walk along the river, returning an hour later. Someone had been with me, I couldn't tell who. It was a warm, companionable feeling which I found undemanding and relaxing. When I couldn't sleep that night, I sat out in the veranda. I dozed off in the comfortable cane chair and when I opened my eyes, Aunt Katherine was there, sitting on the steps outside. *Come on out Sean, there's something I need to tell you. Don't be afraid.*

I sat down without looking at her. *What is it?* I asked.

If you want to learn how to love and be loved, you first have to learn how to trust. Even if all you have seen and experienced is betrayal.

She got up and walked away from me and I sat there till the air became dusty grey and catfish leapt and splashed in the lake. *Today,* I said, *today I'll speak with Lorrie.* But that day passed and the next after it and there were just two days left for our return to school. So after a set of tennis I asked her if she'd like to use the air rifle.

Sure, she said. *My parents are out of town, you're welcome to come over to my place for a fruit cocktail after that if you want.*

So we had a shooting session, this time using a large coin as target. She hit it twice out of ten shots.

At her place sometime later, she invited me up to her room which overlooked the river. *Come on out,* she said, opening the door on to her balcony, *I love sitting here. The river seems so close I can reach out and touch it.* Then she threw a few cushions on the floor. *Relax, I'll go fetch a drink.*

I sat there, looking out at the river, thinking of the complex relationship I shared with it. It was the same Hooghly I had rowed down as a child with my family returning from the Botanical gardens, the same I had lived beside and nearly drowned in, the same that had flooded and carried away a mango grove. The rich muddy fragrance of the water rose to meet me out on the balcony.

She brought back two tall glasses. *I call this Pear Drop Mint. It's got the juice of pear, lemon and ginger shaken with crushed ice and a dash of honey, topped with mint. One of my latest inventions.*

What are the others?

The fish kiss, she said, putting down the glasses and kissing me. Then she drew back, looking into my eyes. *Thank you,* she said, *for accepting my trust.*

We spent the evening looking out at the river, watching the lights of fishing boats float by in the dark, disembodied voices of fisherman riding on the wind. *I'm all ears,* she suddenly whispered, all ears. *I'm listening. I know you have something to talk about. Out with it.*

And so I spoke, pouring words out in a gentle stream, there was no intensity, no drama, nothing, just words finding their own way out, uncontrolled. She listened, holding my hand. When I had finished, she ran her fingers through my hair and kissed my forehead. *I accept your trust,* she said.

Thank you.

I could have sat there all night, holding her close, but I had to leave. Dad would be home, expecting an overnight visitor. He would want me to be present, like some sort of showpiece.

This, said Dad, with a flourish, *is Dorothy Tindal, winner of numerous beauty contests. She was selected as Ponds Fresh Face when she was sixteen, then she was chosen as the STOPA Queen—you know what STOPA stands for don't you? St Thomas' Old Parents Association. And lots else. Tell him, sweetheart.*

The woman waved his compliments aside and offered her hand to me. I walked over and shook it. That startled her. *This isn't a chip of the old block as you said he'd be. He's a real gentleman, not a rogue like you, you naughty man!*

Dad laughed and brushed aside her comment. *But seriously Sean, tell the truth, isn't she beautiful?*

I was so taken aback by the question that I didn't know exactly what to say. I looked at her sitting there with an awkwardly fitting red gown, overly made up face with false eyelashes and fingernails painted a bright red, and asked myself, *where the hell has he picked this one up from?* Then I lied through my teeth. *She really is.*

Dad looked pleased. I had to excuse myself so that they wouldn't see the expression on my face. *So this is what the tom cat brought in,* I told myself.

Dad took the next day off and spent it locked in the bedroom with her. Kamaluddin rolled the food and drink trolley in and out of the master bedroom.

I found an extra thick envelope of pocket money waiting for me on the sideboard, before I left for school. Lorrie and I sat in the last row of seats in the van, holding hands all the way.

The rest of school term was a race against time to be prepared for the board examinations. I had never been a particularly good student and had struggled to move from class to class. Now the final examinations loomed ahead of me like some sort of iceberg that I was sure I'd crash into and sink.

When they were over, I was ready to burn my books and flee into the sunset. But before that could happen, we planned to celebrate at a friend's place. His parents were out of the country and he had the huge apartment all to himself. So a group of us who were done with the final exams landed up there one morning and spent the day feverishly preparing for the evening. Beer, soft drinks, music and mounds of kathi rolls and bowls full of Chinese delicacies were laid on. Lorrie coordinated the female contingent and I coordinated the boys. We tried our best to prevent a surfeit of unattended singles.

As the night wore on, the party became increasingly boisterous with Saul doing the dance of the seven veils till he was stripped bare, after which he pranced off into the dark. The problem started when Tony discovered that Angela, his girl, had made off into an adjoining dark room with someone else. He banged the door down and soundly thrashed the boy. Three others, having had too much beer, leaned out of the open window and threw up on the neighbours' lawn below. Lorrie and I sat on the floor singing along with the Beatles *All You Need Is Love* blaring out of the speakers.

Then the door bell rang. Lorrie heard it despite the noise. She jumped up and went to the door and opened it, turning the volume lower on her way. The man outside looked anxious. *I've come for my daughter Camilia. Is the party over?*

Yes and no, she replied.

What do you mean yes and no? Is there a problem? Where's Camilia? He sounded agitated. *Are you drunk, young lady? Where is Camilia? Camilia!*

I heard the shouting at the door and rushed out to settle the matter.

Relax, I tried to calm him. *Relax, I'll just get her.*

Don't tell me to relax! I'm coming in. Get out of my way. Camilia! He pushed me roughly. I could feel my pleasant beer buzz evaporate into irritation. I reached out to grab his arm.

Hey, I said I would get... before I could finish my sentence, he punched me in the face. I stumbled backward and the man charged in. Lorrie looked stunned.

Camilia! Where are you? Put on the lights or I'm calling the cops, the man yelled. *What the hell is going on here?*

An incredulous voice emerged from the dimly-lit interiors. *Daddy? Is that you?*

When the lights came on, the man stood dazed amidst a wild crowd of young people surrounding him. Someone had a cut lip, a few had vomit-stained clothes. Everyone was blinking stupidly and some were even swaying and giggling drunkenly. Saul stood in front of the man in someone's little yellow skirt with feathers behind his ears, grinning like a fool. And amidst the chaos stood Camilia with her blouse hastily buttoned wrongly and her hair a dishevelled mess.

Camilia, how dare you? her father looked shocked.

Daddy! Camilia looked equally shocked. Her face crumpled as she dissolved into tears. Her distraught father led her away, swearing that he would send for the cops for sure. Half an hour after he had left, the revellers slipped away. Even the fellow whose apartment it was took to his heels. Lorrie and I were left with piles of untouched food, empty beer bottles, and a royal mess of a house. We went into the master bedroom, and fell into each other's arms, asleep in just moments.

In the morning, we cleared up the mess and got the hell out of there. It felt like Loretta and I had just been through some kind of test. We had passed...with flying colours.

The Showdown

It seemed that whenever I went home, Dorothy Tindal was already there. I didn't get an opportunity to spend even a little time alone with Dad. He was all wound up and preoccupied with his new woman and was happy to give me whatever I asked for so long as I stayed out of the way and left him to do whatever he chose to do. The woman sat in a purple gown with an unusually large sparkling pendant around her neck and her face caked in dark makeup. It looked as if she was all set to go to a masquerade of some kind. Dad was togged up in a Burlington pin striped suit. *When will you be back?* I asked him.

Back? We're not going anywhere. Dorothy likes dressing up in the evening, even when she has no plans of going out. I'm keeping her company.

Well, we are *all dressed up,* Dorothy pouted. *Can't we go to the club?*

I'm not in the mood to socialise, he replied. She shrugged her shoulders and poured herself a drink. When he left the room, she leaned forward and said conspiratorially, *I want to have a word with you, when's a good time?*

Any time. Is it something important?

Very.

I suspected that she was going to pump me for information which she needed to lay her hands on. But Dad rarely left us alone that evening. At ten he guided her off to bed and I was left to mind my own business. After a walk along the river I climbed into bed, flicked off the light and lay there in the dark. I was sure that when Dad hit the sack, she'd slip out of bed and check if I was awake. And that's exactly what happened. There was a tap on the door and it creaked open.

Are you awake?

I flicked on the light. *What's the urgency?* I wanted to know.

Even though there was an armchair nearby she chose to sit on the edge of the bed instead. She remained there for some time, looking at me.

What's the matter? Something wrong?

She sighed. *You know I'm not a loose person. I come from a good family who gave me a good upbringing. I've hurt no one, I've cheated no one. I don't fool around.*

Why are you telling me all this?

Because I want you to know you're going to have a good mother.

I have a good mother.

Thank you, she smiled, *thank you for the compliment. But you can say that after we're married.*

Who are you marrying? I didn't like where this was going.

Why, your Dad of course! Who else would I like to spend the rest of my life with?

But he is still married to my mother.

Darling, your Dad has told me the whole story. Dorothy looked at me pityingly. *She died when you were little and he says that you still imagine that she's alive. I can understand how much you loved her. I'll do my best to take care of you and treat you as my very own.*

I was almost too stunned to speak. *She's not dead. You're never going to be my mother.*

Oh come now, she said, reaching out and putting her hand on my chest then sliding it gently down to my stomach. *I'm here, I'll take care of you any way you want, believe me. I'll do anything for you.*

Anything?

Yes, anything. Her eyes gleamed.

Get your hand off me.

She patted me on the thigh and stood up with a tight smile. *Are you sure your mother is still alive?*

Yes.

She left the room.

The next morning I was shaken awake by raised voices from their bedroom. There was a banging of doors followed by crying and then raised voices again. I covered my head with a pillow and forced myself to go back to sleep.

Around lunch time, my father returned from work and took her to the railway station. Before he left he pulled me aside.

You and I are going to have a man to man chat this evening, you hear me? Cross my path again and I'll settle your hatch, he snarled.

That evening after I finished a set with Lorrie, we stood chatting beside the courts. Dad walked over to me, *I'll be waiting at home. I expect you there in ten minutes.*

Something the matter? she asked after he had left.

Yes, I think there's going to be a showdown.

But I didn't get into it with Lorrie.

He was waiting for me when I got home, pacing the sitting room, whiskey in his hand. *Maybe you'd like to change into something comfortable. We've got a long night ahead of us.*

I'd prefer to get over with it now.

Alright, suit yourself. Sit down.

I'd prefer to stand, I insisted.

I don't care a damn about what you'd prefer. Sit down.

That's always been the problem. You've never cared a damn about what I preferred.

He looked a little surprised. *What did you just say?*

You don't really care.

I don't care? After all that I've spent on you? After all that I've spent on you? That's all you have to say? I don't care?

Are you doing this because you want thanks? Dad, Nora ran away and got married, Phillip is probably drugged out of his mind, in the clinker or dead, Mum is hanging around with Big Mummy. And I'm all you've got to answer for. I was surprised at what I was saying.

Great speech, talking like a prosecuting attorney. Put your father in the dock, convict him and then put him away. Clever way of avoiding the real purpose of our discussion.

What is the real purpose?

What you told Dorothy.

What did I tell Dorothy?

He put down his glass and walked up to me, staring cold and hard. *That she should stay away from me because I'm married. Who the bloody hell are you to talk to my woman like that?*

I didn't back off from him but stood my ground. *I didn't say that. She said that you had told her Mum was dead and you were making plans to marry her. Did you say that Dad? Did you?*

Your mother is dead where I am concerned. I have nothing to do with her. I'm free to do what I want.

But you are still married to her. Aren't you going to divorce her or are you planning to have two wives?

Careful how you talk to your father, you ungrateful wretch. I'll do what I want.

Then tell your woman to stop trying to make passes at me. She walked into my room and sat on my bed and made a pass at me. That's the woman you are going to marry. What does she expect to get from you? Two birds with one stone?

His lips began quivering. I wasn't sure whether it was with rage or he was about to burst into tears. *I didn't realise that you hated me so much. I thought I was doing alright taking care of you and providing for you and being your Dad. I was wrong, wrong, terribly wrong. What was the point of all my effort?*

Have you done the same for Mum? Or cared to find out about Nora and Phillip? Think of where we were as a family and where you are now. You could still provide a decent life for them, but have you tried...

Now you watch your bloody step, he snapped. *Don't cross the line, Mum's got nothing to do with this. Neither has Nora. Or Phillip. This concerns you and me. Just you and me...*

You lied to Dorothy that Mum had died and you promised to marry her. And in the end you'll do with her what you did with Carol.

Sean! I am your father. I am your father, you can't talk to me like this! He stepped forward, wild-eyed and took a right swing at me. I deflected the blow. Then predictably came his left hook which I sidestepped and blocked. He lost his balance and stumbled forward and was about to fall when I grabbed and steadied him. Holding him there, his face close to mine, I looked into his eyes and found them flooded with tears. I led him back to a chair and made him sit down and handed him his drink. *This will help you feel better. Nothing else will.* When he emptied his glass, I poured him another.

We waited in silence. Each of us waited for the other to speak. Neither did. He crumpled forward, looking like a broken man. *I am sorry for being me. I am sorry for everything that I am. I am sorry for letting down your mother. I am sorry for being such a useless, helpless father. I am sorry for trying to buy love and affection. I am sorry that I am your father. You deserved someone better. If I only had the courage to really sit down and tell you who I really am and why I am this way, I would. I would tell you everything, every single thing. I really would.*

What's stopping you? I wanted to know.

My whole life is a lie. I don't know what's true and what's false any more. I don't know where to start.

Why don't you start with why you married Mum.

I didn't want to marry her.

Then why did you?

I was forced to.

So they put a gun to your head and dragged you to the altar?

I did love your mother. She was beautiful and kind and good and pure. When I first saw her I said to myself, 'Dear God, is that my guardian angel'? It was in a department store in Madras. She stood across the counter when I saw her and I went over and stood staring at her and she asked me, 'Sir, you want something?' And I replied, 'You' and she blushed, 'Sorry I'm booked'. One thing led to another and I started visiting the store every day and took her out for tea and walked her home until it was time for me to return to Kanpur because my training was over. But I couldn't get her out of my mind and returned and proposed. She was sixteen and I was nineteen and her father put his foot down and her mother begged me to go away as your mother was already engaged. But we insisted, so the engagement was broken and then three days before we were to marry I fled. I was afraid. I wouldn't be able to handle the responsibility. I didn't want to put my head into the noose. But your mother conned me. Said she was pregnant. It was a matter of keeping the family honour, I didn't dare ask for proof. Reluctant and scared, I married her only to discover that I'd been cheated. She wasn't pregnant. Our relationship was destroyed right from the start. Her angelic beauty began irritating me. Her goodness appalled me. Her shows of love and affection irritated me. So I played the role of husband and carried on scenes on the side. I didn't want the responsibility of a family, I was scared. And yet I could not, did not have the strength to resist your beautiful mother. When Nora arrived, I could have shot myself, when Phillip arrived I regretted that I had not shot myself, when you arrived, it was the last straw. I was never meant to be a family man and I have had to live with the mistake I made. I keep asking myself why I didn't have the courage to say no when they were forcing me to keep my word and marry your mother. What's the worst that could have happened? What? When I look at you Sean, I can't believe that you are my son. You are so strong and independent.

I stopped him from continuing. *Listen Dad, you don't have a damned clue how hard I have struggled to get here and be what I am. You don't have a clue of all the pain and anguish and hurt and loss and emptiness that I have had to experience. You don't have a clue of what I have had to live with. All you were concerned with was yourself. All you are still concerned with is yourself. You dumped me in Mathura and didn't even bother to tell me the truth about why you had left me there. You carted us like wandering beggars from place to place, living off other people's generosity. You didn't care...*

He poured himself another stiff whiskey. *You say I didn't care but the truth is that I was helpless. My family had caged me, had trapped me, had made me desperate.*

So we made you violent? Your family was to blame? You're trying to make me feel guilty? Nothing you say or try to say will change anything. You have damaged all of us. I didn't even have a childhood Dad. Even before I was a teenager, I had become an adult. Was that my fault Dad? Tell me. Was that my fault? I don't know if I will ever be able to forgive you for what you have done.

But you still live off me, son.

It's my bloody right now that you are able to take care of me. It's my right. I could feel my anger rising.

But I'm not a loser. I have a steady job, I am respected, I live in a beautiful home, I dress well, I eat well, I have intelligent and influential people around me, I am a success.

That doesn't make you a winner. Beneath all this, you are still what you are and always were. It's too little, too late.

By then, he was an emotional mess, sobbing and trembling. I stopped myself from getting up and going over to him to console and forgive him. Instead I sat there watching him. Waiting for him to respond.

So all this effort to be who I am today, to work hard and honestly and earn my keep means nothing at all? he asked.

I didn't respond.

Sean, I'm asking you a question. Do you hear me?

Still no response.

Listen, I know you aren't ever going to forgive what I have done to your mother...but try and understand that that's between your mother and me. It didn't work out between us. It just didn't.

True, I responded, *but we suffered.*

He downed his drink and poured himself another. *So then, that's me. Okay, now what about you?*

What about me?

What are you going to do with your life?

It's my damned business, I replied.

But it's my money.

And your responsibility. I didn't choose to be here. It was your choice. But now that I am here and I've got this far...

He cut me short. *Okay. Now that you've got this far...what have you thought about? What do you want to be?* He had begun to slur, lost in a haze of whiskey. *What do you want to be son?*

Silly bloody question, I thought to myself. *How the hell would I know what I want to be? You didn't bring me up, you dragged me up, living from moment to moment.*

He asked the question again, *What do you want to be?*

I did not answer him but took the glass and bottle out of his hands and left them in the kitchen. When I got back I discovered that he had passed out. I called Kamaluddin and we half carried him to bed, took off his shoes, covered him with a light blanket and shut the door. I sat down and ate alone.

That night, I sat out in the veranda listening to the restless water birds in the trees.

Bloodsports

The next evening, I was in no mood to spend time on the courts but sat on the sidelines instead watching Lorrie thrash her opponent Minty Kapur. The poor girl chased the ball which seemed to constantly elude her and by the end of the first set she was ready to throw in the towel, her heavy legs almost buckling under her.

You look like shit, said Lorrie sinking into the chair next to mine. *Have you slept at all? I would love to spend the evening with you, but Dad has been behaving a bit strangely and Mum has been asking me about you.*

What about me?

Just the usual mother worries. What happened about you and your Dad last evening?

What do you think happened? The worst. It's all become quite messy. I really need to spend time with you this evening.

I'd love to be with you but Mum wants me home before Dad returns from work.

You aren't a child, Lorrie.

Easy for you to say. It's different for men. Sorry Sean, I won't be able to make it this evening. Maybe we shouldn't see each other for a while. She sounded quite tense.

I'm sure your parents have laid their hands on some piece of gossip or the other about me and my family, that's why they are behaving like this.

Come on, don't start getting paranoid.

I'm not. I'm confused and upset. Your parents don't even know me and they've already decided that I'm not the sort who you should be seen with. Just because my mother is not here and strange women sneak in and out of our house, I'm an untouchable.

I don't think it's really about you. It's about me and boys...there are stories that I still haven't told you.

What stories? Where is all this coming from? You haven't said a word about all this before...is this all a game to you?

Don't raise your voice at me. Minty Kapur is looking most interested.

Let's get out of here. We need to talk.

Some other time Sean. I can't. She took out a small blue envelope from her satchel and quickly handed it to me. *Read this.* Then she left. I stuffed it into my pocket.

Minty caught my eye when I was leaving. *In a hurry today?*

Not exactly. Just a change of plan, that's all.

I'll still be here, she said, *in case you want company.*

Walking back alone down the avenue of flowering trees, my mind went blank. At home, I avoided Dad, ate dinner hurriedly and slipped away for a long walk along the river. That usually cleared my head. Back home, I tore the letter into tiny pieces and flushed it down the pot. I lay in the bathtub and let the warm water ease over me. Just when I needed Lorrie the most she had shut the door in my face. I was angry, hurt, confused. When I recovered from my rage, I regretted having torn the letter up. What had she wanted to tell me?

I never saw her again.

She's gone, your Lorrie, said Minty one day.

What do you mean?

She left for France. She's gone to a finishing school there.

Finishing school?

Yes, one of those places where they turn bad girls into decent young ladies. Ha! Isn't that a joke!

I kept quiet, fearing the worst.

She was having it off with Sanjay Tyagi, you know. Minty was clearly enjoying herself. *Can you imagine? He was old enough to be her father! Oh, but you knew that already, didn't you, Sean?* She batted her eyelashes at me. *Well, everyone knew... except you, I suppose.*

The next morning, I took out my air rifle and climbing over the fence walked along the line of trees, shooting water birds off the branches. Being with a weapon was refreshing, it gave me a renewed feeling of power and control. In the days that followed I left the environs of the Mill and crossing the nearby railway track, I wandered through the fields and bamboo groves. Along the pond, I picked off stray snipe and pheasant tailed jacanas and in the fields I shot as many as thirty-two doves and pigeons. It was on one of those shoots that I met Bhombu for the first time. His real name was Bidhanchand Mukherjee.

Bhombu was on his way back from a duck shoot with an empty bag. We got chatting and exchanged weapons. His Holland and Holland over and under, thirty two inch barrelled, twelve bore was a delight. Light as a feather, it was perfectly crafted. When I dropped half a dozen green pigeon with the first shot, he was impressed. He brought down a few blue rock pigeons with my air rifle. *My gun doesn't like me,* he said sheepishly. *Your gun does.*

That was the beginning of a brief but meaningful friendship. During that time we roamed the wooded areas of Howrah district, travelling on as far as the flower gardens of Bagnan and the wild marsh lands of Birshibpur where the lonely cries of curlew haunted the air and a fine mist hung mysteriously over the desolate expanses. We spent entire days paddling down the glowing waters of the Damodar river, dropping lines as we went along, hauling in fish. At dusk, we'd hitch a ride on a long distance truck back towards home.

I soon discovered a romance and adventure in all that slaughtering. I felt primitive, real, in touch with a darker self.

Noticing my enthusiasm for shooting, Dad appointed me the official pigeon executioner at the power house of the Mill. Hundreds of birds roosting inside the complex had started becoming a menace, their droppings corroding the metal surfaces, their feathers filling the air with mustiness and covering the floors with messy down. He said that they had tried everything in the book to chase the birds away but hadn't succeeded. This was their last resort—to start exterminating them till enough fear was spread to drive them away.

Like a professional killer, I spent a day taking stock of my potential victims: where they roosted, their escape routes, the levels to which I could climb to get a decent shot at them, where they'd fall and the pattern of firing that would be necessary to bluff them into perching despite their fear. The night before the slaughter, I went through the whole ritual of methodical cleaning the weapon and polishing the butt and stock, almost like an executioner sharpening the blade of the guillotine or testing the strength of the noose.

I kissed the butt of the rifle before I left home.

At the power house, the Manager welcomed me with a big smile and wished me luck.

My strategy was to position myself on a low stool at ground level and start picking off birds sitting on the ledges midway. I was sure this would push them upwards. I'd planned to wait a while after the first spray of shots for them to fly upwards and settle, then climb a metal staircase to the first level and start shooting at them again. After another pause to give them the opportunity to move higher and settle, I had planned to go up to another landing and open fire. By that time, I had hoped to have caused so much havoc that the remaining birds would flee.

I sat there on a stool and pinning my sights on the nearest bird, squeezed the trigger. It staggered back a bit and then plummeted to the ground below with a thump. The bird next to it didn't know what had happened and peered over, bending down to check, losing its head with the next pellet. After twenty-five birds had been picked off the ledges there was chaos. Wings and feathers were everywhere as frightened birds bulleted around the place and blood streaked the grimy walls.

Then silence.

When the birds had settled I quietly climbed the metal staircase to the next level and opened fire at those perched on the higher ledges and bars. What followed was a rain of birds and blood.

The final assault was deathly, with pigeons dropping from great heights to the unforgiving concrete and metal below.

All through the firing, I had become so cold-bloodedly deadly that I didn't miss a bird. Every shot spelt death. It was exhilarating.

Standing at the railings almost near the ceiling I looked down at the scene below. There were birds everywhere, many lying still and some twitching and fluttering helplessly. Then I descended to the ground level and walked out, spattered with blood and covered with feathers, my heart slamming against my ribs, the taste of copper filling my mouth.

A recklessness had taken hold of me and I permitted it to propel me on. There was no reason to be tender any more. No reason to be a nice guy.

I set up a match with Minty Kapur and allowed her to win the only set we played. I drank lemonade with her till it was dark and then walked her home, stopping behind the huge karonda bush to kiss her on the mouth and let my hands wander across her yielding body. We played tennis every evening for a week, ending each session the same way. After that we stopped meeting at the club and spent time alone on the far side of the lake, among the roots of a wide spreading tree. There was nothing refined about her so preliminaries weren't necessary.

It was just what I needed to turn my life around and give me a new lease of strength and stamina. I didn't have to bother any more about whether I had a family or not, what my mother or brother or sister was doing with their lives, whether my Dad would ever change for the better. What was 'the better'?

Life had to be lived to the last drop, the last breath, the last gasp, the last thrust, the last cry of triumph.

When my high school results came out, I discovered that I had just about scraped through and no college would even consider giving me admission with the pathetic scores that I had eked out. The only course

I managed to get admission into was a B.A. with English Literature and History. It was a joke. I disliked books, considered studying literature and history a waste of time. I found the Jesuit college in Calcutta far too serious for my liking. What relevance was all that learned seriousness if the world around was in a mess? Calcutta was burning. Unemployment and injustice had driven thousands of young people beyond the limits of desperation to join the Naxalbari movement. In the name of the cause, innocent people lost their lives and any person in any position of authority or power found his or her life threatened. Banks and business establishments were looted; petty businessmen were shot, stabbed or beheaded.

I really couldn't understand why all this was happening because I wasn't into politics and was virtually clueless about why so many people my age were ganging up to set out on killing sprees. From my understanding of all the fracas, the poor and defenceless were ruining the happiness of the rich. There were heated debates in the college canteen and in tea shops but I was always the observer, sipping hot tea from a chipped cup and pulling on a bidi. For quite a while since the chaos had started in the city, I had not actually witnessed any shootout or murder. I had only heard people talking about bloody events, read a bit on the front page of papers, saw shattered glass and dried patches of blood on pavements, saw an ambulance leaving with the injured...until one afternoon in Coffee House on College Street.

Halfway through my cup of coffee, I looked up and noticed that everyone around me had stopped talking. There was a deathly silence and stillness. The man sitting at the table nearby had folded his newspaper and got up to leave when there was a loud bang and he was thrown backwards against the pillar behind him. He slid down in slow motion and the next shot blew off a segment of his shoulder. He fell, grovelling about on the floor, trying to grab the marble top of the table with the hand that still worked. He knelt there for a moment, his eyes rolling in their sockets, focussed on me and his mouth opened to say something. The third blast blew away his face. Then his body slipped down and sprawled on the floor.

So violent was the impact that my face and shirt were splashed red.

There was chaos. People were screaming and scrambling for the exit. Sirens whined. I dropped to the ground and crawled for cover behind the pillar, close to the corpse that was still twitching. I sat there watching the pool of red expanding. The cops burst in firing recklessly, and innocent people caught in the fire were knocked off their feet.

When the shooting subsided, I crawled out between chairs and tables and down the stairs, into the street, walking most of the way to the hostel.

I was rushed to the infirmary because they thought that I had been injured but when I was stripped bare they got a bit of shock. *Where's the blood from?* Father Shriver, the Warden of the hostel wanted to know.

There was a shoot out, people were killed.

What did you have to do with it?

Nothing.

Don't leave the campus, Sean. The city's on fire and we've lost so many of our students. You're lucky you never got shot or picked up and put away. Don't leave the campus, you hear? Don't leave the campus.

I'll try.

Where did you go? Where did this happen?

College Street Coffee House.

Why did you go there Sean? You walked straight into a hornet's nest. Are you sure you're not mixed up with that no-good lot? You come from a good family Sean.

I'm not mixed up with anyone.

Then what were you doing there?

I wanted to know what's happening out there.

And get yourself killed in the bargain? Why?

It's silly being cloistered here and not know what's happening out there. I grew up in this city. I know the streets like the lines on the palms of my hands. I belong out there.

So you were out there looking for trouble. Unbelievable! Now you go and have a hot bath, a bowl of chicken soup and go to sleep. You'll be fine in the morning. No point you lying around here in the infirmary.

The next day I slipped out again, determined to witness the death throes of the city. But outside, the city struggled to stay alive as a few shops opened and people huddled on the streets in scattered groups. At the corner of Wellesley Street and Colin Street, three victims of a shoot out lay inert. A group of beggars crowded around them to strip them off their belongings. One took off with a pair of shoes and another with trousers. I threw stones at them and chased them away then turned and walked down Colin Street, Junkie Gully, overwhelmed by the terrible silence that hung over its narrow, crooked, lane. Even stray dogs and cats that frequented these quarters had gone into hiding. A flock of crows descended suddenly and alighted on a dustbin, cawing hysterically. I stopped myself from peering in.

A feeling of nausea swept over me and I wanted to get out of there as fast as I could. *What am I doing here? What am I doing here? What the hell is wrong with me? Am I going crazy?* I quickened my pace down the street, suddenly panicked and started running. I took a sharp turn between buildings and landed up in someone's backyard.

What're you doing here? A voice growled from behind shuttered windows on the ground floor of a crumbling apartment block. *What're you doing here? Get out of here, or else I'll hammer you. Do you hear me?*

I'll leave, I'll leave, I responded hastily.

When I turned around I was facing three fellows with metal pipes in their hands. I slammed the first with a right cross that sent him into a washing line. The other two ran away. I walked up to the fellow tangled in a white cotton sari and kicked him a few times till large patches of red appeared on the fabric, spreading quickly. Picking up his metal pipe I walked out to the street. A group of cops stood at the head of the road. One had a megaphone. *You! Drop your weapon!* he called out. I broke into a run in the opposite direction and heard shots being fired. Speeding up, I reached Free School Street and headed on from there to New Market where I sneaked from one alleyway to the next. I kept running, only slowing down when I reached the green expanse of the maidaan. In the distance I heard dull explosions as plumes of smoke rose up from among the buildings. The city was at war with itself, cutting its own wrists, breaking its own bones and suffocating on its own fumes.

By the time I finally reached the hostel, a posse of cops had already raided the place, searching for weapons and explosives. When they found nothing, they had picked up a couple of students and taken them away for questioning, bringing them back an hour later, dazed, bruised and bleeding. I hid the pipe amongst the plants in the small garden behind the dormitory.

In The Shadow of His Hand

A few days later at the breakfast table Father Shriver and I got talking.

What do you get from roaming the streets? he wanted to know.

I don't know.

If you don't know then why do you do it? It seems to me that you're challenging yourself, daring yourself. Are you trying to convince yourself that life has no meaning? Why is a Catholic like you doing this? You do go to church, don't you?

Yes.

And to confession?

Sometimes.

And receive the body of Christ?

Yes.

Then what's the problem?

I don't know.

I'm sure you do but you're just not willing to talk.

I shrugged my shoulders.

I won't persist. Sorry. It really is none of my business. But I'd like you to come with me to Nirmal Hriday, a home for the dying and the destitute, where the unwanted of your city die with dignity.

There is no dignity in dying, Father.

Come with me Sean, I'll show you.

I'll find my own way there some time.

Before I could even contemplate doing that, the Bangladesh war of liberation broke out I joined a group called 'SLAY' (Students' Liberation Army), inspired by the exploits of Che Guevara. One thousand five hundred of us from four colleges in Calcutta, set out for the border... only twenty reached, the rest changed their minds and went home when they witnessed a dogfight between Pakistani Sabre jets and Indian MIGs. Fifteen chickened out when they saw streams of shocked and wounded refugees crossing over into India with their bundles and heard some of their tales of torture loss and death.

That left five of us. It was a cruel joke when I think of it now. Five young, unarmed men, out to fight alongside the Mukti Bahini with no experience of combat whatsoever. Down Jessore Road we went, five fools rushing into a ravaged land that angels had already abandoned. We were too proud to turn back and went headlong into the smoke, tripping over the remains of the departed.

When the euphoria of potential martyrdom subsided we were frightened out of minds as the war became increasingly furious and brutal.

Pradip, the only son of a trader from Burra Bazaar, was sure that he would never return home alive. Neelkanth, the rabid revolutionary took out his notebook and began writing a last message to his girlfriend who had already ditched him and married someone else. Shailain, the protest poet, kept repeating *poetry can no longer be written.* Charu kept finding weapons with no ammunition or unused grenades. He pulled the pin of one threw it away hastily. It landed somewhere without exploding.

I had given up hope of ever returning and kept plodding through the rubble, ducking and dropping flat every time there was an explosion.

We spent nights in abandoned bombed out homes and on two occasions narrowly missed getting shot. Finally, tired, thirsty and hungry, we were picked up by a young Indian Army officer who was leading his equally young soldiers into combat. Two got themselves shot when they lost their nerve and ran into a crossfire.

After Major Gurjeet Singh Ahluwalia was convinced that we were in fact Indian students, we were bundled into an ambulance along with a pile of half dead infantrymen and sent behind the lines. Three days later we crossed the border. We were so relieved that we were alive that we enlisted in the refugee camps as volunteers. When all five of us were laid low with severe dysentery, we had no option but to return to Calcutta. We did the journey back in the bogey of a goods train which chugged along through the Bengal countryside, stopping for hours at a time. Whenever we wanted to empty our bellies, we'd hop off, do what we had to in the bushes and then run alongside the snail slow train to our bogey and climb in. On one occasion, the train picked up speed so I had to run alongside with my pants sliding down. I'd stop, yank up my trousers and break into a run again. Fortunately the train finally stopped and I climbed in.

We returned to the hostel as heroes. Dad had the cops out in search of me and was relieved when he heard that I was in one piece. When I told him what I had experienced he said, *I don't believe you.*

The dysentery was treated and knocked out of my system and my body limped back to normal.

Father Shriver hugged me. *Good to see you back alive. Did you really cross the border?*

I nodded.

I'm impressed, Sean. I'm not sure what you did there but you showed your solidarity. He was a compassionate man who encouraged me to feel comfortable with who I was. *Now I wouldn't have done what you did but it was your choice, your calling...to go out there and witness man's inhumanity to man. That alone has its value Sean. I think finally all that matters is to listen to what your heart tells you to do.*

Father Shriver was interesting company and soon I found myself attending early morning mass at the Carmelite chapel down the road. It was a small chapel with a patch of a garden and a white marble statue of Theresa of the Little Flower at its entrance. Old man Lazarus sang to the tune of a wobbly organ from the loft during mass. No one could bear his singing but Father Shriver continued to encourage him.

He's got cancer, he once said to me, *let's help him to go out singing.* And when the man passed away, Father stood by his coffin before they buried him, and presented a little reflection on the quality of the man's singing. *He may not have had even a decent voice but he surely had a lot of faith and Christian feeling. We suffered his singing because we knew that he meant every word that he sang.*

After we buried the yodeller, I went with Father to Nirmal Hriday for the first time. *The neglected old and sick can die here with dignity,* he said. *I get solace here, and it's here I know that I'm not alone.*

What about when you are offering mass?

That's another sort of experience, an elevated one. It's beyond the physical. This is emotional, it's physical, it is comforting in a very real way. Be here a day and you'll understand what I mean, Sean. Just one day.

There really wasn't much time to reflect on the cool quietness of the home and the gentle care of the women who shuffled between low cots tending to the dying, bathing them, cleaning and dressing sores and wounds, praying with them, talking to them, helping their spirits to let go and move on. I was given a bucket of disinfectant and water with a broom, pan and swab. *Start from there, brother,* said the dignified nun, pointing to the far end of the large room where light streamed in from a small window and washed over sleeping figures.

So I started from the floor area below the window and began sweeping with the soft broom, gathering the dust and unwanted bits and pieces into the pan and tossing it all into a waste bin. The difficult part of an otherwise easy job, was when I had to go down on my knees and stretch the broom underneath a bed. My face would come close to a reclining body and the unmistakable odour of decay would hit me. Sometimes I would even find a face staring at me, eyes haunted with imminent death. I'd struggle to smile. After a few repetitions, I began to reach out and touch the person to connect and acknowledge the nearness.

The swabbing began from the other end of the room but I had hardly cleaned a small patch when I heard a still small voice behind me. *Brother, why do you want to die young? Are you fed up with the life you have?*

Without looking back I replied, *I've seen more than I've needed to in the few years I've been alive sister, but I'd like to live a little more if I'm given the chance.*

In that case, maybe you should use a mask, that's what intelligent people generally do when they work here. Take this mask and put it on.

I turned around and looked up from my crouched position at the nun holding out a cloth mask. Even though she was slightly built, a gentle power emanated from her. Mother Teresa's smile was unmistakable. *You clean well, brother, bless you for what you are doing. Bless you. Helping the neglected and abandoned to die with dignity is what we try to do here...but not everyone who arrives here wants to die. The ties with life are so strong that some people hold on to a straw to stop themselves from drowning. Letting go isn't easy. God truly loves us, we should trust him enough to rest in the shadow of His hand.*

I watched her weave her way between the aged and dying and dissolve into the shadows around the corner.

Mother says you can stop now, another volunteer will take over from you. Go out to the back there, they want a volunteer to cut hair, said a nun who seemed to have materialised out of nowhere.

So off I went to play barber, cropping hair from a boil infested head. Someone handed me a bowl of antiseptic and a sponge and I cleansed the dripping mouths of each swelling. *Why am I here?* I asked myself, without stopping what I was doing. *Why am I here among the dying, washed to the edge of life?*

Come on Sean, Father Shriver said later, patting me on the shoulder, *time to go.*

We left, the smell of the dying receding behind us and the smell of the dead rising to meet us as we passed the burning ghats. *Ever considered answering the call?* he asked as we walked towards the bus stop.

What call are you talking about?

To the Order.

No. That's not my line, I responded.

It's not a line Sean, it's a calling.

I know, that's what they say. But I haven't heard it. And anyway what good would I be? Ask me to box, I can do that. To run, I can do that. To shoot, that too. But to be a priest? Why would someone like me be called?

I was a porter in the Alps. What good was I but to carry loads on my shoulders? But I was called. It's got nothing to do with who you are or what you are. It's got to do with that divine being inside.

Why would any divine being want to live in me Father Shriver? My life so far has been one big mistake.

That's what happened to the Prodigal Son.

He went away and then came back but I've gone nowhere, I'm stuck here, trying to make sense of my life.

You know best, I suppose. I'm not the sort who tries to make people believe that they have been chosen. I'm not one of those sorts who go around thumping the Holy Bible and searching under my chair for the Lord.

But something had touched me because I returned to Nirmal Hriday a few times a week, giving whatever I could of myself to help the dying let go in peace.

Am I becoming obsessed with death, violence and suffering? I asked myself one day.

I couldn't find an answer so I let the experience stay hanging over me like a heavy bellied dark cloud that refuses to rain, like a shadow that refuses to go away even in the dark and I can feel it there, slowing me down, like a constant taste of copper on the tip of my tongue, like tartar on my teeth that can't be brushed off, like an embarrassing memory that keeps presenting itself at the most unexpected times. Like living with a wound because I survive on the blood that I draw from it.

Yes, I survived my wounds and I survived because of them.

The nurse tells me that my sponsor, my benefactor, the one who has made it possible for all this medical support and the room in this hospital is here, waiting outside.

May I bring him in? He's been waiting out there for an hour already. He didn't want to disturb you.

Sure.

The man walks in and stands at the foot of the bed, looking at me. *Hello Sean, I am so happy that we meet again after all these years.*

I look at him standing there before me, immaculately dressed in a deep blue suit, his mop of wavy grey hair brushed back, high cheeked bones and eyes more prominent than before.

Remember me, Sean?

I feel a cold wave of nausea wash over me. *Yes. Uncle Prem. I remember you. How could I forget you?*

There is a long awkward silence.

Listen, I know this is painful and confusing for you. I mean all that you've gone through with this terrible happening. And then you see me here. Me. Someone you can never forgive. You can't bear the thought that I have been paying your bills, that I've put you here.

Get out. I don't know how you've turned up. I don't care if you want to be generous with me now, I don't care in the least. Just get out. I'll pay back every single rupee that you have spent. I'll pay it back, just get the hell out of here.

You don't have to get hysterical. I'm not going to harm you.

You? I'll kill you. How I've dreamed of killing you. I'll kill you now.

Be reasonable Sean. I know you hate me for what I did, but I just want to be of help to you now.

To pay for what you did? Do you think that your money is going to wipe out the memory of what you did to me? Do you? I sob.

Yes because it's not only going to pay your bills but it's also buying you out of the trouble you are in. My money is going to get you off the hook. Have you noticed, your guards haven't come in here to escort me out, they're sitting out there. You're shouting your head off and no one is coming in. Sean, you'll always be a part of me and I'll always be a part of you. We share the same shame. Aunty died and I married again. I have children now, three of them, all grown up. I'm a different man now. Those were difficult times for me. It's different now.

But it's the same for me, I snap and I can feel the bile rising up my throat, heading for my mouth. *It's changed for you, great, but I can't get rid of the wound, I can't. I was abandoned and needed your shelter. Instead of offering me the shadow of your hand, you filled me with your darkness. You are never going to be a part of me. Never. You are the dirt that sticks to life, dried and hard...I can't remove you.*

You have no option but to accept my generosity, Sean. I will walk out of this room and you will never see me again I promise. And remember, I want nothing back. He walks out, leaving me nauseous and confused. I start puking and the nurse rushes in. She cleans me up, bathes and dresses me.

Why is this man so powerful?

Prem Sir built this hospital and has major shares in it.

I lie there wondering how to react. If I was able I would have bashed him against the wall, thrown him out of the window, put his head in the toilet bowl and kept flushing it.

But I couldn't.

I was helpless then. I am helpless now.

The doctor comes in and gives me a shot that calms me down. I can feel my body going limp and my joints loose and my senses disintegrating and all I have is my memory that flows like that stream of blood across the floor in Coffee House. I can feel myself spreading, the years stretching, flowing one into the other and once again I drift back to those Nirmal Hriday days.

In a strange way, my visits to the home helped me to learn how to be tender, to learn how to give, to learn how to heal, to learn how to love without expecting love in return, to learn how to look at my face in the mirror and reassure myself that I was alive.

Dad walked in and out of my life during those years, as he had always done before, preoccupied with his own well being, his own ambitions, his own sense of right and wrong, his own expectations, his own joys and fears and hopes and memories. After our confrontation that night at home, he kept me at arm's length. He seemed to be wary of even displaying more affection than usual just in case I suspected him of insincerity. Our relationship turned predictable and slipped into becoming formal. We even started shaking hands when we met.

Mum's letters were few and far between. I found it difficult to reply to them because they seemed to have been written out of habit. My replies were occasional. Her last letter had mentioned that Big Mummy had died painfully, but she never explained the cause. The family house was being sold and she was leaving Coimbatore. Even though our ties had snapped, I nevertheless felt an aching sense of incompleteness. She was a part of my childhood and I had left her behind and walked into my adulthood without deep feelings for her. I thought of her with affection and a tinge of sadness. Life had overtaken her and left her waiting by the roadside. Maybe I was afraid of going back to her as numerous other ghosts would surface again.

There's this fellow in Nirmal Hriday who claims to know you, said Father Shriver. *He says he's seen you there but you never recognised him.*

He's a volunteer there?

He's dying. Last stages of TB. Do you want to meet him?

Reluctantly I made my way to the home with Father Shriver and was taken to the bedside where a bag of bones lay. He was covered with a light sheet and his breath was laboured. Father uncovered his face and I looked into Phillip's eyes.

I didn't know what to say, what to feel. I cried holding his hand. *You've won,* he said. Then he closed his eyes and turned over on his side, away from me, breathing heavily.

I spent the night on a small stool beside him and in the morning they covered his body and praying over it, carried it away to join so many others on the ghats.

I really don't know what to think, what to say, what to feel. Phillip, I never expected to find you there among the many derelicts of the city, reduced to a bag of bones, at the end of your life. To me you were always the tough one, the fighter, the survivor, never scared to say whatever you wanted to say, even to Dad. You stood up to him and faced his anger. You had what I didn't have—strength. And I don't think you were ever appreciated for that. You needed that strength to survive my arrival. I am sorry for spoiling your pitch, for ruining your place in our family, for being loved by Grandpa and Aunt Katherine and Big Daddy. I'm sorry I was their bundle of joy. It's strange, usually it's the younger siblings that have to fight for their place in the family but it was quite the opposite in our case. I displaced you. I'm sorry Phillip, I'm sorry that I did that to you. I didn't mean to. Believe me. I didn't choose to be born. But you're gone now and I can do nothing about it. How I wished to have been nearer to you, for you to be my real elder brother, to learn from you...and when that didn't happen, I wished that we could at least be friends. Remember that day at the Botanical Gardens, Phillip? I never wanted it to end.

Phillip's passing threw me off course and even though my final exams were precariously close, I couldn't get myself to concentrate. Sensing my confusion, Father Shriver did his best to try and help me through but seemed to get increasingly exasperated when I didn't respond.

I know you want to help, I finally said to him, *but this is my grief, I have to work my way through it...please Father, don't throw the Good Book at me.*

I'm not throwing the Good Book at you Sean. I'm only trying to help.

Yes, but you will never really understand our relationship. Letting go must make sense to me.

Sorry, he said graciously and stepped back whilst I went through my own purgatory.

Phillip's presence permeated my waking and sleeping hours. He appeared and disappeared. Until one night I awoke in a cold sweat. He stood there at the window, looking in at me. I sat up and looking in his direction said quietly, *I'm letting go now, Phillip, I have to move on...*

It rained heavily that night and I lay awake listening to the storm heave and rumble in the night and the wind break branches of trees out in the garden. And then there was silence and a stillness. It was as if the storm had whisked my brother away. Exhausted, I slept.

The next day I slowly began my return to the reality of my examinations. I realized that I had to get through. I had nose dived twice in the second year exams and just about scraped through in the third attempt. And now the final exam. I dreaded sitting there in an examination hall trying to make sense of the printed questions in front of me. But when the examinations arrived I fought my way through each paper and emerged a wreck, crawling back to the hostel to sleep for days.

Dad wanted me home but I kept delaying my departure. When I finally packed and was ready to go Father Shriver sat me down with a mug of tea. *What are you going to do now?* He wanted to know, *now that your finals are behind you. I don't see you studying any more. What do you want to do?*

I'm not sure.

You're the sports type right? I've always wondered why you had to suffer studying literature since you disliked it so much. Now that we know each other well, I know you well enough to make this suggestion. Why don't you train to be a sports teacher? And while you're doing that I can fix you up as an assistant to a senior sports teacher in one of our schools. I could try Don Bosco's or any of the others. Do you want to give it a try?

Are there prospects in that field?

For you? Of course. He was emphatic.

I surprised myself by agreeing to his proposition.

What about going home?

I'll go back and explain things to Dad. If he doesn't see the light, I'll do what I want.

The Beginning

Predictably, Dad put his foot down. *A sports teacher? Over my dead body! Absolutely not.*

I'm no good at anything else. Dad, what's wrong with being a sports teacher?

You've got to be joking! Are you serious?

Of course I'm serious. If you don't let me train to be one I'll walk out.

Don't challenge me.

I am challenging you. What are you going to do about it? Are you going to support me or not? I stormed into my room, slamming the door behind me.

Sean, open the door, you hear me? Open the door! We can discuss the matter in a civilised way.

You think that you are capable of discussing anything in a civilized way, Dad? All you will try to do is convince me to do what you want me to do. You don't want the whole world to know that I am incapable of higher studies. Don't try and live through me, Dad. It's not going to work.

Stop behaving like a child, Sean. This isn't being mature.

Do you think that you are mature?

If I wasn't, would I have reached where I have? he asked.

That's for you to decide.

Suit yourself, I'm cutting you off. Don't expect any support from me for your grand designs. It's over.

How convenient. You've finally freed yourself of all responsibilities.

By the way, you'll never have to worry about Phillip suddenly showing up and embarrassing you. He's dead. He died pitifully in Mother Teresa's Home. He was a bag of bones when I saw him. And now he's dead.

I choked up. Dad was quiet. When he spoke, his voice was thick with grief.

What are you... I don't understand...Why didn't you tell me? You saw Phillip? Why did you keep this from me? He was my son! My son! He died in a home for destitutes...oh God, dear God..

I could hear him weeping. *Dad, that drama won't get you anywhere. You'll get it all back in full measure.*

Sean, please. Please open the door.

I switched off the light and throwing myself into bed, went to sleep. He banged on the door a few times in the morning before he went to work and then gave up. After he left, I packed my clothes and then went over to the post office and withdrew all the money that I had saved. Two hours later I was in Father Shriver's office.

Well, I've done my bit, he smiled. *I've got you a one year contract in St George's as Assistant Sports Teacher; that is, if they think you're worth the offer. They're a boarding school so you'll have a place to stay and food to eat. So here's who you have to meet. The sooner you meet the person, the better.* He handed me a card.

Sure, see you...and thanks for the hand up.

Hope this works out.

I caught the first bus in that direction and forty-five minutes later was in the school office to meet the Vice Principal Sylvester Ghosh, a portly gent with a tufts of white hair growing out of his ears and a smile that was disarming. He stood at the door reprimanding a scruffily dressed teenager. *Look at your collar Hilton, like a crazy butterfly, your hair like a thatched hut. And your shoes!* Hilton looked at his toes sticking out of the front of his shoes.

Sorry Sir, the shoes got torn...and

You were up all night due to the ragging...

No, Sir...

Then why are you looking like something the cat dragged in?

The boy was quiet.

You can go now. Run along and clean up.

When the boy had left, he said to me, *It's not his fault poor thing. It's the ragging.* After a pause, *are you the sporty fellow?*

Yes. I'm Sean Varma.

Follow me.

We took an instant liking to each other and I got the job. *There's a room for you beside the laundry section on the second floor. It's got an attached bath and a small balcony facing the playground. You don't have any attachments, do you?*

No.

The matron's quite pretty, that should keep you busy. He started laughing when he saw the surprised look on my face. *That was meant to be a joke. She's on her last legs, well past retirement. But she's a real dear.*

My career as a sports teacher began, making its way through a host of other schools. I managed to complete an advanced course in physical education on the side. I was ready for a position of some worth. But the city was too small for me, too full of my past. Everything was stale, old, used, repetitive, the sounds, sights, smells, the people, everything.

Time to move, I said to myself, sipping a beer in a bar off Bentick Street. *This city weighs me down. It stands for all the past that I have tried to forget—my shame, my poverty, vulnerability, hopelessness, defeat. Even though I am actually doing well for myself, it's like being in hell all the time. What do the people here find in it? Desperation to give their lives passion? When the physical world closes in on you, assaulting your senses, eating into you, you have nowhere to go to but into yourself in order to feel secure. And from inside there you rebuild the city you inhabit, making it into some place that's not just habitable but welcoming, all-encompassing with its voluptuous maternal glow. Dirt and chaos is transformed into soft blue nostalgia, giving places and people a mysteriously warm humanness that is both stupid and divine. Decay appears to be almost beautiful. It's easier for you to cope with the city then and learn to love it if you live in your head and heart. I am not capable of doing something like that. So it's time to move, snap the cord and drift away.*

After twenty-two professional years in the city, I quit my job, moved to Bombay and did the rounds of schools, looking for a job. It took a while to land it but when I did, I was more than just satisfied. The Bombay Bastion was a formidable school with an enviably large playground and a well equipped gym. Fifteen hundred students, a battalion of teachers and funds enough to experiment with new approaches to almost any educating experience. The only hitch was that the presiding deity Deborah Reuben was a mammoth Baghdadi Jewish lady who controlled the collective destinies of all from her ancient study filled with memories of her 'glorious youth'. She sat there in a large cushioned chair behind a delicate wrought iron table with a glass top, sipping black tea flavoured with almonds and raisins. A black lace veil fell delicately over her face, protecting its white horsiness from the eyes of the world.

One had to be in her good books to get anywhere far in the school. She gave me the job because she liked my voice, apart from being impressed by my credentials. *Can you sing?* she asked at the interview.

No Ma'am, I can't.

Why can't you? You have such a naturally melodious voice.

I'm a sports teacher, a physical instructor.

I know but what's wrong with a sports teacher who is a singer? Our Maths teacher is an actor, he does the drama in the school. You must meet him, he is there in the outer office. You should meet him. Ezra, Ezra Luddy. I want a word with you.

A dishevelled, rumpled looking man came stumbling in. *This is our resident genius, Ezra Luddy, a Maths whizz and a Shakespearean eyeful. Ezra, this is Sean Varma. Take him under your wing. I want him to sing in one of your productions.*

Ezra looked at me and I looked at him and it was evident that we didn't want to have anything to do with each other. He mumbled a greeting and left. *It's the tradition in this school. I'm a dancer. Of course, not anymore. I'm quite plump now because I live a sedative existence.*

You mean a sedentary life, I understand.

I mean a sedative existence, she insisted.

I didn't pursue the point further and smiled.

I have films of my dance performances. We show them on Founder's Day. Always a big hit. I won't bore you any more, Varma, she finally announced. *I'll ask the Head Master Mr President to introduce you to the rest of the staff.* The Head Master entered on cue. *This is our Head Master Richard President. He'll take you around.*

He was a solemn looking fellow with a crew cut and a goatee. *Come along*, was all he said and left the room with me behind him. On our way, he said, *The physical education and sports department is in a mess. The last teacher who was in charge made a business out of special coaching and neglected the work he was being paid to do. The one before that was obsessed with football, his predecessor with cricket and so the story goes. I hope we can expect some good from you.*

Of course, was all I could say. I kept my word and revamped the physical education and sports department. That year, the school won a number of sports meets and even got a few notices in the city newspapers. My colleagues became uncomfortable with my popularity amongst the students and began to isolate me. Eventually, it stopped bothering me and I started enjoying my time at The Bombay Bastion. What I enjoyed the most was the once a month trek into the hills around Khandala with groups of senior students.

I remember the first outing. There were eleven of us and we took an early morning train to Khandala in the Western Ghats. The monsoon was ripe and the driving rain hammered the green hills at right angles, dislodging rocks and sending torrential streams of muddy water down their sides onto the highway, across and down the other side, cascading into the valley and joining the swelling streaming below. It was dangerously wide when we reached it, after trekking along a ridge and down into the valley. My city slicker companions who had hardly soiled the soles of their walking shoes till then, stood quaking at the sight of such elemental fury—the rushing stream before them and the rain-slammed hills around joined in an unsettling roar.

They suggested that we turn back, check in at one of the small hotels near the station, clean up, rest and set out again the next morning when the downpour had subsided. Instead of agreeing I took them on a long walk through calf-deep slush to a small stone bridge half submerged in the flood. *We cross here,* I said, leading the way and they followed half-heartedly. Once over to the other side, the climb began along a rising path that had been occupied by the steady swish of rain water working its way down the hill towards us.

No, said Santosh, *I don't think I'm going to make it. This doesn't make sense. This path belongs to the stream now, we have no right to be here. I'm turning back.*

You're walking on, straight up. You wanted to join us, I said, *you can't back off now.*

If you want to, added Murtaz, *You can find your own way back.*

Everyone agreed.

Santosh stopped, holding on to the trunk of a young tree, breathing heavily.

It's your smoking, someone commented, *that's why you've even stopped running.*

Don't pick on him now, if he wants to stop for a few moments, let him. It happens to me sometimes. Go on Murtaz, lead the way, I called out *and when you reach the open ground of the tableland head for the rock shelter to your right. We'll be there soon.* I called out. They continued on their way and slipped out of sight. A cloud of mist descended. When it lifted, Santosh and I continued till we reached wild clumps of lantana alive with large blue and black butterflies. And behind the clumps the land levelled off, electric green and glowing. Far to our left a rainbow formed and peacock could be seen almost beneath it. Santosh looked at me and smiled and we headed for the group waiting in the rock shelter.

Are we camping here? someone asked.

I pointed upwards to the crags half hidden by the dense forest. *There. We're going there, after we've eaten.*

After an hour, we set out again, entering the lower tree line, quickly trailing the path till we were out the other side, crossing carpets of glowing green and into the next fortress of trees. Hours of persistent walking and climbing released in each of them a knot of energy and enthusiasm and when we hit the last lap of the trek there were no complaints.

Standing there in a small clearing in weak sunlight, amidst ghostly trees dripping wild orchids, questions came at me from the group.

Where are we checking in?

Will there be hot and cold water?

I need to crap. Where's the loo?

What about dinner?

There, I said, *around the bend of that path is where we're going to spend the night. We'll cook our own food. Get stuff from the village.*

Our residence for the night was a large crude hut put together from slabs of stone brought down from the ruins. Even the wooden and rusty metal door with chains had its origins in the ruins above. Since the caretaker living in the nearby village had been informed days in advance that we were coming he had placed a large clay pot of drinking water and two kerosene lanterns with trimmed wicks in the centre of the room. Everyone settled in quite easily.

A couple of them came with me to the caretaker's home in the village and we bought three fowl, onions and a large ball of finely ground spices and took a cooking pot on hire. *There's enough fire wood in there,* he assured us. *But you'll need to order rotis.*

Back at camp we discovered that the wood was slightly damp and got smoked out whilst trying to light the fire. Once we got that under control and finally produced a tender but spicy curry, the long wait for the rotis began. When they arrived, the boys thought they were plates because they were so large and stiff.

Later, after laborious chewing and chomping, dinner was over and the pot was licked clean and put out in the rain to soak, they stacked the remaining rotis near the fire to keep them warm for the next morning. A couple of the braver ones stripped and bathed in the rain whilst the others splashed their faces, hands and feet.

With lanterns low and the room warm, they rolled into their sleeping bags and slid into a deep, dead, sleep leaving me with the night. Outside, the rain had stopped and I stepped into the open allowing the damp air to hug me with its cool body. Strings of fire flies draped themselves from the branches of the dark greenery around me and rooted me in the moment. There was nothing more important than that moment, swollen with the joy of being alive.

When I returned indoors, the rain came down again, clattering on the roof hysterically and the wind banged against the door, rattling the chains. Deep into the night, the rain finally subsided and the wind went to sleep. Only the owls in the trees were awake.

At dawn, we climbed the upper slope to the ruins of the fortress and spent the morning exploring. At noon we made our way through the village and down the slope of forested green to the plains that stretched to Karjat. And by evening, we were chugging along in the train, back to Bombay. No one spoke. We were full with the experience of green, tingling and tired.

One trek followed another and the groups multiplied as rock climbing was added to the experience. Weekend camps were started and Bombay Bastion led the way in adventure sports, quickly expanding its activities and hiring a team of assistants and specialists. As my work became more and more administrative, I resigned, granted myself a month's holiday and reorganised my apartment in Malad, a suburb of the city.

Initially, I padded about the place, listened to music and went out for an occasional beer and biryani. When that became too much of a routine I turned one room into a mini gym and strung up a punching bag to bang away at whenever I felt like. Then that stopped too as I found myself becoming increasingly inactive. Lying about and listening to music and watching television took hold of my life.

A month dragged into two and three and four and one day when I decided that I couldn't be on holiday anymore and had to either go out and look for another job or leave the city, a series of bomb blasts ripped through the metropolis and Bombay was never the same again. I put off my decision and stayed where I was, becoming increasingly restless and lonely.

I began to accept that I was actually a solitary person, incapable of making friends. Everyone I had known was associated with my professional life, even women. What was wrong with me? Was I sending out the wrong signals? Or was I so preoccupied with myself that other people had become incidental? An inner compulsion which I could not comprehend was keeping me away from others.

Was I afraid of a relationship? Scared of being hurt? I felt unable to shed the darkness that had haunted me since childhood. *Am I like my Dad who tried to get away before his marriage so he wouldn't have to take on the responsibility?* I threw myself into one night stands and multiple relationships, sinking into the warmth of bodies and the transient tenderness of hopelessly brief encounters. I got whoever I wanted.

But eventually, I knew I had to tear myself out of myself, throw out the wreckage, dig out the dark seed, empty myself.

The Haven

Deciding to look for a job in a beautiful place somewhere far from the city, I remembered with fondness and nostalgia the trip Phillip and I had made with Big Daddy from Coimbatore into the hills. The Nilgiris would be a place I'd like to live in.

In a fit of enthusiasm and determination I placed a small advertisement in a southern newspaper, offering my services as an experienced sports teacher with an impeccable record of service. I got seven responses from schools in the Nilgiris and landed in Ooty a week later. After a number of successful interviews, I couldn't make up my mind which school to choose so I convinced two schools to take me on part time. Then I rented The Haven, a cottage in Kotagiri and spent a month overhauling its interiors, repairing its roof and redoing the garden.

The cottage stood on the edge of Longwood Shola, a forest of old trees and shrubs inhabited by wild hare, the Malabar flying squirrel, barking deer, mouse deer, a leopard or two, a herd of bison and an assortment of smaller animals and birds. To its right was a small tea estate and to the left the land sloped down into the valley where a village lay. After working through the day on putting the house and the garden in order I'd take a long walk in the evening down the narrow path through the forest. The fragrance of mud and leaves and fruit was rejuvenating and I'd give myself up to the wholesome experience of the wild.

Since there was still a month or so for me to start work in the schools, I headed back to Bombay to pack my belongings, hand over the keys to the owner of the apartment and return to the hills. Gratefully, that wasn't much of a stressful experience. I focussed on the task at hand and got it over with as quick as I possibly could. The Haven welcomed my return early one morning with a barking deer and three wild hare grazing on the lawn and a flock of scarlet minivets decorating the orange trees. *This is the life I have chosen, I will make it work,* I kept telling myself as I set about creating a familiar and comfortable space for myself.

The next day started with a heavy downpour and I sat out in the veranda watching the land all around me whipped by the savage lashes of rain. By afternoon, only a grey drizzle remained and a brain fever bird went wild in Longwood Shola, filling the air with its cries. Slipping on a rain jacket I headed for the forest.

You're in an awful rush, a voice said from behind as I walked the slushy track.

Going for my evening walk, I said, turning around and facing the owner of the voice. She was tall and broad shouldered, almost manly, wearing black wellingtons and a mackintosh down to her calves. The hood half covered her face.

I didn't ask you to stop.

I stood there waiting for her to catch up to me. When she did I discovered that she was far older that she had first appeared.

So you're the new resident of The Haven. Not at all like I'd imagined.

What did you think I'd look like? I wanted to know.

Like some sort of city slicker. I thought you'd be playing loud music and have friends visiting from Bangalore and leave empty beer bottles and garbage all over the place. And that you would end up either getting lost in Longwood or gored by a bison.

I had to smile. *That's quite a detailed description! Why would a bison gore someone without provocation?*

These creatures are unpredictable. There are fourteen heads in that herd and there's a loner. Francis Pinto, the retired naturalist who lived out in Coonoor got himself gored by this fellow in the clearing behind The Haven. He was standing out there looking at two Malabar squirrels feeding on the edge of the sholas when this crazy animal charged out from nowhere and knocked him off his feet with an awful thud. Each time poor old Francis tried to get up the bison would knock him down again. This went on until the animal finally trampled on him and left.

And he's still around these parts?

Francis? Every single bone in his body was broken beyond recognition. He died.

Oh dear. That's tragic. But I meant the bison.

Sure. If we're lucky we'll get a glimpse of him in a while. Anyway, what's your name?

Sean Varma.

What a lethal combination.

Why?

An Irish and an Indian name.

What's yours? I asked in response, as we walked along.

Stella Sundaram. I came out here from England years and years ago to do good. Hah, what a joke. To do good. I'm a doctor. So I went around offering my services for free to people who belong to tribal communities here. Finally, I started an NGO along with some well-meaning Indians and we've been running a service. But then you probably know better than me about NGOs and their politics.

No, I don't. Nor do I know anything about these tribals you are talking about.

And you are an Indian?

Of course. But I don't know anything about NGO politics. I'm a sports teacher.

You mean to say you know nothing about anything else apart from physical education? Her response may have sounded a little insulting, even to her. She softened up and asked me another question. *How have you put together such an interesting garden?*

I'm comfortable with plants and trees and flowers and all that...and I know a lot about birds and animals and their ways...

Where have you got all these interests from?

I used to go out into the wild with my Dad when I was young. On shikar.

All of that is banned now and if you're caught killing any creatures here you'll be fined, possibly even jailed.

I'll remember that, I replied sarcastically.

We walked on in silence with the sounds of Longwood around us... the creaking trunks of red gum, the swishing of branches as squirrels leaped from tree to tree, the call of the scimitar babbler, the gurgling of a distant stream and the sudden sound of heavy rustling to our right.

Stand still, she whispered.

Amongst the trees, heading on to the path ahead of us, were a small herd of bison. *Should we turn back?* I asked.

Look over your shoulder, what do you see? I did and there on the path behind us I saw a massive beast, easily six feet at the shoulder. He was so close that I could smell his musky animal scent. He snorted.

Don't move Sean. That's a sign of respect. He'll watch us for a while and leave. And this lot, they'll go on their way.

Dusk began colouring the air when the lone bison finally stumbled off into the forest. The herd had left long before that. *I'm turning back now,* she said decisively and I walked with her on to the road beyond The Haven. She climbed into her black Ambassador and drove off. *We'll meet again for sure,* was all she said.

And we did. She was at my gate the next evening. *Sean? Care for a walk?*

Sure, I called back from inside.

And we set off again, this time going further into Longwood till we reached the swamp which lay at the foot of the slope. *This is my favourite place,* she said and settled down on a large boulder. We sat there absorbing the spirit of the ancient woods. *There are powers here that are beyond our comprehension, Sean. Often when I have sat here alone I have felt a presence in the air.*

She had hardly finished her sentence when suddenly all the sounds of the forest fell silent. It was the trilling of a golden backed woodpecker that snapped that magical moment five minutes later and we were thrown back into the buzz of the moment. Though it had lasted just those few minutes, it seemed like ages had passed...and she began talking again in a voice that was so soft that it was barely audible. *You'll find this presence in other places in these blue hills too. If you set off by yourself, trekking through the hills, you'll not feel alone. In lonely glades, under ancient trees, on desolate mountain slopes, besides gurgling streams flowing between flowering rhododendrons and wherever the hidden forces seem most pronounced, you will come across sacred stones of all shapes and sizes. Who knows...maybe this boulder we are sitting on has a story too. The past and the present is here...it's in the forests, grasslands and the air.*

I'm not too sure I understand what you are talking about, I interrupted her.

That's what I was saying... you are a city slicker, she smiled.

But I've seen the wilds, I insisted.

Yes, but through the eyes of a city slicker. You must live in a place and get to feel its rhythms and breathe them in and become part of them. I did. That's how I survived the passing of Vijay, my husband. I was working among the people who belong to the Toda tribal community then. They're a pastoral community living on the high grasslands of the blue hills who believe that the entire region represents their sacred land. Haenn was the first Toda. According to legend, he came from Heaven with his wife Thoovi Thirke. At that time no one lived here on earth. So they came down to earth and started a family, producing three sons and two daughters. Haen ruled for three hundred years and went on to rule Amunore, the land of the dead with one of his sons. Porshaey, one of the daughters, was responsible for the creation of all the other munds or settlements; she divided the clans, buffaloes, human beings, shastras...everything. She was the maker of these things. The conical temple, called Moonbow Porshey, made from grass and reeds and wood in Muthanad Mund marks the place of their creation. In fact not far from there is a stone circle which marks the place where Porshaey created the Toda buffalo. When a Toda dies, a buffalo is sacrificed so that the spirit of the animal may accompany the person on the long journey to Amunore and live there, providing milk and butter.

So where's their Land of the Dead?

Right here. I know where it is. It changed my life.

Where is it exactly?

It's up in the high grasslands beyond the upper reaches of the Bhavani river. To get there, the spirit of the dead person must start its journey along with the spirit of the buffalo from a place called Mulli Mund and travel across a mysterious landscape. On the way it passes sacred places where it has to perform certain rituals. It's a real landscape, I know, I have been there. Not all the way to Amunore but have done the journey with a group of Toda elders, following the Spirit Path and came quite close to the land of the dead. Of course even though we did not reach the Land of the Dead we saw it from a distance, shrouded by clouds.

I don't understand, how did it change your life?

I felt I was travelling with Vijay.

But he wasn't a Toda, was he?

Certainly not, but to me he was because he was so loved by the community and had done all he could to help their people. Sorry Sean, I didn't mean to put you through all this.

Am I complaining?

I know you're not, but...

A barking deer called from the thicket far down to our left and another answered from beyond the swamp. *Let's leave,* she said quickly, *there's something coming our way.* So we followed the path as it climbed along the forested slope to higher ground and eventually on to the path which ran along the periphery of Logwood. Mist had descended and we waded through. Suddenly she stopped. *What really brought you to these parts?* she asked.

It's a long story.

I'm sure it is. You have attachments?

No.

Then I suggest that you should get yourself a dog. You need one. Come over to my place and have a look at my German Shepherd Cleo's litter. I'm not selling them but giving them away to deserving homes.

As her car moved away and the cloud of mist closed in behind it, I turned back to head for The Haven, only to be met by the lone bison standing outside the front gate. He snorted and tossed the turf with his front hooves. I stood still and waited, making no attempt to run away or move forward. *We have to learn to live with each other, we're neighbours,* I said silently.

A while later, he swung his head away from me and made off towards Longwood, snorting as he moved. I watched him disappear and the mist move in curls and swirls with the eddies of breeze that played over the tops of the tea bushes and licking at my face, dissolve gently into the night. Somewhere in the distance, a great horned owl called, a long eerie *uh hoo, uh hoo.*

I stayed up all night, wondering whether I'd ever want to walk the spirit path. Perhaps, when I was ready. But first, I needed to heal wounds, build bridges, make peace, put together the fragments of my life into a whole, not brush them on to a dust pan and throw them out. The next day I sat down and wrote to Father Shriver. I felt the process had to begin with him. How right I was.

Dear Fr Shriver,

Here's a voice from the past—the fellow who once walked the burning streets of Calcutta and not satisfied with that, went off in search of the horrors of war and didn't know why; the one you helped by opening a door. Yes, it's me, Sean, writing to you after all these years. I am sure you must have given up on me and written me off as a rotten egg because I fell out of sight and never kept in touch. You will never really know how sorry I am for being so insensitive after all that you have done for me.

The last time I wrote to you was when my fortunes in The Bombay Bastion changed for the better. You replied, I remember but I didn't respond because I had got so carried away with my own sense of self importance. So much has changed since then and as I write to you now I feel as if it's from another life altogether, another world. I left Bombay and have set up a base for myself in Kotagiri, in the Nilgiris and will be starting part time work as sports teacher in schools in these parts.

Everything around me is calm and green and bursting with life and I am ready to start my life all over again with a new feeling of blessedness.

How are you Father? I would love to hear from you, even if it is a small note.

Thank you for all that you have done for me.

With peace and respect,

Sean Varma

His response came a few weeks later.

Greetings Sean,

Thank you so much for your loving letter and the considerate words that you have used so meaningfully.

I had tried for some time to get in touch with you but all my letters came back undelivered. Finally when I managed to get in touch on the phone with The Bombay Bastion the people there were most unhelpful. And I was forced to abort further attempts. And now, praise be Christ Jesus, here is a letter from you out of the blue.

The reason why I was so frantic about getting in touch with you is because your father passed away on the 14th of last month of a massive heart attack one evening in Blue Fox. He was out alone. The Manager happened to know where he lived but didn't know who to inform as there was no one at home. The police were called in to track relatives and none of his brothers wanted to have anything to do with his remains. Anyway, they got hold of your mother's old address in Coimbatore but were told on enquiry that she had sold the property and left. Finally they set out looking for you and arrived at my doorstep.

By the grace of God I was able to represent the family and you and handed over all his papers to his lawyer Mr Bankim Chandra Mazumdar. I have had someone clean the apartment. The lawyer now wants to meet you. Caroline, a woman who claims to be a family friend from Allahabad, came and met me. She asked after you and I told her that I did not know where you were. Now I do. Praise be Christ Jesus, that I have found you.

Please get in touch with me as soon as you read this letter.

In Christ Jesus,

Fr. Shriver

I stood there, hands trembling, in the veranda at The Haven, wondering how I should respond. *As a man and as a son,* I told myself and went in to pack my bags.

A day later I found myself knocking on a large dark wooden door. An old priest opened it. It took me a few moments to realise that he was Fr Shriver.

Sean? he said, surprised, *Just look at you! What amazing grace that you are here! Come on in. Yes, put your bag there...and sit. I'll get you some coffee?*

Don't worry about all that, please sit. There should be no formalities between us.

Stop this nonsense, I'm getting you coffee. Sit down Sean. Don't try and organise me. Seems like you've been alone far too long. Sit. As I sank into his comfortable deck chair, he went off to get coffee from the refectory, returning soon with a mug of the steaming brew and a small glass plate of ginger biscuits. *Your favourites,* he said.

Later, we met the lawyer and initiated all the formalities. *I can get all this completed in a few days,* he said looking at me over the dark horn rims of his spectacles. *Meanwhile here are the keys of your father's home. Now it is yours.* At the door, he turned to Fr Shriver and shook his hand I looked at the small bunch of keys in my hand. I felt nothing.

Embers

The apartment was two floors above Carol's old place. It had three bedrooms and a large balcony that overlooked the street and faced a view of the Calcutta sky wedged between buildings. He had left the place along with his savings and investments to me in his will. Considering I hadn't seen him or been in touch with him for years, it was an odd thing for him to do. A part of me didn't want to have anything to do with the inheritance and the other felt that it was my right, a compensation for all I had been put through. I swung like a pendulum between the two. One moment I wanted to sell the place with everything inside and hand over the money to Father Shriver to be used for a worthy cause and the next I thought of selling it and buying property in the Nilgiris...and the very next—to keep the apartment as my Calcutta base. Then the idea struck me that the right thing to do would be to hand it over to Carol since she had been such a support to Dad.

Where was Carol? What had she done to me that I had shut out her memory? The more I thought about her, the more she began to grow on me, spreading through me, filling me, touching me. It was as if she was coming alive, as if after a long sleep I had awakened to her.

I stood in the centre of the room and looked around me. There was a fraying carpet, arm chairs and a sofa, bookcases, a liquor cabinet, a bar with high stools and two paintings by an unknown artist on the wall. There was nothing here that really reminded me of Dad, apart from the bar and the cabinet. It was all quite impersonal.

I headed for the first bedroom to my left. It looked like a hotel room. Everything was neat and tidy and in place. The cupboards were empty, devoid of any kind of lived in smell. The other bedroom facing it was identical. That left the third bedroom, the sanctum sanctorum, the master bedroom. I opened the door and stepped in. Three walls were lined with enormous gleaming teak cupboards, deep enough to sleep in. Initially, I was reluctant to open them because it would be like intruding into his world.

I opened the first cupboard and discovered that it was filled with row upon row of brand new shoes; another had shirts and trousers, the one beside it had suits. The opening of each new door revealed other collections. It was like a storage room of a departmental store. Finally, I came to the last cupboard—the largest and widest one. It contained his past, photographs of his marriage, a few of our family together, torn letters, and a host of other bits and pieces—little windows to his life now past. On one long shelf lay my air rifle, boxes of pellets, a box full of photographs of shikar trips with me standing among the adults and a shoe box which was labelled *Sean.* It contained two gold coins and a metal whistle in a paper packet. With a start, I recognised the coins that had been given to me by Grand Mummy. *Where did he get these from? I thought I had lost them. Had he stolen them from me?* I would never know the truth. At the bottom of the cupboard was a large box with letters from women addressed to him, mostly from Carol. They were embarrassing in their candour, almost sticky with desire. I sat on the bed and read a few of them. I was obsessively jealous for those few moments and struggled the rest of the night to get her out of my mind. Early in the morning, I drifted to sleep and by ten I decided to go down and ask the neighbours if they knew her whereabouts. One of them turned out to be an acquaintance of hers. *Carol's staying at a friend's place near by.*

I took the address from her and turned up there. I rang the bell, my heart racing. No one answered. I stood there for a long time with my forehad leaning against the door.

Do you really want to meet me, Sean? Carol asked from the other side of the closed door.

Please open the door.

And there she was, after all those years. I felt tears spring to my eyes. She looked a lot older and care worn; she had put on weight, but not enough to make her look out of shape. Her eyes were still the same and so was her mouth. I wondered what was going to happen next. She served me a cup of tea and two buttered toasts.

Sorry, there isn't much in Geeta's fridge.

How long are you going to be here? I asked.

A week more and then I'm going back to Allahabad. I had come here to look at a possible flat. I'm planning to buy a place here in Calcutta. I've inherited part of the family property in Allahabad and we're selling so with my part I want to buy something here. Then I heard about Gordon's passing. I wasn't there at his funeral. Even if I had got to know in time I don't think I would have gone. I wouldn't have been able to handle it,after all that has happened. I was scared that I'd be happy that he is gone. Anyway, that's over now. She sounded dry, wrung of all emotion.

You can have his apartment if you want it. He owes you that after all that you did for him. Take it, Carol.

Are you bloody joking? I'm not a beggar. I don't need his money, I don't want compensation for what I did. I loved the man, Sean, I really loved him. It didn't work out so it didn't work out. What has come to you has come to you. You need to be compensated more than me.

We sat in silence for a few moments after her outburst.

I better be going, I said, sensing her discomfort. I stood up to head for the door.

Don't, she said suddenly and hugged me. *Don't. Please.*

That evening she brought her bags over to the apartment. We ate out and then took a long rambling walk up to Park Street and all the way across Chowringhee, along the avenue of trees towards Red Road.

I have a confession to make, she said softly. *I hadn't come to Calcutta to look for a place to buy. I have no inheritance. We lost our property in Allahabad to repay loans. I came back to Calcutta to start again. I am sorry I lied. It was difficult to admit, considering you are flush with inheritance and possibly now have your own life somewhere else. I didn't want you to think that I want any sort of 'compensation'.*

I said nothing and we walked the rest of the way in silence, back to the apartment and my father's bedroom. We lay there side by side, two lives entombed in a dead man's apartment, in a room lined with cupboards full of shoes and clothes and memories, crying in the dark, hugging, whispering stories of the past, confessing, feeling the warmth of our bodies passing from one to the other.

The next morning we began talking it through and by evening Carol agreed to come back with me to Kotagiri. Neither of us wanted to return to Calcutta. The apartment had to be sold. The lawyer turned out to be more resourceful than I had imagined and in a matter of days had lined up a Bombay based buyer. We decided to fly down to Bombay, sign the papers, collect the advance and then travel down to the Nilgiris from there. The final settlement would be done two months later.

I visited Fr Shriver before we left and told him what I had planned. I didn't mention that Carol was a part of it and he was discreet enough not to ask.

Don't look back, walk on. God bless you, son. And don't forget to visit your father's grave before you leave.

It was a warm afternoon when we reached Circular Road Cemetery. A few trees were in flower and flocks of sparrows pecked busily, tossing up dust in the shade. *I'm not sure that I want go in,* whispered Carol. *You need to be there by yourself.* She didn't wait for a response and sat down on a stone bench at the entrance. Walking down the middle path that cut across the middle, I took the third left, following Father Shriver's directions, and arrived at the foot of a freshly set mound of earth. A small white plaque bore his name.

There was a caretaker standing near the grave. He smiled, flashing a set of nicotine-stained teeth. *Friend or family?* he asked.

Family.

We will be working on the tombstone when the grave has settled. Father Shriver has made the arrangements. Sensing that I wanted to be alone, he walked a short distance away and sat down on his haunches, facing in the opposite direction.

I looked at the simple tombstone. *So finally Dad, your struggle is over and you don't have to prove anything to anyone anymore. Thank you for all that you have given me, particularly those little moments of caring and sharing when we were out in the wilds. Remember that question you once asked me and I never got a chance to answer? 'Sean, what's your biggest wish?' My biggest wish, Dad? That we had a 'normal' family. I'm not blaming you, I'm not...I wish you were my hero...*

As that poet, I don't remember his name, wrote in his poem on his father's death...

Do not go gently into that good night,
Rage, rage against the dying of the light.

My eyes swam. I turned away.

The caretaker's two children had joined him and the three of them sat staring at me, waiting for a tip.

The koels called frantically in the trees, small clouds of sparrows rose from the shades of trees and chirped their way through the dappled air, vanishing over the boundary wall. I fell into Carol's arms and hugged her close.

That evening, we went for a long walk down old familiar streets and bylanes, then collecting our bags, headed for the airport. I didn't turn back.

The few days that we spent in the Bombay were filled with precious moments which made the stressful experience of dealing with a Bombay businessman more than just bearable. I took Carol to all my old haunts in the city.

Sorry to say this, she said, but *you've inherited Gordon's habit of spending recklessly. I'm going to help you kick this habit.*

I don't spend recklessly, I insisted. *Finally I have someone to share my life with. Let's not talk about money now, we're not short of it. I've never been this happy.*

She held my hand and squeezed it gently. *I won't talk about money after this. You do the talking till we get to the Nilgiris. But we're aren't flying to either Coimbatore or Bangalore. We'll take a train.*

Have it your way, I smiled.

Two days later, the deal was through and we packed our bags then set off for a late lunch at Leopold's, staying on for a while after eating, people-watching and sipping beer.

Are you sure you won't get bored with me once the novelty has worn off? Carol asked.

What novelty?

Of being with your father's lover.

Before I could react, she laughed. *Don't take me seriously, I was joking. That was long ago.*

I know, I lied, pushing my irritation to the side. I realised that my father's ghost would stay with us for a long time to come.

We walked back to Hotel Cowies which is in a lane just down the road and took a cab later to the station. Once past the gate on to the platform, we sat waiting for the arrival of the train. Other platforms began filling up until the station swelled with people, bustling, shouting and pushing.

Sitting beside Carol I felt safe, an island of calm washed by turgid waters. She hummed a medley of her old favourites and then got on to Buffy Sainte-Marie's *Up Where We Belong:*

Who knows what tomorrow brings / In a world where few hearts survive / All I know is the way I feel / When it's real I keep it alive...

And as she sang, I let the lyrics carry me along, lifting me and dropping me gently and then lifting me up again. I wanted to hold her, really hold her close and thank her for coming back into my life.

You really do justice to the song, I whispered but she wasn't listening to me because the words had taken her to a place from where I couldn't get her back.

Time goes by / No time to cry / Life's you and I / Alive / Today.

Suddenly there was a loud bang followed by another and another and another. In the blink of an eye, there was chaos; bodies were littered everywhere amid pools of blood. People were screaming and running. We were so stunned that we hadn't moved. The lyrics were still hanging suspended from Carol's lips. *Run,* I shouted, *duck and run.*

What about the bags?

Leave the bags, come on Carol, come on! I dragged her into a corner behind a pillar. *Sit there behind those crates. Go on, there's place for one, go on Carol.*

What's happening? Don't leave me Sean!

Don't argue Carol, just sit down. I'll be right back, I promise. When she finally sat down and was out of sight, I stepped forward and peered around the pillar. A group of armed policemen ran towards me, hoping to get cover behind the pillar. I watched them mowed down by automatic fire. The last just about managed to crawl up to my feet and began vomiting blood as his body went into convulsions. I stripped him off his weapon and his ammunition and stepped out and opened fire at three figures coming in my direction wielding weapons. One fell and two dodged out of sight only to emerge again before vanishing out of range again. I went after them but the rifle jammed so I ran across to one of the bodies and yanked out his machine pistol, dodging fire and trying to get back to the pillar. That's when I saw Carol run out. *Don't leave me here, I'm coming with you, I'm coming.*

A burst of fire erupted and she was thrown off her feet and landed in a crumpled heap, her legs twitching.

I could see them ahead and charged at them firing. Another body fell and a policeman caught in the cross fire also joined him. A tremendous force threw me backwards and I fell. I knew I had been hit. An intense heat seared its way through my body. I tried to get up but couldn't so I began dragging myself towards Carol's bullet-riddled body.

Later, much later, after what seemed like ages, they carried our bodies away. In the ambulance, I shut my eyes and prayed that it was all a horrible nightmare.

I keep wondering whether I am alive or dead. Did I bleed to death on the station platform or die under the surgeon's knife or quietly in my room whilst the world was asleep…or am I alive, having survived the terrorist attack and the surgeon's knife and the horror of realising that Prem once more had me at his mercy even though this time it was to make peace?

Yes. I am sure I am alive because everything is so real, throbbing with energy, my senses are awake and responding. Or is death a hyper-reality…a continuous state of being? Where are these thoughts coming from? Where are these feelings coming from? It is all so pure and clear. Like a mountain stream, crystal in the light. I feel lighter. The past has fallen away like dry skin; the dark, bitter seed inside me no longer remains. It is as if the tree has shed its leaves and the clear spread of branches is all that remains. I do not know how I survived the investigation, the court hearings and the frightening glare of public curiosity. I do not know how I survived the cameras and the front pages. I do not know how I finally reached here, back home to myself.

The Spirit Path

And now, the time has come. I know it is time for the spirit walk. Stella's friend, Thaethli Kuttan, a Toda elder has already told me where to meet him when I am ready. I stuff a backpack with bare essentials and head out to Mulli Mund in a hired jeep and spend the night in the mund.

Early the next morning we set off on foot across an open field and up a path of thorny bushes covered in tiny star-like white flowers, eventually reaching the base of the hill. He walks ahead, leading the way as the climb becomes steep and the path gravel strewn. My feet can't get a firm footing, and I slide down faster than I move up. I am so absorbed in the act of climbing that I do not realise that the landscape has begun to change. The deeper we penetrate into the thicket, the cooler it becomes. Forests give way to grasslands and grasslands to mossy glades where strangely beautiful butterflies flash and wild flowers exude a heady fragrance. Everywhere there is the music of the wind and streams as they cascade around us, singing in harmony.

We stand at the base of an enormous forehead of granite jutting out of a grassy hill. *This is Mettine Karsh, Steps of Stone, the place where the spirits of women climb with an* oarskh, *or grinding stick, in one hand. And up above there is Koche Arre, Bangle Rock, where the spirits crawl, dragging their bangles along the surface of the rock. Let's move on. If we stay long we'll block their path.*

Moving up along the side of the hill, I glance down to see dust understand what they were saying. Somewhere among them I heard Carol's voice singing:

Who knows what tomorrow brings / In a world where few hearts survive / All I know is the way I feel / When it's real I keep it alive

I closed my eyes and listened. Then, when silence surfaced again I walked back, up on to the path and made my way through clouds of fireflies back to The Haven.

Now it's dark and I'm not alone. The blue gum air is heady with the blessedness of being. The wind dances with a crowd of leaves and spreads them at my feet.

RANDHIR KHARE is an award winning poet, writer, artist and teacher who has written more than twenty volumes of poetry, fiction, translations from tribal dialects and cultural documentation. His work has inspired national and international puppet theatre productions, been performed along with various traditional and contemporary musicians and bands, set to music by A.R. Rahman and has been translated into Bengali, Marathi, Bulgarian and French. He has had five solo exhibitions of his pen and ink drawings and paintings and has illustrated a number of his own books.

Among his numerous awards is The Gold Medal For Poetry (by the Union of Bulgarian Writers), the Sanskriti Award For Creative Writing and the Winter Cultural Festival Poetry Prize.

The author wishes to thank the Sahitya Akademi for the special grant bestowed on him under the Writer In Residence Scheme to make it possible for him to work on this book.